Bones Behind the Wheel

Bones Behind the Wheel

A HAUNTED GUESTHOUSE MYSTERY

E. J. Copperman

CROOKED
LANE

NEW YORK

Copyright © 2019 by Jeffrey Cohen

All rights reserved.

Published in the United States by Crooked Lane Books, an imprint of The Quick Brown Fox & Company LLC.

Crooked Lane Books and its logo are trademarks of The Quick Brown Fox & Company LLC.

Library of Congress Catalog-in-Publication data available upon request.

ISBN (hardcover): 978-1-68331-887-3
ISBN (ePub): 978-1-68331-888-0
ISBN (ePDF): 978-1-68331-889-7

Cover illustration by Dominick Finelle
Book design by Jennifer Canzone

Printed in the United States.

www.crookedlanebooks.com

Crooked Lane Books
34 West 27th St., 10th Floor
New York, NY 10001

First Edition: January 2019

10 9 8 7 6 5 4 3 2 1

For every reader of every book I have ever written

Chapter 1

"This is no walk on the beach."

Against all evidence to the contrary, I had to agree. Katrina Breslin and I were, in fact, on the sand behind my massive Victorian home/business and we *were*, indeed, traveling by foot, but you couldn't possibly have mistaken what we were doing for a nice, relaxing walk on the beach.

"We just need to get a little farther down toward the ocean and the other houses," I suggested, pointing south. "There isn't quite so much heavy equipment down there."

The state of New Jersey in its infinite wisdom (and this might be the time to remind you that the National Language of New Jersey is Sarcasm) had decided to do some—it said—necessary excavation on parts of the shore in Harbor Haven, the town where I live and run a guesthouse. The state had noted that Superstorm Sandy (we're not allowed to call it a *hurricane*) had done considerable damage to the area just a few years back and erosion had also taken a toll, so bolstering the dunes was necessary, and apparently that was done by moving huge amounts of sand around in what appeared to be a completely random pattern. I didn't see how using bulldozers and other huge machines to move sand from one place to another was going to protect anything, but oddly, I had not been consulted. I had been nice enough to let the foreman, Bill Harrelson, and his crew use my bathrooms while they were here, with the provision that they make sure to keep them clean and not abuse the privilege, which they had not. They'd been conscientious visitors.

If I'm going to be fair—and there is no reason to expect that I will—it made sense for the work, if it was really going to be done, to take place now. November is hardly peak tourist season on the Jersey Shore, although Senior Plus Tours, the company that steers a number of guests in my direction each month, had still sent three this week. They weren't here so much for the lovely beaches (now being bulldozed) or the amusement piers (closed for the season except, for some reason, on Thanksgiving).

They were here for the ghosts.

Perhaps I should explain.

A little over four years ago, I was a newly divorced single mother who had just won a lawsuit against a previous employer whose hands hadn't remembered his marriage vows and whose ears had been deaf to my refusals until I decked him. Sorry, until he slipped on some spilled copier toner and bumped his head on my fist. That's what it said in the depositions.

I decided to take charge of the changes in my life instead of letting them be imposed upon me, so I moved back to Harbor Haven, where I'd grown up, and bought the Victorian, not in spite of but because of its having far too many rooms for me and my then-nine-year-old daughter Melissa to inhabit. I wanted to own and run a guesthouse in my home-town and got a deal on the place because it needed a *lot* of repairs and renovation.

In the midst of doing those—my father had been an inde-pendent contractor and had taught me how to do home repair work so I wouldn't be taken in by contractors less scrupulous than he was—I met with an "accident" and was hit on the head with a bucket of drywall compound, which I can tell you hurt quite a bit.

When I regained what few senses I had, I could see two people who I'd have sworn had not been there pre-bucket. As it turned out, they were Paul Harrison and Maxie Malone, and they had recently *kicked* the bucket in what was now my new house. They were ghosts (go figure) who wanted to know who had killed them (which, in retrospect, was probably rea-sonable) and wanted me to help them find out (which was not, even in retrospect).

That's a story told elsewhere, but suffice it to say we found Paul and Maxie's murderer, and I think all of us expected that would propel them to some other area of the afterlife, what with the "unfinished business" on this planet completed. But no. Paul and Maxie were still here in the guesthouse four years and change later.

We had worked out an arrangement: Paul had been a pri-vate investigator just getting started when he and Maxie had met their end (if you want to call it that), and he still wanted to investigate things. Problem was, he needed someone in the living world to go other places and ask the questions, because the vast majority of people couldn't see or hear him and at the time he was unable to move past my property line. He has since overcome that last restriction, but only a select few, including Melissa and my mother, can see the ghosts. Liss and Mom always could and had chosen not to tell me about it because they thought I'd feel bad. That was something of a miscalculation on their part, but I will admit I probably would have at least taken my daughter to a psychotherapist if I'd heard she could see the spirits of the undead and was fine with it.

Paul wanted me to get a private investigator license so I could help him with what he saw as his detective agency. I had discovered that some guests actually *want* to be in a house with ghosts and that that could help my business. So I agreed to do as Paul asked if he and Maxie would put on "spook shows" for the guests twice a day. Senior Plus provided the guests who wanted some interaction with the deceased, and I did the occasional work with Paul, which so far had not once worked out profitably for me. But we make the bargains we make and move on.

So now I was a newly remarried single mother and innkeeper/extremely part-time private detective, walking on the beach with one of my guests who had observed that what we were doing was certainly no walk on the beach.

Katrina looked down the beach in the direction I'd indicated. "I don't think it's that much better down there, Alison," she said.

She had a point. The earth-moving equipment was located in every location as far as the eye could see, and when you're on the shore, you can see pretty far. There aren't any private houses near mine because much of the beachfront has been bought up by businesses, and some of it is just municipal territory to lure the tourists, which I appreciate. The previous owners of my house (with the exception of Maxie, who had occupied the place briefly before her demise) had held fast against the commercialization of the beach, although I imagine the seven bedrooms in the house hadn't been put there just because they'd decided to have a large family.

"Maybe it's just not a good idea to stroll out here," Katrina said. You could hear the unspoken *today* at the end of her sentence, because she clearly knew this wasn't getting any better before she ended her vacation and went home in three days.

"I'm so sorry," I told her. "The town didn't tell us the dates they'd be working on our property specifically, so I couldn't warn you too much in advance."

Katrina turned toward the guesthouse and started in that direction, so I followed her. "It's not a big deal," she said. "I wasn't expecting to go swimming or anything." That was fortunate, because the heavy cardigan she was wearing would no doubt have weighed her down once it was saturated. "I came to get away from my life for a while and maybe see some ghosts." She smiled.

Of course, Katrina and the other guests, a couple named Adam and Steve Cosgrove, had not seen and would not see Paul and Maxie. They wouldn't see Maxie's husband, Everett, or my father when he dropped by with my mother, who was thankfully not yet a ghost. They'd see what we wanted them to see of the *results* the ghosts have, which consist mainly of carefully planned objects flying by and effects (pretty cheesy ones) we put together for entertainment purposes. We never scare the guests, largely because Paul and Maxie et al. are not scary people. We've discovered that people are pretty much who they are, and death doesn't change that so much as make them considerably less tangible.

"Have you been enjoying the shows so far?" I asked. It's always good to get feedback from a guest during the stay if you can, because if there's something that's bothering him or her, you can fix it rather than read it on a guest evaluation form after they leave.

"Yeah, more than I thought I would, to tell you the truth." Katrina stopped for a moment to regard me with an amused smile. "That Maxie is a riot."

It's not the word I would have chosen—Maxie and I have a complicated relationship based on mutual irritation—but the customer is always right, and Maxie's heart (if she still had one) was in the right place. I was pretty sure. I'd check at the Harbor Haven Cemetery.

"She has a style," I allowed, and started walking again toward the house, letting Katrina follow this time.

We reached the edge of my property, and I stopped—for lack of a better word—dead in my tracks.

The excavation being done in what was basically my backyard had been carefully described to me by the construction firm the town had hired to handle the erosion issues. It was going to take six days, I'd been told, and would inconvenience me only by having the huge bulldozers and other beasts of sand-moving parked behind my house. The actual amount of earth displaced (that was their word) this far from the ocean would be "minimal."

So the enormous hole now occupying about a quarter of my backyard was something of a surprise.

It hadn't been visible when we were approaching because of the ginormous excavator that I thought had been idly parked on the spot but now was clearly digging something out of the crater it had dug in the sand. *My* sand. (I can show you the deed.)

I stood there stunned for a moment while Katrina, stopping at my side, said, "Wow."

No kidding.

I opened and closed my mouth a couple of times, something I often do with sound coming out. That didn't seem completely possible at the moment. This violation of my property was enormous and clearly going to take a *while* to restore. I hadn't been this angry since any time ever that I'd seen my ex-husband, The Swine. (It's not the name on his birth certificate, but it's much more descriptive of the man he had become.)

When I could start breathing normally, or close to it, again, I noticed Bill Harrelson, the foreman for my section of the project, trudging from the side of my house toward the Grand Canyon that had suddenly been deposited where a placid beach had been before. I reminded myself there was a guest present (you need to watch your language under such circumstances) and headed for him.

"Bill," I managed. There were so many other words that could have been.

He held up his hands, palms out, feigning innocence. "Hang on, Alison," he said.

"Hang on? You told me you were parking some equipment, and now I have a bottomless pit in my backyard. You want me to hang on? I might trip and end up on the molten core of the Earth."

"I don't know what happened either," Bill protested. "I just got a text to come back here. Let me see what's going on."

Okay, so I could hang on. For a minute. Tops.

Bill walked to the side of the extractor, whose arm was extended deep into the crater. Katrina looked over at me. "Good thing it's not the summer, huh?" she said.

Now, I liked Katrina. Truly. She had seemed, in the short time I'd known her, to be a very nice and level-headed person. So I made a concerted effort not to scream at her. I'm a good hostess.

"Yes," I said. It wasn't terribly original, but it avoided snarling. That was something.

"I mean, it would really have hurt your business then, I'm guessing," Katrina continued. She was clearly operating under the assumption that I had not understood her point.

"Yup." I saw Bill talking earnestly with the extractor operator and then, shaking his head, walking around to the front of the big machine and looking down into the pit, which was something I didn't think you were supposed to do unless you were in a Vincent Price movie. And even then it generally didn't turn out all that well for the person leaning over the edge.

"Because a lot of people come here for the beach." Katrina, no doubt spurred on by my terseness, was now explaining the appeal of the Jersey Shore to me. I needed to let her off the hook but I was busy watching Bill, who didn't exactly recoil from what he saw in the hole but did seem to move back a couple of feet instinctively. "You know, not just for the ghosts."

"I know, Katrina. Sorry, but I have to see if there's a problem. Excuse me, okay?" Like most people, I did not wait for a response and walked past Katrina toward Bill, who took what appeared to be another incredulous look down into the gaping hole (whose repair bill I was already mentally sending to the state) and then stood up straight again, a look on his face that indicated wonder and some unease.

"What's the problem, Bill?" I asked. As I walked to his side, I could see more of the crater and the arm of the excavator digging into it. The machine had clearly unearthed material other than sand, material its operator hadn't been expecting, because the claw appeared to be dragging something out of the ground. Something metal and large.

Bill wheeled to face me, a sign that he hadn't known I was lurking behind him. "Alison!" I gave him a moment—that was certainly my name, and I didn't see any reason to dispute it. "There's something down there."

"Yeah, I get that. What is it and why did your guys start digging here? I'm not on the list for major excavation." The lawsuit I was planning could lead to another renovation of the guesthouse, maybe add an outdoor swimming pool. Because there are, believe it or not, some strange people who like to come to the beach and then swim in a pool. I know.

"One of the guys had a divining rod and read some metal vibrations," Bill said. "He thought it might be a rare coin or something."

I glanced down toward the tremendous maw they'd opened up but didn't get any closer. I have this thing about not falling into bottomless pits. "That's bigger than a coin."

"Yeah. It's a Continental."

Of course it was. What was a Continental? "A what?"

"A Continental." He saw the confusion in my eyes. "A *Lincoln Continental.*"

I confess; it took me a second. "It's a car?"

Bill nodded fervently. "Yeah. By the look of it, I'd say midseventies, maybe. A Continental sedan. Green."

Well, the color made all the difference. "What's it doing down there?" I asked. It seemed like a logical question. Forget that Bill's crew had been scavenging for change on my beach like some tinfoil hat prospector and they'd chose to dig for a quarter with a shovel the size of, well, a Lincoln Continental. "Why is there a car buried in my backyard?"

He spread out his hands, palms out. "I wish I knew. But . . ."

I didn't hear what he said next because the man operating the excavator decided to start it up. You sort of get used to the noise from the construction equipment after a day or . . . never . . . but usually you're not as close to the big machines as I was right now. The scoop on the front of the rig moved, down, digging under the frame of what I guessed was the car's rear end. Bill motioned me away from the pit, and I was happy to walk back in the direction of the ocean, whose roar was considerably more soothing than that of the Caterpillar equipment causing yet more damage to property that was described in detail in my deed.

Katrina, whom I'd left perhaps fifty feet away, was

watching the earth-moving machine quite closely with an expression on her face indicating she'd seen something incredibly wondrous. It's not that I get to see tremendous trucks carve out part of my property every day, but her look was more in the area of having seen a genie create a palace of gold using some straw and a used fez.

Then I realized she was taking in the spectacle that was Bill Harrelson.

Bill wasn't really my type, but that was okay because I was married and needed only one man in my type. But to Katrina, Bill was clearly a type in and of himself. I considered standing back but remembered I wanted an explanation about the vintage sedan now being brought out of my property, so I stopped as soon as I thought speech would be plausible and looked at Bill.

"But what?" I said.

Luckily Bill wasn't in the mood to play coy. He'd been shaken by what he'd seen in the hole, and now it was coming out to be seen by all. So he had to come clean right away. "There's something inside the Continental, I'm pretty sure," he said.

I didn't like the way he said the word *something*, but I didn't get to ask right away because Katrina, stars in her eyes, was nudging me in the side. "I haven't been introduced," she said.

She would continue to not be introduced for a moment, though. I didn't like Bill's ominous tone. "What's in the car?" I asked him.

"It looked a lot like a skeleton," he said.

Chapter 2

Usually when I call the Harbor Haven Police Department I talk to Detective Lieutenant Anita McElone (just go with a rhyme for macaroni), but apparently vintage car with a human skeleton in it was only enough to merit uniformed officers. So I stood on what was once the beach behind my house with Katrina, Bill Harrelson, Bill's excavator operator Jim . . . something . . . and Officer Mark Canton, who was holding a tablet computer and taking pictures of the Continental with the extremely dead person in it.

"It looks like this has been here a while," Officer Canton said, looking into the abyss and assessing the discovery Jim had made while he was searching for loose change in the sand.

I had not ventured a close look into the unknown because I liked it remaining unknown to me. The cops could figure out what they wanted and move on. But Paul, who had materialized with the first flashing red and blue light (there was clearly no need for sirens), had actually taken a dive into the hole to do his own reconnaissance. He'd come back looking thoughtful, which is Paul's go-to expression under any circumstances.

"I'd have to concur with the officer," he said despite there being no one there who could hear him except me. He held his hand to his chin. This wasn't a full goatee-stroker of a problem yet but he was covering his options. "Parts of the car are rusted through and although the windows were closed the person who was inside has clearly been deceased for a number of years at least."

I nodded just a little so he would stop before going into a detailed description of the body's decomposition. I hadn't had lunch yet and wanted to keep that open as a possibility after this was finished. I looked at Officer Canton while Katrina kept up her intense study of Bill Harrelson, who didn't seem to notice.

"So can the crew take it away now and start filling in my backyard?" I asked. "Does anybody need to come and study the scene any more than this?" My priority was on getting the guesthouse back to what passes for normal if you don't look too closely.

"Let me get this video back to the lieutenant and she'll let me know," Canton answered. That told me a couple of things. First: I wasn't getting my backyard restored anytime soon. Second: McElone was still afraid to come to my house unless she absolutely had to. She has a problem with what she calls "the ghosty stuff." "I need to look up and see if there's any record of a car being buried here legally sometime in the past. And we need to get the registration number on the car to trace it. There are no license plates, at least not on the back, so that might mean they buried the guy in it after he died."

"You think somebody killed him?" Jim . . . somebody . . . asked Canton.

The officer made a face that indicated he thought that unlikely. "Some guys just want to be buried in their cars," he answered. "But until I find out more my job is to get the facts to the detective if there's going to be one working on this."

"Does this area have any history with organized crime?" Paul asked. This was New Jersey, so it was a silly question, but Paul is from Canada and was born in London, so we allow him some lack of knowledge on the history of our home state. "It is possible the victim was murdered and then buried here to cover up the crime."

"It seems unlikely someone would be able to bury a whole car in the sand without really big excavating equipment like this." I pointed at the machine Jim had been using. "Not the kind of thing a killer would be able to do real quietly. But what I really want to know is when can I get my beach back?"

Bill tilted his head to the right a bit. "That depends on when I can get my crew back to work. We're still scheduled for another two days, Alison."

Of course. Body or no body, Bill and his men would continue to be moving sand around back here. The only thing the police might do at this point was prolong the process, which I could certainly live without. I turned my attention again toward Canton.

He held his hands up. "It's not up to me," he protested. "I'm waiting to hear from the lieutenant."

I pulled my phone out of my pocket and hit the button for McElone. That's right, I have the chief of detectives in my town on speed dial. It's not as big an advantage as you might think.

She no doubt saw my number on her Caller ID and ignored the call. That's what I mean about the whole "advantage" thing. McElone sees me—and I can understand it—as something of a nuisance, an innkeeper who occasionally gets involved in investigations and isn't exactly Sherlock Holmes. Guilty on all counts, but I wanted the Deathmobile and its occupant off my land as quickly as possible.

McElone had left me with no choice. I played my ace and called my friend Phyllis Coates.

Phyllis owns, runs and occasionally cleans the offices of the *Harbor Haven Chronicle*, the only newspaper to exclusively cover my hometown, although the "paper" part becomes more academic every year as Phyllis moved her news online in keeping with the fickle attitudes of consumers. At least she didn't link local stories to things like *Which Kardashian Are You?* These days that is a serious news organization.

Phyllis, unlike the lieutenant, saw my name and picked up on the second ring. "This about the cops in your backyard?" That's Phyllis for "hello." She is constantly monitoring her police scanner. Twenty years working for the *New York Daily News* had taught her not to worry about the niceties and never to take anything for granted. She hasn't written about my ghosts only because she can't verify their existence to her own satisfaction.

"Yeah. They found a car with a body in it buried under my beach," I told her. "And for some reason Lieutenant McElone doesn't want to take my call."

"She'll take mine," Phyllis said, and hung up.

I put the phone back in my pocket, satisfied that Phyllis

was on the case. I looked over at Katrina and Bill Harrelson, who were now bonding although Bill didn't know it. He thought he was answering Canton's questions. Katrina's eyes indicated she thought otherwise. Who was I to argue? If that made her vacation more enjoyable, it was part of my service. I decided.

"We usually don't go down that deep but once they saw there was something that big there they kept digging," Bill was telling Canton. He looked to Jim for help. "Isn't that right?"

The excavator operator nodded. "We thought it was something little, like a buried treasure or something, but it turned out to be a bumper," he said.

Canton's eyebrows danced around on his forehead a bit. "A buried treasure?"

"It's been a long project," Bill told him.

I stepped forward because I didn't care that much about the car other than to get it to go away. "What did you hear from the lieutenant?" I asked Canton. "Can I have my yard back yet?"

"Lieutenant McElone said I should question the witnesses and get back to her," he reported. "I'm questioning the witnesses."

I figured that included Bill and Jim, and Katrina because she wanted to be included, but not me. I hadn't seen anything happen and didn't know what I could add to the discussion. So I headed toward the French doors leading into my den. I had innkeeper stuff to do. Paul, however, was fascinated with the investigation—as he would be by any investigation of anything in history—and told me he'd be inside shortly. We'd already had the morning spook show so I wasn't that concerned with Paul's punctuality. He's a free spirit. Literally.

But Canton called to me before I could make it past the carcass of the car with the skeleton of a person in it. "Hang on, miss!" he called. I stopped because I haven't been called "miss" in a while and found it refreshing. I turned to look at him. "Officer?"

"I'll be needing to question you in a minute," he said.

"Well I didn't see anything," I told him.

"Even so. The lieutenant was real clear about that." McElone was getting at me long-distance.

I groaned but not loudly enough for Canton to hear. "Okay, tell you what, officer. I need to get some stuff done in here for my guests. When you're ready for me you come on in and I'll be happy to tell you the little I know. Okay?"

Canton didn't look happy about it. "The lieutenant said I'd be better off if I didn't go inside," he said.

"Really. Did she say why?"

"She wasn't real clear about that, no." Canton was a nice young man but he looked like he'd graduated high school in the past half hour and didn't want to make his superior officer angry with him.

"Tell Lieutenant McElone I gave you special permission to come inside," I told the kid. "I'll take responsibility for your safety, okay?" Without giving Canton a chance to reply I opened the French doors and walked into my den.

The usual state of barely controlled chaos was in full swing when I got there. Melissa was at school and my husband Josh was at his store, Madison Paints in Asbury Park. But that didn't mean the place couldn't be bustling with people. It's what a guesthouse is all about.

Maxie was just now descending from the ceiling, having "recovered" from her arduous tasks at the morning spook show. Maxie puts on a bigger show about how hard she's working than the actual show she's putting on. That's Maxie. Now she was floating aimlessly about four feet off the den floor wearing her usual sprayed-on jeans and another in a series of black t-shirts. This one bore the legend, *I Know I Am*. Which didn't even make any sense.

"What's going on outside?" she wanted to know. Maxie spends a lot of time on the roof of the house looking out on the beach in one direction and the town of Harbor Haven in the other. Wherever she can cause more consternation to the living, mostly me, is where she'll concentrate her attention. She must have seen the brouhaha going on behind the house.

"The construction guys found a car buried in the sand," I told her. "They think there's a skeleton in it."

Maxie looked interested. "Anybody I know?" she asked.

"They haven't figured that out yet. Where's Everett?" Maxie's husband, who married her at the same time I was marrying Josh except that the person officiating at the ceremony wasn't talking to either of them, had been a mentally ill homeless man when I'd met him at the end of his life, but had reverted to the more stable, fit, military version of himself when he'd made the transition. Sometimes that happens. Dying had done wonders for Everett.

"He's at the gas station, patrolling." Everett died in the restroom at the local service station and still feels an obligation to protect the area, so he goes there to stand guard some days. Other times he just likes to guard Maxie, but he's also very serious about keeping the guesthouse and its residents safe, which I appreciate. "Said he'd be back but not before the next show."

"That's okay. You and Paul can handle it alone." I straightened some pillows on the large sofa and started in fluffing up the easy chairs and the loveseat. Appearance means a lot in the inn biz. This was the common area where many of the activities I plan for the guests take place when I have more than three of them in the house at a time. During weeks like this I could concentrate on the library, which was smaller but cozier.

"Yeah." Maxie was being quiet, which was disquieting. She's usually so in-my-face that I have dreams where Maxie is hovering over my bed. I *think* they're dreams, anyway. "I'm thinking maybe I'll be taking . . . a break from the shows for a while."

That caught me off guard and it wasn't because I was so delighted. I turned to look at her. "What do you mean, a break?"

"Well . . ." Maxie was twirling her hair on her right index finger. Coy Maxie was a bad sign; if she didn't want to come right out and say what she meant it was going to be a problem. For me. "I've been thinking about our deal."

Deal? What deal? "I don't understand," I told her. Best to make it look like I wasn't on edge. I straightened a picture that didn't need it. Yeah, that would definitely project the right image.

"You know, about how you go and detect stuff for Paul

and so he and I do these shows to draw people to your hotel."
Maxie liked to say the guesthouse was a hotel because she
knew it irritated me. "I've been thinking about that."

"Yeah? What have you been thinking?" No sense in delay-
ing the inevitable.

"What's in it for me?"

It took a good deal of effort to refrain from rolling my
eyes. We'd been through this a number of times before. "Look,
you know what I'm going to say. Paul's the one who negoti-
ated with you on this. I have no idea what kind of bargain the
two of your struck, but you didn't seem to have any objections
at the time and I don't see how anything has changed. If you
want to complain, go complain to Paul."

"I did. He told me to talk to you."

So Paul was ducking responsibility and leaving me with a
disgruntled Maxie. Not that I'd ever seen Maxie completely
gruntled other than when she was marrying Everett. "I don't
get why this is coming up now," I said. Yeah, it was a deflec-
tion but it gave me time to think.

"Paul gets to be a detective because that's what he wanted.
You get to run this place because that's what you wanted."
Maxie began doing slow laps around the ceiling. The faster
her pace picked up, the more agitated she'd become. Or the
other way around. "So how come I don't get what I want?"

I knew I'd regret saying it but I just couldn't stop myself
in time. "What do you want?" I asked Maxie.

"You know." Her pace picked up a couple of miles an
hour.

"I really don't. What do you want?"

I heard the front door open, which was slightly odd. I knew Adam and Steve were out exploring the mostly deserted boardwalk and were going to have lunch in town. I don't serve food at the guesthouse. Melissa was at school. Katrina was in the backyard, or what was left of it. My mother was coming for dinner, but that wasn't for six hours. Nobody else who came through here used a door. I looked toward the front room but the door didn't open immediately.

I was about to ask Maxie to go see who had come in—nobody could do anything to *her*—when two things happened: My husband Josh walked through the door to the den and Maxie said, "I want to be a designer again."

One of those was a good thing and I kissed him when he reached me. "What are you doing here?" I asked.

"Oh no," Maxie said. "You don't get to duck out because he came home." She was getting faster up by the crown molding.

"I decided to take lunch and come see my wife," Josh answered, holding me a moment longer. "What's with all the flashing lights and stuff back on the beach?" He craned his neck to look past me through the French doors.

"You have to answer me," Maxie intoned. She sounded ominous and was beginning to be a little blurry with speed.

"The construction guys found a car with a dead person in it," I said to Josh. "Excuse me." I looked up toward Maxie, as much as I could make her out. "So you want to design something. Who's stopping you?"

Josh looked at me and mouthed, "Maxie?" I nodded.

Maxie had been a budding interior designer when she was poisoned at the age of twenty-eight. She hadn't ever said anything before about wanting to take up her old career although she was generous in her distaste at the way I had decorated the guesthouse.

She slowed down considerably to look down at me. "You serious?" she asked.

"A dead body!" Josh was already heading for the French doors.

"Who's watching the store?" I asked him as he crossed the room.

"Sy. Don't worry. I can leave him for an hour and a half." Josh's grandfather Sy was the original owner of Madison Paint and still came in to work most days. He was in his nineties and said coming to the store to talk with the painters and contractors kept him alive. I wasn't going to argue with him.

I had no desire to get into a row with Maxie, either. "Sure I'm serious. Since when has anybody told you that you can't design stuff if you feel like it?"

"Well, I can't get any clients. Paul finds ghosts who want stuff detected but I can't just redo a house that someone's haunting." She stopped circling completely and contemplated the sentence she'd just said. "Can I?"

"No. You can't," I told her. The last thing I needed, in a town where I was already considered the crazy ghost lady and had a sign on my business that read, *Haunted Guesthouse*, was for people to hear spirits were renovating houses in the area. They'd be at my front door with pitchforks and torches. "But you can just design stuff for fun, can't you?"

"Fun." Maxie looked annoyed. "Fun."

I didn't think I wanted to know what that meant so I

didn't ask. Besides, my phone buzzed and Phyllis was on the other end.

"You're going to have a car in your backyard for a while," she said. That, too, is Phyllis for "hello."

"You spoke to McElone," I said. I'm really perceptive.

"Yeah, and she says if there's a dead body in the car they're going to keep it there until they can be sure it wasn't just put there an hour and a half ago."

"It's a skeleton," I reminded her. "Besides, I would have seen someone digging enough sand to bury a car. I do live here."

"I don't make the news," she told me. "I just report it. Now, what can you tell me about this car?"

"Nothing. I didn't get close enough to look. They tell me it's a Lincoln Continental, probably from the Seventies."

"That's a big vehicle," Phyllis said.

"Yeah. My luck this bunch of bones couldn't get buried in a Smart Car. They could have pulled it out with a pair of tweezers."

Phyllis waited. "That's it?" she asked.

"Yes. Oddly I didn't get the make and model of the tires. What do you want from me, Phyllis?"

"You're my reporter on the scene. I expect more."

I sighed audibly because that's the only way you get the point across. "I'm not a reporter, Phyllis. I'm an innkeeper and very occasionally sort of a private investigator. And I'm not investigating this thing for two very good reasons. First, I don't have a client who wants it investigated."

"What's the second reason?"

"I don't feel like it."

Maxie, hovering near the chandelier (it's really just a four-bulb light fixture with a publicist), muttered, "I don't feel like it."

Phyllis, who wouldn't have heard Maxie even if she could hear ghosts (their voices are not audible over a telephone), said, "I need to write a story about this and you don't feel like it?" Phyllis believes, simply because I delivered papers for her when I was thirteen years old, that I am an aspiring journalist. Phyllis is wrong.

"Feel free to come over and report the story, Phyllis. I'm off the case."

It was Phyllis's turn to sigh and she did so in a fashion that could actually be described as "crusty," if that's even possible. "I'll be over in a while. Don't let the cops leave."

"Don't let them? I couldn't get them to leave with a hefty bribe."

Phyllis disconnected the call. That's Phyllis for "goodbye," and I promise that'll be the last "that's Phyllis for" comment you'll get from me.

"So what about my decorating?" Maxie has waited close to half a second after I got off the phone, which was a remarkable display of restraint from her.

"I give up. What about your decorating?"

I saw Officer Canton appear near the French doors. No doubt he was going to ask me about stuff that I didn't have answers for, which is always a highlight. I turned my back on the French doors so he couldn't see that I appeared to be talking to myself.

Maxie said, "I want to do some decorating and you won't let me do it in other people's houses, so how about here?"

Here? In my guesthouse? After I'd spent more than four years getting it into the kind of condition I'd envisioned when I'd first taken the tour with the Realtor? "Nothing here needs decorating," I said. I knew it wouldn't stand up but it gave me time to think.

Canton opened the French doors and called in without stepping over the threshold. "Miss?" he called. You had to love this kid.

I turned toward him. "You need me, officer?"

"You're having that bullet hole fixed soon. I could redo the den," Maxie said. It was true that my contractor friend Tony Mandorisi and his brother Vic were coming to replace a beam between my kitchen and the den where a bullet had . . . never mind, but the beam needed to be replaced and the Mandorisi brothers were coming to fix it. The ceiling and at least two walls would have to be repainted. I really wasn't in the mood for a complete redecoration, particularly in the famed Maxie Malone style of "more is more."

"Not now," I said between clenched teeth.

"Did you say something?" Canton asked. "Miss, the lieutenant is here."

I looked at him. "Lieutenant McElone is here?"

"Yes, miss."

That couldn't be good.

Chapter 3

"I'll have the car out of here as soon as I can get all the forensic evidence out of it that I need," Lt. Anita McElone was saying.

The scene in my backyard, to which I had been persuaded to return because McElone is a scaredy-cat, was not the one that was in my guesthouse brochure. The suspect Lincoln Continental's trunk was sticking out of a gaping hole in the ground, held up by the excavator Jim . . . somebody . . . had been operating. Jim was sitting on the excavator's track, staring off at the ocean and looking upset. Maybe the shock of finding a seriously undernourished corpse in the ground was starting to have an effect on him.

Bill Harrelson was off to the side, contemplating the excavator and oblivious, it seemed, to Katrina's attention no matter how extravagantly she might be lavishing it upon him. He nodded every once in a while when she took a breath.

My husband was standing at the edge of the bottomless pit, peering in like he had stumbled across an amazing treasure and was trying to figure out how to get it out of the ground. I've seen him look happier, but not often.

I had moved the picnic table up to the deck, which was where McElone and I were now sitting. This was as close as she would allow herself to get to the inside of my house. That idea was especially amusing because Paul was just to her left. He loved watching law enforcement at work and as long as McElone didn't know he was there she would be very professional.

"How long will that be?" I asked.

"Usually I'd say there's no way of knowing, but since you're going to badger me until I give you a more specific answer I'd guess sometime tomorrow," McElone said. She looked at me with eyes that dared me to complain.

I've never been one to turn down a dare. "Tomorrow!" I said. "How am I supposed to run a tourist business with a great big hole in my backyard that has a huge car and a dead person in it?"

McElone regarded me carefully. "You getting a lot of beach traffic these days?" she asked. "We had a high of fifty-two yesterday."

"People like to walk on the beach."

"There's a dead person buried in a car on your beach," McElone reminded me. "That's a police matter. If I want to I can quarantine the place until the ME makes sure whoever it was didn't die of a communicable disease. So do you really want to push me over one day?"

I hate it when she has a point.

"Good," the lieutenant said when it was clear I wasn't going to object any further. "Now we get to the part where *I* ask the questions."

"All my answers are going to be, 'I don't know,'" I told her. "Because I honestly don't."

"Humor me. Let's start with, how could you have not known there was a great big car buried under your beach?"

That was what we were going to *start* with? "I think it's pretty clear it was here long before I showed up," I told her. "How *could* I have known it was there? The survey before I bought the place didn't look for buried Lincoln Continentals, oddly."

"Any of your *ghosty* pals know anything about this?" McElone's voice dropped in volume despite there being no one she knew of who could have heard what she was saying. Paul looked amused.

"Tell her I'm from Canada and don't have a New Jersey driver's license," he said.

I decided against taking his suggestion. "Nobody knows anything about it. They didn't get here all that much before me."

The lieutenant nodded but didn't make eye contact. She didn't like having to broach the subject. "Can they ask around?" she said.

"You're admitting that you believe I have ghosts in my house?" McElone had steadfastly refused to put words to the thought although it had been clear she was convinced some time before.

"I'm following any possibility that might help," she said, which of course wasn't an answer at all. "Is there any chance they could find something out?"

I looked at Paul, which was probably something I shouldn't have done. McElone noticed the movement and turned swiftly to see what I might have been looking at. Luckily Josh was climbing the steps to the deck in that general direction so she wasn't too alarmed as far as I could tell.

"Without a name at least it would be hard to check about the person in the car," Paul said. "I need more information."

Paul is able to communicate sort of telepathically with other spirits, a system we call the Ghosternet. But if he wants to send out a message he needs to know who he's looking for and if he wants to receive one in any way other than randomly, he needs another ghost to ask.

I relayed Paul's answer to McElone without being clear that it had come from someone other than myself. She scowled but nodded, understanding. "We're going to do some forensics on the car. I'll have the body out of your yard before tonight, anyway. Once we can get DNA we might be able to get a match but it'll take weeks. Maybe they're carrying a wallet with ID in it."

"How would you know it wasn't planted there to give you the wrong idea?" I asked. Paul, looking impressed, pointed a finger at me like a gun.

"I don't," the lieutenant admitted. "But it would be a place to start. You and I both think that car's been down there for quite some time. This could be the coldest case I've ever seen."

Josh walked over, through Paul although he didn't know it. Paul looked amused. He was in an amused mood today. "What have you found out, lieutenant?" he asked when he got to us.

"Not much," McElone groused. "Since you're here I might as well ask if you've ever seen that car before."

Josh shook his head. "I never even heard about it before I came home for lunch today."

"Lunch!" I said. "You haven't eaten. When do you have to go back?"

"Pretty much now," my husband said. "I'll get a sandwich on the way. Don't worry."

"I feel like a bad wife."

Josh leaned over and kissed me on the cheek. "You are the opposite of that," he said.

"I'm a cop." McElone stood up. "I don't have to put up with this kind of stuff."

"I didn't invite you over," I reminded her. "This was your idea."

Josh looked over his shoulder at the car, suspended by its back bumper as apparently it would be for another whole day. "It's really fascinating," he said. "You have to wonder what this was all about."

"Good question," McElone said. She didn't sound nearly as enthusiastic as my husband did.

"I know, right?" Josh kissed me again and headed into the house, no doubt to walk through and get into his car again.

McElone let out a long breath. "I really hope the person in that car died of natural causes," she said. "That would be nice."

"You say that like you don't think it's what you'll find out," I said to her.

The lieutenant started toward the steps back down to the beach. "That's because I don't," she answered. "You don't bury a car in the sand because some guy had a blood clot. You do it because you don't want the body found for forty years."

I watched as she approached Bill, who seemed glad to have something to do. "Tomorrow, right?" I called after her.

McElone turned and looked at me. "There's no way of knowing," she said.

Chapter 4

McElone stayed another hour, re-interviewing Bill and Jim. Katrina was infatuated but not obsessed and came into the house after a bit to warm up and take a shower. The lieutenant had asked her two questions, she said, and determined there was no terribly useful information to be had from Katrina. At least on the subject of the buried car.

I went back into the house and immediately encountered Maxie, who was still waiting, intent to keep hectoring me about redecorating part of my house. As soon as I was back inside she took up the challenge again.

"The way I see it, I have been doing these shows for years for absolutely nothing," she said before I could manage to make my way to the coffee urn. I put out a cart every morning with urns for hot coffee (regular and decaf) and hot water for tea. It was now time to wheel it back into the kitchen but not before I took an especially caffeinated cup for myself. It had already been a long day and I hadn't even had lunch yet. "You owe me."

Maxie should have known better than to challenge me when I needed coffee. I turned toward her and stopped moving entirely. "I *owe* you?" I said. "You stay in my house, you met your husband because of me, your closest friend is my daughter and I *owe* you?" Maxie was the spoiled teenage brat I was hoping I would never actually have in my family.

"Okay, maybe *owe* isn't the right word." That was a rare concession on Maxie's part; this must have been an important point for her. I started wheeling the cart of the den and into the kitchen again. "Maybe it's more in the area of fairness. Maybe I'm just saying that the one thing I really liked doing when I was, you know, like you, was creating interesting spaces. And now I'm looking at not being able to do that *forever* and it's getting me down."

The worst thing about Maxie is that she's not actually a bad person. Ghost. Whatever. She does care about the people she cares about and even if her tactics are often as irritating as you can possibly imagine (and maybe more irritating) she can be counted on when you really need her. She has saved my life at least once. She has also driven me to distraction pretty much every day since I have known her. It's a strange dichotomy, which sums up Maxie perfectly.

Actually, any phrase with the word *strange* in it has a fighting chance of summing up Maxie.

"I get that," I said. I did understand that she was looking at a very, very long time that needed to be filled with something. "I'm concerned about you indulging yourself too much. This isn't the house you bought for yourself, to show off your talents. It's a public house for people to come and spend a relaxing vacation. You can't paint the walls black, you know what I mean?"

I pushed through the kitchen door and rolled the cart to the corner near the sink. I'd clean out the urns with enough time for them to dry before I had to refill them for the next day. I knew Maxie was following me into the kitchen despite the fact that her movement made no sound at all and I wasn't looking in her direction.

But I could sense her enthusiasm level spiking even before she swooshed herself over my head and looked me straight in the face. "You mean I can do it?" she squealed, every inch a nine-year-old who had just been given permission to attend a sleepover at her best friend's house. "I can decorate the den?"

That hadn't actually been what I'd meant but walking it back now would be a severe miscalculation. Never get a poltergeist mad at you if you can avoid it. I'm going to have that embroidered on a pillow.

At least now I could appear to agree while managing to pivot away from having Maxie do whatever she would do to my most public room. "Tell you what," I said. "The ceiling beam being replaced sits right between the den and the kitchen. Why don't we start with you making some designs for in here and we'll see where it goes from there?"

If she were in her normal state of mind Maxie might have noticed that what I'd done was get her to work in the room that guests see least often in the house, other than Melissa's bedroom and the one I share with Josh. But she appeared to be downright giddy now, and spun around the circumference of the ceiling a couple of times in celebration.

"I'm doing it!" she exulted. "I'm decorating again!" Maxie rose like a shot up into the ceiling and vanished. Which was the best possible outcome for me.

But that was just one ghost down. Paul phased himself through the back wall of the kitchen and he was stroking his goatee. That wasn't promising; it meant that he was thinking seriously about an investigation and I knew we didn't have one to think about right now. My best tactic would be to cut him off at the pass.

"We're not looking into the person in the car," I said. "McElone is on the case and you know for certain that we have no client, so we're not."

"I had no intention of suggesting that we should," he answered, in a tone that clearly indicated he'd had every intention of suggesting that we should. "I am not entirely convinced there is anything to investigate. The person in the car might very well have requested such a burial, although it would be interesting to see if there were any record of such a thing taking place on this property."

"If you want to do that you can do it on your own time," I told him. "You're capable of moving around now. Catch a ride to the real estate records at the county offices in Toms River. It's not exactly around the corner but you can probably find your way there. Just don't involve me; I'm not interested. Got that?"

Paul tried to avoid looking like I'd just made his month and failed miserably. "Of course," he said.

Then I got a truly wicked idea. "Why don't you just

get yourself into town—I'll drive you the next time I'm going—and just follow McElone around? You'll know everything she knows and that will get you information you've never had in an investigation before."

Now Paul's inner child was going to Disney World. "I think that's an excellent plan!" he said. "When can we go?"

I nodded toward the back door. "I'm not even sure she's left yet," I said. "You could start now."

"Very good thinking, Alison!" Paul practically flew—no, he *actually* flew—out through the back wall and headed in the general direction of McElone as I reminded him we still had the afternoon spook show to do in two hours. He made some perfunctory sound that was supposed to assure me he'd gotten the message but I made a mental note to see if Everett could come back from the gas station should it become necessary.

I had a very brief, contented time when I went around the first floor and straightened up. I would have gone into the kitchen to start baking an apple pie, but then I remembered that I can't do anything with food except eat it and that Melissa is the cooking genius in the family. It was just as well because then I'd have to clean up the kitchen and who needs that?

As it turned out I wouldn't have gotten past peeling the first apple anyway because my front door opened and closed. I don't lock it during the day despite the guests having spare keys I give them (and scrupulously gather upon their leaving). I heard the activity in the front room and looked up from the library. Someone had come in and was walking around the house looking for me . . . or something.

Sure enough Phyllis turned the corner at a full trot and

pretty much charged into the den when she saw me. "Alison!" she blurted. Phyllis blurts more than she talks.

"The cops are in the backyard," I said, pointing in a general direction. "McElone might still be here. Go talk to her."

"First I want to know what you've found out," she said, sitting down on one of my armchairs. "Tell me about the skeleton in the buried car."

"I haven't found out anything," I told her, wondering where she might have gotten the idea that I had. "Go ask the cops. I just happen to own the land the car was buried in."

"Nothing?" Phyllis demanded. "What am I paying you for?"

"You're *not* paying me."

"That's not the point."

I looked down at her as I straightened a shelf of paperbacks. "Phyllis, you need to pay attention and hear me for once. I don't work for you. Aside from throwing papers onto people's porches I have never worked for you. I have no ambition to be a reporter and I have no talent for it either. I'm just your friend and that's all."

When I glanced down again Phyllis was scrolling through emails on her phone. "I know, dear. I know. But with you on the scene I expect to get more than *that*."

It's a lesson I learned at the one and only high school reunion I have ever attended (at the insistence of my best friend Jeannie Rogers): People never change. You think they will, but they won't. They will be who they are and just get older doing it. It has been a real source of comfort for me because now I don't have any expectations and I am almost never disappointed in anybody.

I shook my head in something approaching amusement and said, "You better get out there, Phyllis. From here I can see McElone heading for her car." I could see Paul following her only a few feet behind like a devoted puppy. This would be an excellent test of McElone's detecting abilities. If she couldn't sense a ghost staying with her all the time from a very close distance, how perceptive was she really? (And if she didn't sense Paul's presence, it wouldn't bother her and I could have some quality "me" time—win-win!)

Phyllis rose out of the chair, not as swiftly as she once had, and mimicked my headshake even if she didn't realize it. "You're just not trying, Alison," she said as she headed for my back door.

"That is exactly right," I told her. She probably didn't take note of that, either. I'd been in contact with two women who had jobs demanding unusual perception and neither of them had really noticed things I had. Maybe I wasn't giving myself enough credit. But I finally had the house more or less to myself, assuming Katrina was upstairs showering (and she certainly was, I could tell by the sound of my water pipes shaking).

As I got down off the stepstool I'd been using, my phone buzzed and I saw a text message from Josh: *Just got back to the store. Have they figured out anything about the bones in the car yet?*

Not exactly the kind of romantic message one might expect from a husband of less than one year, but I've learned that you can't anticipate people and besides, he's a really good husband even without much practice. I sent back: *Not yet. McElone thinks it wasn't just a burial.*

Why we weren't having this conversation on the phone or when Josh got home from the store tonight was a mystery but I'd decided I wasn't going to be solving any mysteries for a while, if ever, so I didn't pursue it. In a moment my phone buzzed again.

Are you going to investigate?

Okay, that got me concerned so I sent back: *Go sell paint.*

I'll take that for a no, he texted.

You are correct, my friend.

I put the stepstool away in the hall closet outside the library and thought about going up to clean the two guest rooms in use, which wouldn't take very long. But apparently my text conversation was not concluded because the phone buzzed yet again with another message from my husband:

Do you mind if I look into it a little?

Chapter 5

"You want to be an investigator?" My daughter Melissa, having concocted a magnificent dinner of garlic/brown sugar chicken and risotto, had received the usual accolades from Josh, my mother and me, the only other people in the room who could eat it. My father, noting the preparation that had been done in the damaged ceiling beam, was hovering near the top of the doorframe and Paul was sitting in/on the stove while Liss's apple cobbler was baking in the oven. I don't know if Paul gets any of the warmth from the oven but he certainly doesn't feel the way I would if I were perched on top of a working oven, let alone inside it.

Josh, chewing thoughtfully, considered the question and shook his head negatively. "No. I'm not interested in doing this more than the one time, like your mom," he said, knowing perfectly well that I'm only (technically) interested in investigations because of the deal I've made with Paul. "I just find this particular thing fascinating, and I figure I can do some research without getting in the way of the police. I don't expect to solve the case or anything."

"That's good," my mother said. "One private eye in the

family is enough." Mom doesn't mind my doing the occasional investigation, and she actually enjoys hearing about the cases Paul makes me look into, but I think she considers it a dangerous vocation and given my previous experience, I can't argue too strenuously.

Maxie dropped down through the ceiling wearing a painter's smock and cargo shorts. She wasn't carrying any tools but she picked up a pad and pencil from the countertop and started sketching the inside of the kitchen door. Her husband Everett, in fatigues, floated in behind her, watching his wife with some admiration and I thought a tiny bit of tension, which is the proper way to view Maxie. "Don't mind me," she said absently.

"Too late," I said. It's just hard to resist a good straight line sometimes. Maxie didn't appear to hear me and no one else in the room reacted. So I had amused myself. That's half the battle.

I hadn't returned Josh's text when he's suggested he might want to look into the car and the bones in the backyard. The bones had been removed now, thank goodness, and McElone had semi-promised the car would be gone the next day. I didn't want to think about my husband taking up with the strange events and objects that had been dug up but I didn't really know why. Was it that investigation was supposed to be my thing? I didn't think so but it had come to mind. I certainly didn't want to take on this question myself but for reasons I couldn't really pin down I didn't want Josh to do it either. Since I couldn't come up with a decent argument against him getting involved I hadn't answered and wasn't raising any objections now. But I gathered he could sense my lack of enthusiasm.

So Paul wasn't helping when he stepped out of the oven and said, "I think the case definitely needs some closer examination. After seeing what Lt. McElone is researching I believe as she does, that the person in that car probably had not died of natural causes."

"What do you think of teal?" Maxie asked from the upper reaches of the room.

Josh can't see or hear the ghosts. So I didn't have to react to anyone who wasn't currently drawing breath if I didn't want him to be included in the conversation. I'd long ago concluded, however, that such a tactic was rude and since I actually do love this husband (we won't discuss the first unless it's absolutely necessary) I had made it a policy to keep him up to date on posthumous chitchat.

In this case, I didn't have to do much. "For the whole room?" I asked Maxie.

"No, just around the door. I'm thinking about other colors for other walls." Maxie was nothing if not inventive. The last thing I needed in my kitchen.

"Might not be the time, Maxie," Everett suggested. He went ignored. Maxie was focused. She can focus better than almost anyone I know.

I didn't answer her. Melissa, who *can* see and hear the deceased (better than I do, in fact), looked over at Paul. "You think the person in the car was murdered?" she asked.

Josh's eyes took on a focus they hadn't had before and he looked at her. "Who said that?" he asked. "Was it Paul?" Josh knows the ghosts' backstories and he has great respect for Paul's investigative abilities. I guess he figures anyone who could keep me alive through a series of murder investigations must have some idea of what he's doing. I think Paul is an excellent observer and interpreter of information and something of a lousy bodyguard.

Melissa nodded.

Paul glanced at Josh, whom he still didn't know very well despite his being in my life for a few years full-time, and noted his interest. "The lieutenant said it seemed unlikely the person would be buried in a car if no one was trying to hide the body," he said. "She was unable to find any records of a burial in a Lincoln Continental in this area and she went back to the car's date of manufacture in 1977."

I saw Melissa, who was sitting next to Josh, lean over to quietly relay the information Paul was disseminating.

"So that would point to the idea that the person in the car was not buried there willingly," my mother said. Mom watches a lot of true crime shows on television. And she hangs around my house quite a bit. After a while everybody who spends time in the guesthouse thinks they're in a rerun of *Law & Order* and acts accordingly.

"It's a theory," Paul said. "But it fits the limited number of facts we have so far."

"What's this *we* stuff, Kemosabe?" I said. "I told you, I'm out on this one. I have no interest in poking around an old car that was buried under sand for forty years. I have a guesthouse to run and a ceiling beam to replace starting tomorrow."

"It's gonna be a tough one," my father added because he

thought he was being helpful. "Some of the wood is bent at a really interesting angle because of the bullet. This might go up higher than we thought." Dad loves a construction challenge. Dad wasn't helping to do the work or paying for the people who were. I adore my father, but his enthusiasm is sometimes a little . . . impractical from my standpoint.

Josh got up and started clearing plates to put into the dishwasher. "I don't want to involve you, Alison," he said. "But I do want to keep up with what's going on. I think this whole thing is fascinating. I mean, a car buried in the ground with a body in it, and right in our backyard!"

"You make that sound like a good thing," I said. My husband had never really shown this kind of fanboy interest in anything before when I'd been around. He didn't even follow a football team. It was a little disconcerting.

"I don't see the harm in it. Everybody likes a good mystery."

That was a matter of opinion. I liked a good mystery fine when Sherlock Holmes or Miss Marple was solving it. Took so much of the responsibility out of my hands.

"I'm not saying there's harm in it." I picked up more of the utensils and dishes on the counter and walked over to the open dishwasher Josh was filling. "I'm saying I don't want to be the consulting detective this time. I want to be blissfully ignorant of what's going on with this investigation as soon as McElone gets that car out of the ground and hauls it away tomorrow."

Josh stopped in mid-dish-placing. He has a better sense of spatial relationships than I do so he can load a dishwasher more efficiently. And if you ever meet him I urge you to tell him I said so. Better for him unloading it, too. "So I guess I'll just have to hear about anything that goes on through Phyllis at the paper," he said. There was almost a wistful quality in his voice. I felt bad about depriving the poor guy his interest, but not bad enough to start poking around bones in a car.

But Paul had already picked up on the problem and seemed intent on providing an answer. He reached into his pocket—the ghosts can conceal objects in their clothing and they won't become visible until they're removed from said clothing—and pulled out the rudimentary cell phone I'd bought for him after he'd developed enough manual dexterity to use it. Ghosts can't be heard through telephones, but Paul could push buttons and that meant he could text.

He did just that, and in a moment I heard a ping from Josh's phone. He looked a little puzzled and reached into his pocket for it, then checked the screen carefully. "I don't know this number," he said.

"It's Paul," I told him.

Josh's face filled with wonder. "Really?" He'd never communicated directly with one of the ghosts before. He looked at the screen, then up into the ceiling, which is where people who can't see ghosts always think they are. And sometimes they're right. In this case Paul's cell phone was clearly visible much closer to eye level, but Josh wasn't looking there. "That would be really great. Thank you!" he said.

"What would be really great?" Melissa asked.

"Paul says he'd like me to work with him on this case," Josh answered. He sounded sincerely honored. I'd worked

45

with Paul on a number of cases now, and the idea of being honored by the experience was something I'd never actually felt. But who was I to burst my husband's bubble?

Paul texted furiously again for a few moments while Maxie considered the ceiling, which she did by becoming horizontal and looking at it from only a few feet away in her best Michelangelo-doing-that-Sistine-Chapel-thing impression. "Royal blue," she murmured. I would have been seriously alarmed but I knew Maxie's first ideas were rarely the ones she thought were best. She would ruminate on every detail of what she believed was her renovation of my kitchen for weeks and then hopefully decide not to do anything. Hey. I can dream.

Josh's phone sounded again and he looked at the screen. "Yes," he said, "I think we can definitely work out a way to communicate but you're going to have to take the reins on this, Paul. I've never been involved in an investigation before." That was only technically true, in that Josh had been involved with virtually every case Paul had forced me to look into with him since we'd gotten together as adults (we knew each other when we were kids but lost touch for a long time). But he'd never been an *operative*, as Paul liked to say, before. "You'll have to tell me what you want me to do." I was sure Paul would excel at that.

Paul, apparently, agreed. "That shouldn't be a problem," he said aloud. Then he texted something of the same general sentiment to Josh, who appeared absolutely tickled about the whole thing.

"Maybe not navy," Maxie mused to herself. "Puce. Could be puce."

"Maxie," her husband said mildly.

"Oh, really!" she sputtered, and vanished into the ceiling. Everett shook his head affectionately and followed her up. Slowly.

"What time is Tony showing up tomorrow?" Dad said. "Maybe I should stay here tonight and help."

I love my father dearly. He has always been a calming and stable presence in my life. Well, almost always, but we were past that now and despite being dead, he had been quite an asset to the guesthouse the past few years, doing minor repairs and spending time with his granddaughter. And the idea of him spending the night was not entirely unwelcome. But the notion of his helping two living, breathing contractors replace a beam in my ceiling crossed the line into troublesome.

"I don't think we need any flying hammers while the guys are working," I told him. "I appreciate the offer, but only Tony knows you're here and he can't see you either."

"I could supervise," Dad suggested. He is at a loss when he feels he's not being useful.

"Feel free to drop by," I told him, "but you have to let the guys do what they do. If you see a better way to do something—and you might—you have to go through me to communicate it. That okay?"

Dad tilted his head this way and that with a thinking-it-over air about him. "Okay. But I'm making your mother drive me here first thing."

"Then we'd better get going," Mom said. "I don't like getting up early if I haven't had enough sleep."

They were out the door in a few minutes. Josh, being given a play-by-play from Melissa, had started the dishwasher and now looked up again to locate Paul's cell phone. So Josh knew his new mentor was still in the room and he had a general idea of where to look. He looked at the phone, which meant he was conversing with Paul's belt buckle, but it was better than nothing.

"What are my first instructions?" he asked.

Paul stroked his goatee a couple of times and mused aloud. "Well, I'm going to be watching Lt. McElone to see what she finds out," he said. "And I assume Josh will still be going to his store each day as usual."

Liss confirmed that with my husband, who looked positively amazed at the suggestion he might consider leaving his business unattended (or attended for more than an hour at a time by a man in his nineties). "I'll still be at the store during my regular hours," he told Paul. "I'll have internet access and I can go places and talk to people evenings or during quick lunch breaks."

That sort of stunned me because evenings were generally our time together, and Josh took lunch breaks in the store when he wasn't coming home, which he did very rarely. I must have made some kind of sound because everyone looked at me at the same time.

"Sneezed," I said. It seemed to placate them and they went back to what they'd been doing.

Paul sucked in his lips a little, thinking. He started

pressing buttons on his phone and Josh's cell buzzed. He looked at it. Then he looked up in Paul's general direction. "Got ya, boss," he said.

"What does he want you to do?" I asked. I turned toward Paul. "What do you want him to do?"

"I thought you weren't going to be involved," Josh said. His tone wasn't confrontational; he actually seemed confused by my question.

"I'm not, but I'm interested in what you're doing," I answered.

"There's nothing for you to worry about," Paul told me.

Josh, not having heard him, said, "I'll take care of it while I'm at work, Alison. Don't worry." The two men in my life, one to whom I was married and one who was deceased, were starting to act disturbingly similarly.

I cleaned off the countertops and Melissa managed to get close enough that she could talk to me without Josh or Paul hearing what she said. "I'll keep an eye on him," she told me.

"Don't you dare," I whispered. "He's my husband and your stepfather. He deserves our respect."

Liss held her gaze for a moment and then shrugged. "Suit yourself," she said.

When I woke up the next morning the car was gone from the backyard so I thought it was going to be a good day.

I was wrong.

Chapter 6

I happened to glance outside while I was filling the coffee urn the next morning. Josh had just left for Madison Paints with a vague assurance that he wasn't going to do anything dangerous for Paul, something I might not have entirely considered if he hadn't brought it up. What could be dangerous about a guy (or gal) who'd been buried forty years earlier?

Sure enough, the hole Jim . . . somebody had dug in my backyard was still there, but the excavator itself had been moved back about thirty feet and the Lincoln Continental was gone. McElone had been good as her word.

For all the adversarial banter the lieutenant and I bandy back and forth, we do respect each other's professionalism, which meant I thought she was a good detective and she thought I owned a hotel for tourists. Respect can have a lot of different permutations. But given that I'd expressed some skepticism at her ability—or willingness—to get the car out of my yard promptly, I thought the fact that she deserved acknowledgement, so I got out my phone and called her.

"What can I do for you?" McElone has the ability to make any sentence sound like it is uttered in irritation. That might happen only when she talks to me. I should pay more attention when she's speaking with others.

"I just wanted to thank you," I told her.

"For what?" She seemed to think I was setting her up for a joke.

"For taking the car out of my backyard," I said. "I'm not being facetious. I really do appreciate you taking my needs into account and working to get that thing out quickly. Thank you."

McElone must not have had her first cup of coffee yet that morning. She sounded confused. "The car in your backyard is gone?" she asked.

That didn't sound good. "Sure is," I answered.

"I didn't do that." I was right; it wasn't good.

"Well you can bet your last dollar that *I* didn't pull the thing out of the ground," I said.

There was a noticeable pause. "I'm on my way," McElone said.

She arrived eight minutes later, which indicated to me she'd had the flashing lights working on her car the whole way before she turned onto my block. McElone pulled the car all the way into my driveway, which gave her quicker access to my backyard and effectively blocked in my ancient Volvo wagon until she left. I guessed that didn't matter. I probably wasn't going anywhere anyway.

I met her at the site of the crater, which was just as large and just as deep but had no product of the Ford Motor Company living in it anymore. McElone did not look happy, even more than she usually didn't look happy. Her eyes were narrow and her lips were pursed. She was trying to figure this one out.

All I knew for sure was that I wasn't going to be much help.

"You didn't hear anything last night?" the lieutenant asked by way of greeting.

I handed her the Styrofoam cup of coffee I'd brought with me and she nodded thanks. "Nope," I said. "I slept like a log, assuming logs sleep, and nobody said anything to me about it this morning. Of course, not everyone is awake yet, but Josh left for the store and I got to talk to him. He didn't mention hearing construction equipment moving around in the night."

"Your daughter didn't hear anything?" McElone has been around my family long enough to know who the most reliable member might be.

"She's probably just waking up now," I said. "I can ask her to come down and talk to you."

McElone nodded again, this time indicating that was what I should do. She took a sip of the coffee and warmed her hands on the cup. November mornings on the Jersey Shore can be pretty nippy. Or it can be seventy degrees. You just don't ever know.

I texted Melissa and she responded almost immediately saying she'd be down in a minute and asking why the lieutenant was here. I didn't answer, figuring that would get her downstairs faster. Teenage girls can be a trifle listless when they first wake up, which I know because I used to be a teenage girl.

There are days I'm not actually certain I woke up from one of those deep sleeps. Maybe this was all a dream.

The lieutenant walked from the hole to the excavator, which was parked and docile at the moment. She pointed to the sand in between. "It just backed up the one time," she said. "There wasn't a bunch of back-and-forth."

"What does that tell you?" I asked.

"I don't know yet."

Before I even turned my head I knew Paul had joined us on the beach. Not having to worry about the temperature at all he was dressed in his usual jeans and t-shirt. At the very least he could have *pretended* to be cold; was that too much to ask?

"I see the Continental has been removed," he said. "But I don't see a tow truck from the county. How did the lieutenant get it out of here so quietly?"

I really wasn't interested in scaring McElone by letting her know a ghost was nearby. She does her best to ignore that type of thing when she drops by, which she does at an alarming rate for a police detective. "So how do you think they got the car out of here?" I asked her.

"They?" Paul said. "The police didn't tow the car? Interesting." He dropped down through the sand and stopped at a point where he was visible only from the shoulders up. "Not much in the way of tracks, either by foot or vehicle. This is baffling." I'd rarely seen his face look so happy.

McElone shrugged. "My best guess is that whoever did this took the car because they didn't want us to find something out, and they were able to smooth over the sand after they left. What's crazy is that nobody saw or heard anything."

"Yes." Paul was agreeing with a woman who couldn't hear him. "Certainly one of us should have been vigilant on the scene. I'll check with Maxie to see if she or Everett noticed anything." And with that he vanished up and into the house in his search for what would be a grumpy Maxie. Ghosts don't seem to sleep, but she still hates getting up in the morning.

That is usually true of my daughter, but Melissa appeared at the French doors and came out quickly, not even carrying a cup of coffee with a smaller amount of milk than she used to drink. She approached McElone and me and assessed the situation immediately.

"Somebody took the car," she said.

"We noticed," I told her. "Did you see or hear anything last night?"

Liss shook her head. "No. And my room is the closest one to the back of the house." It was true; the attic ran all the way from the front to the rear, but Liss's bed is nearest to the beach side of the house because she likes to hear the sound of the waves when she's trying to sleep. It had been chilly the night before so her window probably hadn't been open.

McElone scowled; she hates it when answers don't supply any new information.

"I'm going to have to get this area cordoned off," she mused. "I don't want the scene being contaminated any more than it already is." She reached for a cell phone in her pocket.

I held up a hand, possibly annoyed at the use of the word

contaminated. "Hang on, lieutenant," I said. "You want to section off this area of my property *again?*"

"We'll need some crime scene technicians out here to get as much evidence as they can," she said, sounding surprised. "You do understand that a crime has been committed here, right?"

Paul arrived from his foray into the house without Maxie or Everett, which he did not immediately explain. "It makes perfect sense, Alison," he said. Just for that I didn't look at him. But Melissa did, and she seemed to be in agreement with the two of them, which irked me more than the contamination.

"I'm already stuck with all this construction equipment back here," I, okay, whined. "Yesterday I had a car with a dead person in it sticking out of an enormous hole and people couldn't walk back here. Then the dead person left, which was better, and this morning—only half an hour ago—I thought you'd taken the car away too, and that was my one moment of relief. Now you want to let a gaggle of cops loose back here for who knows how long and I can't let my guests walk on the beach like it says in the brochures. How is that fair?"

The three of them stared at me and I could tell they were just trying to find a way to stop the crazy lady from talking anymore. Finally McElone said, "Gaggle?"

I didn't have a response. I didn't have an answer to any of it. I had guests—admittedly just a few—and I had to be a hostess at a beach house with, for the moment, no beach. At least there were still ghosts. I turned my back and walked back up to the porch and through the French doors into the house.

Adam Cosgrove, in a sweatshirt with Oberlin College's logo on it, was just reaching the landing on the first floor when I made it to the den. "Good morning, Alison," he said. He looked into the den expectantly. "Is there coffee?"

Rats! I'd gotten caught up in the drama outside and hadn't finished taking care of the urns. "Give me just a minute, Adam," I said. "I'm really sorry. I was dealing with . . . never mind. It's not your problem." I headed for the kitchen.

Adam was protesting that it wasn't a problem and he'd just head out to the Stud Muffin for breakfast but I felt I'd let my guests down and that is the worst feeling you can have as an innkeeper. But his forgiveness was more appreciated when I made it into the kitchen again.

Tony Mandorisi and his brother Vic had already covered my center island with a drop cloth and looked up from the blueprints they had spread out on top of it when I walked in. Their van was visible through the kitchen window. Tony smiled. "Alison." Tony and I go way back. I actually introduced him to Jeannie, now his wife and the mother of his two children. But he still likes me. "Ready for some inconvenience?"

Since I felt I already had some inconvenience, it seemed an irrelevant question, but my mind was fixed on making my guests happy. "I was going to get the coffee urns going," I said. Surveying the kitchen and the obstacle course of tools and equipment the Mandorisis had strewn around it, I added, "Can I do that?"

Tony looked a little startled at my unusual lack of

conviviality, but he looked around. "We brought a Box of Joe from Dunkin Donuts," he said. "Is that good enough?"

I looked behind me to the kitchen door. Adam hadn't followed me in. "Adam," I called. "Is Dunkin Donuts okay?"

There was no answer so I walked to the door and opened it. Adam was nowhere to be seen, undoubtedly on his way to the Stud Muffin even as we spoke.

"I guess," I said to Tony. Great. I already didn't serve food at the guesthouse. Now I wouldn't be able to provide coffee and tea in the morning until Tony and Vic had finished the work I actually wanted them to do. And my guests couldn't walk on the beach because McElone was in the process of calling in the cast of *CSI: Harbor Haven* to cordon off my backyard.

Tony walked over and put a hand on my shoulder, so I turned to face him and saw he looked concerned. "You okay?" he asked gently.

It was a good question. "I don't know," I said. I wasn't going to cry. That was key. I would not cry. I wasn't that kind of woman. You know, who cries.

"What's the problem?" Tony said. "Can I help?" He's a sweetheart, really.

"There's nothing you can do," I said, quite noticeably not crying. "It's just that it's been a really long day."

"It's only seven-thirty in the morning," Tony said.

And that's when I started crying.

Chapter 7

I had managed to get myself back together before Melissa walked into the kitchen and gave Tony a hug. Of course she had remembered the Mandorisis would be here working today even if I hadn't. Tony, who had tried valiantly to calm me down when all I really needed was the release, was being wary of me and went to work with his brother on their preparations for the beam replacement.

Liss gave me a look of concern and asked if I was all right. No doubt the puffy red circles around my eyes had given me away. "I'm okay," I said. "Feeling a little allergic. Is Lester up in your room?"

Lester is Melissa's puppy and always will be a puppy because he's a ghost. Liss adopted him a while back and even though Lester, a happy little dog, is no longer visible to most of humanity, I can not only see and hear him but be affected by his fur as well. I'm allergic to dogs. But this time I knew Lester wasn't the source of my watery eyes; I was.

"Yeah, he's not going anywhere," Liss assured me. "I don't think he knows he can walk through walls. You sure you're all right?"

"Absolutely. Go get ready for school." It's a useful mantra for the parent who's lying to her daughter.

Liss scowled at me a little, but not because she didn't want to go to school. She liked the social interaction even if classes—in which she excelled, thank you—were not at the top of her list of fun things to do. Now she knew I was evading her concern and she didn't like it, but couldn't prove anything was up.

She took a cup of coffee from Tony and Vic's box (with their permission) and maneuvered her way to the refrigerator where she could find milk to add to it. As she walked to the kitchen door she asked, "Do you want me to tell Josh what's going on with the car in the hole?"

That was an odd question. "I can tell him when he gets home," I said. "Go get ready."

"I'm already dressed, Mom. Getting ready will take five minutes."

Tony and Vic, possibly anticipating another female emotional moment, leaned over their blueprint a little more intensely.

"We're getting out of your hair," I called to the Mandorisi brothers. "Let me know if there's anything you need."

I walked out of the kitchen with Melissa right behind me. And was very surprised to find Paul in the den when I got there, floating almost exactly in the middle of the large room and stroking his goatee enough to indicate to me the mystery of the vanishing car had somehow gotten more baffling while I was having an emotional catharsis.

Melissa also noticed Paul's body language (without the

benefit of actually having a body) and looked up at him. "Did we miss something, Paul?" she asked.

Paul's concentration was jarred; he looked down at Melissa and seemed to notice, suddenly, that he was very close to the ceiling. He lowered himself to a more neck-friendly level for us. "I'm sorry, Melissa; I was thinking about something else. What did you say?"

"You seemed like you were thinking about a case," I said. "Is it something with the car in the backyard that isn't in the backyard anymore?" I had promised myself I'd have no involvement in investigating the questions related to that Continental and here I was initiating a conversation. I should probably have gone down the hallway and straightened the movie room. Adam and Steve had spent the previous evening watching a 1985 Glenn Close movie Maxie especially enjoyed.

"Yes. The lieutenant found something that appeared to puzzle her when she examined the scene of the digging," Paul said. "She's out there now overseeing the crime scene investigators. They're sealing off the area." Swell.

"What did she find?" Melissa asked.

Again Paul seemed distracted. "What? Oh, yes. She discovered what appeared to be bicycle tracks, although the sand had clearly been smoothed over with a rake or broom after the car had been extracted and removed from the area. But what was truly baffling was a small pouch made of velvet that had been left behind in the excavation crater."

* * *

"You mean there was a pouch in the hole?" I asked. I thought that was what Paul had been saying, but he was saying it in the original Paul and that made things more difficult to understand to us foreigners.

"Yes, and when the lieutenant examined it she was quite startled, if I was reading her properly," he answered. "Of course I couldn't ask her about what she'd found and I wasn't able to get close enough to see the contents of the pouch for myself before she had placed it in an evidence bag and put it in her pocket."

"Did she say anything when the crime scene people showed up?" Melissa asked. "I guess she didn't say what was in the pouch or you would know, right?"

Paul lowered down a little more to look Liss in the eye. She's not little like she used to be, but the ghost had started pretty far up in a room with high ceilings. "You're correct, Melissa. I saw the lieutenant and the bag over to the CS investigator, but she didn't say anything other than to suggest it be placed into an evidence file. But there was one thing."

He was trying his darnedest to make us feed him straight lines. It was my turn, I guessed. "What thing?" Not my wittiest bon mot ever but I still hadn't had any coffee today.

"I'm not sure the evidence bag the lieutenant gave the other officer was the same one she had pocketed. I don't think it had the velvet pouch inside."

That was weird. "You think McElone is withholding evidence in an investigation?" I said. "I can't believe that."

Paul shook his head, I think in wonder of befuddlement. "Knowing the lieutenant I would agree it's extremely uncharacteristic of her. I wasn't paying very close attention when she reached for the evidence bag but I believe it was from the same pocket in which she'd placed the one with the pouch. Perhaps she just retrieved the wrong bag."

"Did the lieutenant bag any other evidence while you were out there?" Melissa asked Paul. "I didn't see her pick anything up when I was outside."

Again Paul shook his head. "I do not believe I saw her tag any other evidence."

I was thinking about the movie room again and realized that should be my priority. "Have I mentioned that I'm not involved in this little inquiry you two seem to be doing?" I said. "I'm a guesthouse operator. That's my job."

Melissa's eyes took on an air of annoyance one sees in a teenager . . . about every ten minutes. Parents are so inconvenient. But she was usually more tolerant of my obvious stupidity, being a more sensible and reasonable girl than I ever was with my mother, certainly. "You don't have to do anything," she said. "I think it's interesting that this happened in our backyard. Nobody says you have to." I believe that may be the most harshly my daughter has ever spoken to me.

So I resumed my juvenile behavior from before and left the den, heading down the hall to the movie room. Neither Paul nor Melissa made any effort at all to stop me, and I wasn't sure how I felt about that. But passing the library I happened to glance through the window that looked out on the beach and saw McElone heading toward the driveway, where I knew her Harbor Haven Police Department-issued Chevy Impala (because you'd never think *that* was a cop car, would you?)

was parked. She had no doubt stayed long enough to oversee the crew currently making my backyard uninhabitable and was heading back to her station.

Should I go back and tell Paul? He'd want to hitch a ride with McElone to observe her day of investigating. It would be a way to get him out of the house and thereby keep me from having to hear more about the mystery of the disappearing car. But it would also mean that Paul wouldn't be available for at the very least the morning spook show, and even with only three guests that would put me at a disadvantage.

So was I going to put the needs of my guesthouse above the interest of my friend, however dead he might be? Could I be that selfish?

Yeah. I could.

I walked down to the movie room and found it almost neater than it had been before Adam and Steve had decided to spend a few hours there the evening before. These two guests were so polite they'd actually carried their own popcorn bags back to the kitchen and disposed of them. There were no stray kernels or butter stains on the floor or the loveseat they'd used. I wouldn't have been surprised if they'd vacuumed the rug after leaving, but I probably would have heard that. I'd thank them later for their consideration, even when they were on holiday. (I'm not British; I just didn't want to rhyme *consideration* with *vacation*.)

This left me with a rather unusual conundrum: I really didn't have to spend much time straightening up the movie room. I didn't want to disturb Katrina or Steve if they were still in their rooms, so cleaning upstairs was sort of off the table now. I supposed I could go out for groceries now that McElone's car wasn't blocking mine in the driveway, but I didn't really need very much.

It's not often in an innkeeper's life that there isn't much to do, so this was the exception rather than the rule. I decided I'd be a nice friend and go tell Paul that McElone was leaving or had left. I didn't see her through the side window of the movie room, where the driveway is visible, but the angle was wrong to be certain.

I had been callous about Paul's feelings and should correct my mistake. So I walked back to the den but Paul and Melissa were gone. Liss had probably gone upstairs to finish her preparation for school. Paul had either caught up with the lieutenant or gone elsewhere to work on his investigation. He was absolutely focused when there was a mystery to solve.

Still, in my house it's really difficult to be alone for long even when you work at it. I was a little surprised to see Maxie descending through the ceiling in the den, wearing the trench coat she uses to conceal objects she's carrying through walls or in this case, floors. Maxie doesn't usually show up until minutes before the morning spook show and even then she complains about having to be active so early in the morning. The show wouldn't start for another couple of hours.

She was barely in the room before the trench coat vanished and I saw she was carrying her beloved laptop computer, the one she uses to do internet research when Paul is working a case or to watch television programs when he's not.

But she didn't seem to be doing either at the moment. She opened the laptop and held it in midair, typing madly with her right hand and staring, as one might expect, at the wounded ceiling beam that Tony and Vic were noisily preparing to attack from the other side of the kitchen door.

"Aren't you in the wrong room?" I asked. "You're doing work in the kitchen."

Maxie didn't look up from her screen. "The work being done in the kitchen is going to affect the way this side looks too," she said, her voice all business. "I have to take into account the impact on both sides. Besides, the kitchen is crowded." Maxie sort of resents Tony for not requiting a crush she had on him a few years ago despite the fact that she moved on to Everett, a man more suited to her because he 1. wasn't married to someone else and 2. wasn't more alive than her. So she either stays out of the room when he's there or makes pointed comments about him, knowing he can't hear her. For his part, Tony is fine with Paul in the room and a little nervous when he knows Maxie is about. He's an intelligent man.

"You'll have to deal with them being here," I informed her.

She waved a hand to declare it irrelevant. Maxie was concentrating. I hadn't seen this side of her very often, and wondered if it was what she was like when she was working as a living designer.

Melissa called from the front room that her ride to school was here and was out the door before I could wish her a good day. Life is so full when you're thirteen and then you realize you really weren't doing all that much.

Tony opened the kitchen door and Maxie's trench coat reappeared as she zoomed into the ceiling again. I guess she wasn't *that* focused.

"Just wanted to let you know we're going to be bracing the ceiling with a bunch of two-by-fours," Tony said. "It's just inside the door, which you know, so you're not going to have access to the kitchen for a while."

"How long's a while?" I asked.

Tony scratched his head. "I'll know better when I get in there, but at least the rest of the day," he answered.

So I couldn't use my backyard and now my kitchen. It seemed the whole property was divorcing itself from me from the back going forward. I probably moaned a little involuntarily, even though been preparing for this for weeks. "You do what you have to do," I told him.

"Something I think you might want to see," Tony said. He gestured toward the kitchen. "Before the door is off limits."

I followed him toward my kitchen's swinging door. Before he pushed it Tony said, "Incoming," just to make sure we didn't hit Vic, particularly if he was standing on a ladder.

"Okay," his brother said from inside.

Tony pushed on the door and swung it into the kitchen, holding it open for me. He's old school chivalrous. But as soon as I stepped through, I could see he'd been trying to protect himself, too, from whatever reaction I might have when I saw the state of my kitchen after the Mandorisi brothers had prepared it.

Everything was covered in clear plastic tarpaulins. They weren't drop cloths, because they weren't made of cloth. You could see through them but that wasn't the point; they were thick enough to protect against the onslaught of dust and debris that would result from the partial removal of the wooden beam and its replacement with something sturdier, which Tony and I had agreed would be a steel beam.

I had anticipated the covers because I've done work in homes before and I spent some time working in a home improvement superstore and a lumberyard before I bought the guesthouse. And my father had sometimes taken me to work when he was fixing people's houses. I'd done a good deal of work on the guesthouse.

I wasn't prepared for the impact it would have on my emotions when I saw all the small appliances and other items I'd left out on the countertops moved to one table in the back of the room and covered in more tarps. It just so wasn't my kitchen—and I don't even cook. I didn't feel like crying again but I think I did gasp. It's never the same when it's your house being disrupted because you know how hard you worked to get it rupted to begin with. The fact that Tony and Vic had, understandably, taken down part of the ceiling drywall to allow better access to the affected beam was not helping.

Still, I held it together. "What did you want to show me?" I asked.

"We found something when we were cleaning out the work area," Tony said.

Vic, who looked amused, was standing near the refrigerator, which was also covered in plastic. The floors were covered with paper and Tony had hung a protective barrier of plastic over the kitchen door but hadn't attached it yet because he'd wanted me to be able to walk inside. "Yeah," Vic said. "We found something." He sounded like a kid with a secret he was desperate to tell.

"Okay." I had enough going on without having to play guessing games.

Tony understood that, so he walked to the nearest part of the kitchen counter and found a small object I couldn't see. He picked it up and brought it to me. "This was taped to a part of the beam that was a few inches behind the wall board," he said. "I think it might be important."

He handed me the object, which was a small pouch with a drawstring holding it closed. It was covered in dust as you'd expect from something that had spent any time at all inside my walls. And it was made of a velvet material, much like the one Paul had said he'd seen McElone pocket before she left.

"Open it," Tony said.

That seemed a logical step. I undid the drawstring and held out my left hand. There was clearly something small and not terribly heavy inside the pouch. So I turned the pouch over and it fell onto my palm.

What sat there appeared to be an emerald. A large emerald. Okay, a *very* large emerald. It was green and big. That's what I'm saying.

"Yup, we found something, all right," Vic said.

Chapter 8

"Where was this found, exactly?" McElone wanted to know.

Given the nature of the discovery the Mandorisi brothers had made, McElone had overcome her resistance to entering my house and was standing in what had once been my kitchen, looking up at the gaping hole in my ceiling. It was like looking behind the scenes at a theme park and seeing how the magic is made. Who wants that?

Tony stood on the second rung of a ladder he'd set up to access the hole in the ceiling and reached his arm up to illustrate. "We were working in here just to clear out the area," he began.

"Please don't touch it again," McElone said. "That area's probably already got more fingerprints than I've collected in my entire career."

Tony withdrew his hand in a spasm, not wanting to disobey the lieutenant. "Anyway, we were reaching in there and found that pouch."

"We?" McElone asked. "Which one of you found it?"

Vic stepped forward. "I did," he said. "I was pulling down some wallboard and felt it next to the part of the beam that the bullet didn't splinter." I sort of wished he hadn't brought up the bullet, even though McElone certainly knew the details of that incident. I just didn't think she needed a reminder just at the moment.

"It was just sitting there?" she asked Vic.

"No. It was taped to a piece of the beam, so the top was attached and the bottom was just sort of dangling. I didn't know what it was so I pulled it down and that's when we found the jewel inside."

McElone looked at the pouch, which was sitting on a makeshift workbench the Mandorisis had set up across two sawhorses. She put on a pair of latex gloves from her pocket and looked inside the pouch.

"Looks like an emerald," she said.

What was she expecting, a lump of coal? "I told you that when I called," I reminded her.

"I'm saying it looks like an emerald," the lieutenant said again. "I'll have to find out if it's a real one or not." She looked at Vic. "What kind of tape was holding it up?"

Vic shined a flashlight into the mangled remains of my ceiling. "Up there, see?" he said. "I don't want to touch it again."

"You're right not to," McElone assured him. She took a step forward to see into the hole more clearly. "Looks like packing tape, like for shipping."

Vic nodded. "Yeah. The clear kind."

That didn't seem to make McElone happy; her face scrunched a little but she appeared to be thinking, not annoyed. "Okay."

"Why would something like that be in my ceiling, lieutenant?" I thought maybe if I could get her talking she would tell me about the pouch she'd found outside in my backyard and this whole thing would start to make some sense.

But then, I think a lot of things. "I have no idea yet," McElone answered, "and if I did, I most likely wouldn't tell you."

"Can we keep working up here?" Tony asked.

"Not until I get a crime scene team in to look it over," she said.

I looked out my back window. "There's still one on my beach," I pointed out.

"Yeah. I can get a couple of them in here to get fingerprints and pictures. Shouldn't take more than an hour or two."

Tony grimaced a little but said nothing. I knew he had taken a serious discount on this job because it was for me, and he had scheduled today and part of tomorrow to do it as quickly as possible. Tomorrow's work would be mostly replacing the wallboard in the ceiling, something I could do myself if he and Vic had to be elsewhere on a real paying job.

"Lieutenant," I said, "I appreciate that this is a crime scene and everything, but do we really even know that this stone is part of a crime? I mean, you already have half the Harbor Haven police force digging up what's left of my backyard. These guys are working here today because they're being nice to me, and any delay will cost them in work they could be doing for people who have actual money."

Lt. McElone is, at her core, a reasonable person. She has respect for people who do honest work and understands that police business in regular lives can be disruptive. She narrowed her eyes a little because I'd sort of challenged her decision, but said, "I'll get them out of here as quickly as I can." She looked over at Tony. "For you."

She turned before I could be snide and walked through the kitchen door, which took some doing around all the protective sheeting Tony had taped up (with blue gaffer's tape if anyone was wondering) on my walls and windows. She left to go talk to the team working on the *other* major crime scene on my property.

Tony looked over at me and shrugged. "I thought I was giving you good news," he said.

I put my hand on his shoulder. "You were. It just was in this house, where everything turns weird."

Just to prove the point, Paul came phasing in through the wall and assessed the room. "What's happened in here?" he asked.

I don't like to talk directly to the ghosts when there are "civilians" in the room, especially someone like Vic who isn't really acquainted with the, let's say, peculiarities of my home. So I didn't answer Paul directly. "How long do you think you can wait to get back to work on the ceiling beam and not lose your entire week?" I asked Tony.

Through the window I saw McElone point at the house to two of the crime scene people, who probably hadn't had this much work all at one time in their lives. Harbor Haven doesn't lend itself to major crimes except when a ghost comes and asks Paul to investigate . . . anything.

"Maybe the best thing is for us to get out of the way and

work on another job," Tony answered. "You can text me when the cops clear out of the room and we'll get back here as fast as we can. How's that?" It was a polite way of saying that he was anxious to get to something that would help pay his bills.

"That makes the most sense," I said. "But you'll come back as soon as I call, right?"

Tony smiled. "As soon as we *can*. Don't worry. Jeannie will kill me if you don't get this done as fast as possible." Vic was already packing up some of their tools behind him.

They were gone before I could muse on the interconnection of humans and their actions toward each other, which probably would have taken a decent period of time, I realize now.

Paul rose up through the floor just as Tony and Vic were leaving, plastic sheeting remaining in place through the room. No sense in setting that all up again when they came back. Paul likes to ruminate on his problems in the basement, away from the traffic particularly when we had more guests than I did today. He looked like he'd been thinking for a while. His hair was a little disheveled compared to his usual look, which indicated to me that he'd run his hands through it. A breeze really isn't going to affect a ghost's appearance at all, and they can't feel it. I've seen Maxie wear t-shirts outside during a blizzard. Of course, I'm not sure she wouldn't have done that when she was alive, too.

"Is there construction going on?" Paul asked. He tends to ignore some of the more mundane details of my life, like anything that doesn't relate to an investigation or a spook show he needs to attend.

Before I could answer the back door opened and two police officers, a man and a woman, entered. They weren't in uniform but instead in the jumpsuits worn by crime scene investigators and they had already equipped themselves with latex gloves. I thought it was a bit much but they have their protocols.

"I'm Sergeant Menendez," the woman said, showing me her badge in a folding wallet. "This is Officer Lassen. I'm told there a crime scene we need to examine?"

"Another one?" Paul had immediately perked up when the cops walked in. He loves cops. In my house he has gotten to see and interact with them far too often for my taste, but it always invigorates him.

"Yes," I said to both Menendez and Paul. "Right here." I pointed to the rather obvious crime scene. I was hoping the cops were better at their jobs than that opening gambit might have suggested.

"I see," Menendez said, getting close enough to do exactly that.

"The police already examined that area." Paul sounded a little disappointed.

"Is this where the emerald was discovered?" Lassen asked, also closing in on the smaller of the two enormous holes that had recently been opened on my property.

"Emerald?" Paul's enthusiasm was rising and dropping like people on one of the serious roller coasters at Great Adventure in Jackson. He rose up to look into the bullet-caused damage to my ceiling beam, which still looked pretty sturdy despite the splintering. Maybe I should just cover it over with wallboard and forget the whole thing.

"Yes. Lt. McElone already questioned the two contractors who found it. I wasn't in the room at the time."

Menendez climbed up the ladder Tony had conveniently left by the scene of the . . . crime? She stuck her head into the hole while holding a small flashlight to better see inside. She pretty much had to go through Paul to get there but didn't know it, and Paul didn't seem to care. Who was I to object?

"There's some tape attached to the beam," she said. "I take it that was what held the small fabric pouch in place."

"That's what the Mandorisis said," I told her.

"What's a Mandorisi?" Lassen asked.

"A small fabric pouch like the one I saw the lieutenant put in her pocket?" Paul asked. He knew there was no way I was going to answer him with the two officers present but he just talks like everybody can hear him. Look, each person has a way of coping with being dead; that's Paul's.

"Those are the contractors working on the beam," I said. "Tony and Vic Mandorisi. And I'm hoping you guys might be able to get done fairly quickly in here so they can come back and do the repair. I mean, not to rush you, but could you maybe rush?"

"That's going to depend on what we find," Menendez said. She wasn't showing any immediate annoyance at what I'd said, but I figured I'd probably sounded more obnoxious than I really am. "The more that's here the more we have to document."

"Well, that could have been there a long time, right? It might not have been a crime at all, or one that has a statute of limitations that ran out?" I knew that wasn't going to be true, but I wasn't supposed to officially be aware of the pouch McElone was carrying around in her pocket so I could make myself sound as stupid as possible.

Lassen, who was holding the ladder for Menendez but also filming her with his phone, looked sharply at me. "Why are you concerned with the statute of limitations?" he asked.

Wait; was I making myself a suspect? And if so, in what? "I'm not," I said, because it was actually true. "I'm just worried about the beam in my ceiling."

"It's not coming down anytime soon," Menendez said. "I can see why you want to have it fixed, though." She looked down at Lassen. "Fresh packing tape, Jason."

"I don't have any. I can check in the car."

"No, that's what I'm finding up here. This thing wasn't in here very long." She removed the tape with a pair of tweezers I suppose she had in her pocket and placed it inside a plastic evidence bag that must have come from the same place. The woman was a veritable Inspector Gadget. She handed the bag down to Lassen, who held it in his latex-gloved left hand.

I felt the way I do when the guy comes to fix the dishwasher: Should I watch the two cops and be available in case they had questions, or should I leave them to their work and go take care of my own business? Actually, I usually stay for the appliance repairman because I like to know how things work. In this case, I really didn't see any utility to my learning about forensic procedure. Besides, Paul, with his head completely obscured in the ceiling, could fill me in later if there was anything at all I would want to know.

I couldn't imagine what that would be. It seemed to me that in this case, the less I knew about it the better. Let Paul have his fun, even if he'd missed out on trailing McElone today. I felt bad enough about that to drive him into town later if he wanted to pick up the lieutenant's trail.

I started to back away toward the kitchen door (which was still thankfully operational) when Menendez said, "Are you leaving?"

So I froze in my tracks. "Do you need me for something?" I asked. "I can stay." Which response would make me seem less guilty? Menendez had a way of making me feel like I'd done something wrong despite my knowing I hadn't. I was pretty sure, anyway.

"No. I just wanted to make sure you didn't get in the way of the ladder." Okay, so maybe some of that inferred guilt was in my own mind. "Go ahead."

So I did. I noticed Paul looking down at me with an expression of complete wonder at how I could tear myself away from such a fascinating spectacle, but somehow I managed and pushed through the kitchen door to the den. I figured that since I hadn't been able to get the coffee and tea urns out for the guests (and since I could hardly finish off the Mandorisis' Box of Joe), the least I could do would be to drive over to Dunkin Donuts and pick up some coffee, decaf and tea for the three people (well, two now that Adam was at Stud Muffin) I was hosting that week.

I'd gone up to my bedroom to get the right jacket for this

weather when my phone buzzed. Josh was texting from his store: *Melissa says the cops are still there. Lt. pocketed evidence?* That was all I needed: my husband trying to figure the motives of a police detective from inside a paint store.

I'm sure she knows what she's doing, I sent back.

She says the car is gone and the cops didn't do it.

I'm not doing this, I reminded him.

Paul hasn't texted. Ask if he still wants me to help. Shouldn't he have been worrying about matte finish versus flat, or something?

I didn't know how to continue this conversation. The thing about texting is that people have lost sight of what it's supposed to be—a way to send one message quickly. Instead they use it to substitute for a telephone conversation, and it only takes about eight times longer.

Still, I didn't want to call Josh back. I didn't want to have this conversation in any form, even by carrier pigeon or telepathy (although telepathy would be cool). Maybe the best thing to do would be to ignore the whole thing and hope it went away. That had never worked before but there had to be a first time for everything.

Paul's not here now, I sent. (I couldn't just not answer my own husband.) *Let you know when I can talk to him.*

Now, that should have been the end of it, at least for now. But I'd never seen Josh quite as worked up about something as he'd seemed when talking about this thing with the car in the backyard. If I told him about the emerald, I was afraid he'd close up the store, come home wearing a deerstalker and carrying a magnifying glass and start saying things like, "Elementary, my dear Kerby." And the last thing I needed was my husband addressing me by my last name.

But he did persist. *Where's Paul?*

I could have lied but I'd already been through one marriage that had a lot of hiding and falsehoods and that had ended with me referring to the father of my child as The Swine. So I try to avoid obfuscation with Josh. *He's got his head up in the ceiling and can't be reached.* That would settle matters, surely.

I picked up the jacket and walked downstairs to the front room, but I didn't make it out the door fast enough. Lassen walked out of the kitchen and called me from across the room. "Um . . . ma'am?" I'd liked it better when Officer Canton had called me "miss." I stopped and looked at Lassen.

"Yes?" It seemed the thing to say.

"Can you come back in here a minute? Sergeant Menendez has something she wants to ask you about."

Those were not the words I had been hoping to hear, but I didn't see a choice. I couldn't make a run for it or try to shoot my way to freedom. I don't own a gun and I've always been a lousy runner. In gym class I used to run backwards so Mrs. Hedgeman would understand why I was so slow. It saved tons of explanation.

Instead, I trudged back into the kitchen, where I found Menendez down from the ladder and Paul stroking his goatee at record rates. None of that was encouraging.

"Ms. Kerby," Menendez said, pointing vaguely upward, "what happened to this ceiling beam?"

Oh, so *that* was it. This would be easy to explain. "I

thought Lt. McElone had told you about that," I said. "It was hit by a gunshot a number of months ago." I knew exactly how many months it had been but I was trying to show how casual I could be about it because . . . I'm still working on that.

Menendez seemed oddly puzzled by my answer. "A gunshot," she said. "*One* gunshot."

Was this in some way a test of my memory? "Yeah. One gunshot." I was the one who had been shot at; you'd think my account of the event could go unquestioned.

"Then something very strange is going on here," Menendez said. "Because there are four bullets here."

Chapter 9

"Four bullets?" Josh looked at me with some confusion. "How could there be four bullets in the beam? I mean, I wasn't there, but I know there was only one gunshot because that's what you and everybody else told me."

"The bullets weren't all in the beam," I said as he took off his pants. Josh was changing after working at the store all day, and was about to get into the shower. I sat on our bed watching him and (mostly) telling him about the events of the day. "Menendez said three of them were just stuck in the cavity next to the beam. She was pretty sure they weren't even the same caliber as the one that had lodged in there and made me give all this money to Tony and Vic." Even with the discount the repair was costing me more than spare change I could find in sofa cushions. And I've looked.

Josh pulled the t-shirt over his head and looked back at me. "So they're not from the gun that got fired at you."

"No, probably not. Everything's in the lab now. Who knows how long it'll take until all the forensics come back. Personally, I'm trying not to think about it."

I was the only one doing that. Melissa had heard the whole

story from Paul when she got home from school. I won't say I'd decided not to tell her about it, but Paul had pretty much cut me off at the pass before I had a chance to make a decision on the subject. Having ghosts in the house, despite what you might have heard, is inconvenient.

Liss was all in on investigating with Paul until I reminded her that eighth grade required her attention on such subjects as pre-algebra, American history, Earth science and English, and she had homework in all of them. She grumbled something under her breath it was probably better than I didn't hear and stomped off to her room. We were having pizza for dinner. She punishes me by not cooking (not that she could have tonight anyway, but it's the gesture that counts).

Paul, meanwhile, had texted Josh but not given him many details. He'd tasked my husband (I was learning now) with finding out from Bill Harrelson and Jim . . . you know . . . exactly what would have been involved in removing a rather large vehicle from a hole in the ground and how it could be done without anyone in a close proximity seeing or hearing anything. He also wanted Josh to talk to Tony and Vic—who had started work well after lunch when Menendez and Canton had finally left after making the hole in my ceiling only twice as large as it had been before. Paul figured Josh would have a rapport with the working guys and he was right, but Josh hadn't had a chance to talk to any of them yet, he'd said.

"This thing just keeps getting more weird," Josh said. He put a terrycloth robe on but didn't tie it closed and picked a towel out of a drawer as he moved toward the attached bath.

"So far every time I thought we were going to get an answer we got six more questions."

"Welcome to Paul's world," I said. Josh walked away with a grin on his face and closed the bathroom door behind him.

I immediately regretted mentioning Paul's name. I heard his voice through the bedroom door, because he never enters this room unless being explicitly invited to do so. "Did you call me, Alison?"

"Not really." I opened the door but instead of letting Paul in I let myself out. "I was just getting ready to order a pizza. What do you want on yours?"

"That's not funny, Alison." Ghosts don't eat.

I started down the stairs to the front room. Steve Cosgrove was in the front room putting on a jacket. "Heading out?" I asked him, because I really love to restate the obvious whenever possible.

"I'm meeting Adam in town," he said. Steve was blonde and tall and clearly, from what I'd seen, devoted to his husband. "I've had a cold all day but I'm feeling well enough to join him for dinner. Any suggestions?"

I do have arrangements with some of the restaurants in Harbor Haven and the surrounding towns. I send customers their way and I get a small (believe me!) percentage of the bill when it's paid. But I never send guests anywhere but restaurants I've tried and feel comfortable recommending. That's how I justify taking kickbacks. It's a mindset.

I gave Steve a couple of the names and he thanked me. He didn't look ill; his nose wasn't red and his eyes weren't watery.

I should be so sick. "I hope the commotion in the backyard didn't keep you awake or anything," I said.

"I didn't hear anything," Steve told me. "I use earplugs when I sleep. Adam snores like a goat." I had no idea how goats snored but I chuckled anyway and Steve opened the door to go on his way. "By the way, the ghosts are still here, right? I didn't miss anything?"

We'd had the spook show in the afternoon, but only Katrina had attended. The performance had been, let's say, something less than riveting but the audience of one didn't seem to mind. "No, don't worry," I said. "There'll be another show tomorrow morning."

"I'm glad to hear it. I was the one who wanted to come see ghosts, you know. Adam is a little scared about the whole thing."

I don't mind hearing that before guests arrive or on their first day, but once they've experienced the guesthouse for a while it's my hope they'll understand there's nothing to be afraid of while they're there. "Still?" I asked.

Steve moved his head back and forth a bit in a *maybe-yes-maybe-no* sort of motion. "I think 'scared' might be overstating it. He's a little weirded out."

"Well, let me know if there's anything the ghosts or I can do to help him with it," I told him. "We all want everybody to be comfortable here."

"We have a case to discuss," Paul tried to remind me. I did not listen because *I* didn't have a case to discuss.

"Oh, he's fine," Steve assured me. "A little fear will do him good."

"Still," I said.

Steve nodded and went outside. A chilly breeze came in while the door was open just to remind me that November is not June. It's not even October.

Before Paul could go on I turned and faced him, probably more abruptly than he had anticipated. "We don't have a case to discuss," I said. "There is no case. I'm not helping. When Josh comes downstairs you can talk to him about whatever you want, but I'm not in on this. Do you get that?"

Paul blinked a couple of times and I knew it wasn't because he needed to get more moisture into his eyes. "I did not mean to suggest otherwise," he said.

"Good. Because I'm not." I walked purposefully—I thought—into the den, where Katrina, the only unspoken-for guest at the moment, might be found. I didn't turn around to see if Paul was following.

Sure enough she was on one of the sofas reading a Sue Ann Jaffarian novel she had probably picked up in the library. She looked up when I walked in. "Hi, Alison." Her voice sounded a trifle raspy as if I'd walked in on her when she was napping.

"How's everything going, Katrina?" Asking an open-ended question like that makes it possible for the guest to bring up any topic she considers important. You find out things about your hosting skills and your guesthouse when you do that. (And I learned all this without a single class in hospitality! Hard to believe, no?)

"Just fine." Her tone didn't match her words.

"Something I can help with?" I asked. It was a dangerous

question because I'd seen the way she was eyeing Bill Har-relson the day before and I've been in situations where guests had asked me to help them with their love lives. I'm remarkably bad at that.

"Just wondering how much longer the construction in the back is going to go on," she said. Bingo. Bill Harrelson.

Katrina was not one of my Senior Plus guests; I'd guess she was in her mid-forties. She'd come to the guesthouse this week from her home in Newark, Delaware (where they pronounce it *New-ark* for some reason New Jerseyans can't completely absorb—we call our largest city *Noork* for the most part) because she'd heard about the haunted guesthouse and thought ghosts would be fun. I try to make sure they are fun—for the guests. This business is all about being selfless.

"I'm afraid it won't be done before you go home," I said. "I hope it hasn't been too much of an inconvenience."

"Oh, no. It hasn't been a problem at all. But the noise last night made it a little hard to fall asleep."

Behind me, even though I couldn't see him, I think I heard Paul stroke his goatee.

"The noise last night?" I asked. Now *my* voice sounded a little raspy.

"Yes. I don't understand why they'd be working so late at night back there, but I heard it from my bedroom at about two a.m." Katrina looked at me like I was being especially obtuse. I was trying to remember what *obtuse* meant.

"Ask her what she heard," Paul said, because clearly he thought I was an idiot.

"What did you hear?" I asked Katrina. But I'd like it on

the record that I was going to ask that before Paul said any-thing. I'm actually *not* an idiot.

"When they took that big car out of the hole last night." Katrina sat up on the sofa and put her book down, with a handy bookmark right where it belonged, on the coffee table in front of her. "You know, with the big crane, or whatever."

The excavator. "Did you see it?"

Katrina smiled a little guiltily. "I did want to see if Bill was outside," she said. "So I put on some clothes and went to the back to see, you know, over there." She pointed toward the French doors.

"And what did you see?" I just kept feeding her the straight lines so she could do the jokes. It's what I do.

"Well, they were pretty much done by the time I got there," she said. "The big hook with the car was driving away down the beach."

"Hang on," I said. "I think you need to talk to Lt. McElone."

"Indeed she does," Paul agreed.

Katrina looked at me wide-eyed. "Did I do something wrong?" she asked.

"No, Katrina. You might be the only person in the house last night who did something right."

Chapter 10

It was too cold for McElone to interview Katrina outside on the deck now that it was dark. So for the second time in one day she was actually inside the guesthouse looking considerably more unsettled than Adam Cosgrove ever had. And Adam had been to at least three spook shows.

By this point a complete attentive audience had gathered for what had turned out to be the evening's entertainment. Josh had showered and dressed and was watching with some fascination, and Melissa had come down in a much better mood having finished her homework. She sat next to me on a loveseat facing the lieutenant but behind Katrina, who appeared a little confused as to all the fuss she was attracting. Paul had not left the room but had retreated a little to get a better view of the whole scene, so he was hovering to my left and up about three feet. Even Maxie, who was zipping back and forth between the den side and the kitchen side of the wall with the bullet in it, was present, although it was unclear if she was paying any attention. Everett stood guard at the French doors, not holding his drilling rifle but in full military regalia. Everett takes his job seriously, even when nobody has asked him to do it.

I was there because Katrina had asked me to be there. I knew McElone better than she did and I was—prepare to be frightened—the authority figure in the house right now. Except for Josh. And Melissa. Mostly Melissa.

"So tell me," the lieutenant said in her less intimidating tone (she has two tones, and one is less intimidating), "what exactly did you hear?"

This might be the point to say that McElone had wanted to interrogate Katrina alone, but Katrina, perhaps hoping Bill Harrelson would show up in the back and come in to corroborate her story, had insisted on staying in the den and having me, at least, present. Melissa and Josh were the only other people visible to the lieutenant, and she didn't raise a serious objection to either being there, although she did warn them sternly not to talk. Like they wouldn't have known that.

"I was just getting to sleep," Katrina said. "I'd stayed up very late, first walking on the beach and then using some time to check things on the internet. I listen to sleep meditations every night before I go to bed, so I had one of those on in my room. It's very quiet and nobody would hear it through the walls. The two other gentlemen in the house have a room that's not next to mine, anyway."

"Nobody is suggesting you were creating a loud noise," McElone assured her. "We don't think you did anything wrong. It's what you heard that's really important, and since you're the only one who heard it, I'm especially interested in your story." Which was a way of saying, *hey lady, answer the question I asked.* But McElone was being less intimidating.

"Like I said, I was just lying down to sleep and was feeling very comfortable and relaxed because of the sleep meditations." Katrina didn't realize, probably, the circuitous road she was taking to the point of her story, but McElone's eyes were spinning just a little with impatience. "So it was especially troubling that there was all this noise coming from somewhere outside the house. I could tell it was the back even though I don't have a window facing the beach." Was that a crack about the room I'd assigned her? I gave her one with a walk-in closet, for crying out loud.

"What did it sound like?" McElone wasn't really that concerned with Katrina's satisfaction in room placement, but I made a mental note to ask my guest about it after this questioning was completed.

"Trucks," Katrina answered, sounding like that should have been obvious. And maybe it should have, given that we already knew she'd seen the car being towed away.

"Trucks?" McElone repeated, emphasizing the last letter. "More than one?"

Katrina, not expecting that question, took a moment before answering. "No. I guess it was one truck. Or one of those big things that move the sand around on the beach."

"An excavator," McElone offered. She'd known what Katrina meant but wanted to get the terminology down so the questions could move on. "So you heard that. Did you know what it was right away?"

Katrina shook her head. "No, but I knew it was coming

from the back where they were working. So I put on a jacket and shoes and went out to see what was going on."

"It must have been odd to hear all that at two in the morning," McElone said. "Why did you go outside?"

Katrina reddened just a bit. "I wanted to see if Bill Harrelson was out there working. Of course it was weird that it happened at that hour, but if Bill was out there it must have made sense, right? Because he's in charge."

McElone wasn't picking up the signals. "You went out to see if the foreman was there? What difference would that make?"

"I just wanted to talk to him," Katrina said. "We met earlier in the day and I thought it would be nice to talk to him again."

Now McElone couldn't miss the subtext. "Ah," she said. "You have a crush on the guy. So you went outside. What did you see?"

"I don't have a *crush*," Katrina protested. "I was just interested in having another conversation. That's all."

McElone didn't react facially or physically. Even her voice maintained its noncommittal tone. "What did you see?" she said again.

"I must have come out when they were finished. Maybe it took me longer to get dressed than I thought or maybe they were just working really fast." Katrina still looked miffed at the idea of her having a crush. "But by the time I got there they had lifted the car out of the hole and were towing it away."

"They?" McElone asked. "How many people were there?"

"Two. One driving the . . . *excavator* and another one in a dune buggy or something with an attachment on the back. He was dragging the sand and getting all the tracks out. He was almost done when I got outside, too. Then he drove away up the beach toward the street."

McElone leaned forward, indicating this question was an important one. "Did you see either one's face?"

Katrina closed her eyes tightly and pulled her lips together. For a moment I thought she was having some sort of stomach pain. "I'm trying to remember but it was really dark out there. They didn't even have the light on the excavator. The guy dragging the sand had his headlights on but that didn't help me see his face." She opened her eyes and relaxed her jaw. "I'm sorry, lieutenant. I can't say I saw either of them really. I didn't get close enough."

Everett had not moved what would have been a muscle. He could easily have filled in for one of those guys outside Buckingham Palace if he'd had the right suit.

"How long did you stay outside after that?" McElone asked her.

"After?" Katrina seemed confused. "I went inside as soon as they drove away. It was cold out. Why?"

"This morning the excavator was back on the beach, parked like nothing ever happened. I wanted to see if you'd been there when it was returned, but you weren't. Did you hear it come back?"

Katrina shook her head negatively. "I went up and listened to one more meditation and then I fell asleep."

McElone looked frustrated. "Okay. Thank you for your

time, Ms. Breslin. I'll be in touch if I have any further questions."

Katrina, understanding she had been dismissed, stood up and shook McElone's hand. "I'm sorry I couldn't be more help, lieutenant. I hope you catch these people soon. If there's anything I can do while I'm still here, please don't hesitate to ask me."

"Believe me," the lieutenant said, "I won't hesitate."

Katrina stopped as she walked toward the stairs, which I figured meant she was heading up to her room. "Are you a homicide detective, lieutenant?" she asked.

"I'm the chief of detective in Harbor Haven," McElone answered. "I'm in charge of any case that requires the attention of a detective. Sometimes that's homicide. Usually it's not."

Katrina absorbed that information and smiled. "It must be very exciting," she said.

"You'd be surprised."

With that Katrina walked out of the den and I heard her start up the stairs. I guessed I wouldn't have to invite her to share the pizza I had not yet ordered.

"That didn't really help very much, did it, lieutenant?" I said. "Sorry if I wasted your time"

McElone, putting away the small voice recorder she'd used to store the interview with Katrina, waved a hand. "It wasn't a waste. We know when the car was taken and we know how. We just don't know who did it or why." She gave me a goodbye nod. "I'll probably be in touch, whether I want to be or not." We have a very warm relationship.

Melissa was the first to break the silence after McElone could be heard closing my front door. "Do you think Katrina was telling the truth?" she asked.

That was certainly not what I had been thinking. "You think she's lying?" I asked.

"I thought she sounded like she was being honest," Josh told Liss. "But that might have been because I didn't see any reason for her to lie."

"Neither do I," Melissa said. "I'm not even sure that's what I think. But it's weird that Katrina was the only one who heard something that loud at two o'clock in the morning. I think I would have heard it."

Maxie stuck her head through the wall over the kitchen door. "Yeah, she was lying," she said. "You can always tell."

"I have made a study of the signals people give off when they are trying to deceive each other," Paul told her. "I did not notice any of the usual signs in Ms. Breslin."

"I am not given to judgments," Everett said, moving out of his corner finally now that the interrogation was over and the detective had left. "But I think her story was kind of hard to believe. I think Maxie and I would have heard that kind of work being done at that hour."

Maxie's head disappeared into the kitchen. She was busy and didn't want to engage in an argument, which is the opposite of what she usually does. She was taking this redecoration seriously and that worried me.

"Still, the Continental *was* gone when he looked outside this morning," Paul noted. "It had to be taken at some point between last evening and just after dawn."

"Either way, the lieutenant will figure it out," I said. "I'm going to order the pizza now. Anybody want to volunteer to go pick it up?"

"That depends," Melissa said. "You want to give your car keys to a thirteen-year-old?"

"That leaves me," Josh said. "Sure. I'll go get it. You order. I need to go find my driving shoes." Josh was wearing a pair of flip-flops at the moment because our house is heated and he is a man. I don't get it, either.

I reached for my phone and Josh happened to be standing just in front of me when his cell chirped. He stopped and looked at it, which made it possible for me to peer over his shoulder. At the same moment I saw Paul put his phone back into a pocket in his jeans.

The text message Josh had gotten read: *We have work to do.*

Chapter 11

"I need Maxie," Paul said.

That wasn't something I had expected to hear. We (that is, the living people) had finished our pizza hours ago. Melissa was up in her room pretending she was going to bed when I knew for a fact she was watching YouTube videos on her computer. I figured that was relaxing enough that she'd get to sleep when she needed to.

Maxie and Everett had vanished to whatever it was they did at night. Sometimes I know she gets him, somewhat against his will, to indulge in some mischief she likes to perpetrate on the living, like it's our fault someone poisoned her when she was just twenty-eight. Her favorite is to go to Dunkin Donuts and rearrange the trays. But tonight she was concentrating on her newfound job and I doubted they would even swap the Sweet & Lows for the Splendas.

Josh and I were sprawled out together on one of the sofas, not watching the television a "generous" reality show crew had once installed on one of the exposed ceiling beams. There are hundreds of channels available through our television package.

We didn't feel like watching any of them. Josh was holding me lightly and I was luxuriating in his arms because it's a very good place to be. He did have his phone out in case Paul wanted to communicate with him directly, but he's grown accustomed to hearing one-side conversations and figuring out the other end of them. He wasn't sleeping, but his eyes were closed. Paint store owners work long days. Like innkeepers.

"You need Maxie?" I answered. "For what?" It was a good question. If I'm being honest there have been a handful of moments when Maxie has been very useful over the past four years, and then there's all the other times.

"There is online research to be done for our case," he said. Paul is uncomfortable with outward signs of affection so he was making an effort not to look at Josh and me. We weren't exactly pushing the limits of PG-13 but Paul is a ghost with some intimacy issues. He hovered essentially directly above my head and was appearing to do a very close study of the hanging chandelier. "I think the thing to concentrate on right now is the identity of the person whose remains were in the Lincoln Continental. We don't even know if it was a man or a woman."

"Go bother McElone," I said. "I'm in the hospitality industry."

"What did he say?" my husband said with a slight rasp in his voice. Josh would undoubtedly be heading up to bed shortly and I had plans to go with him because I, too, had to be up at the first sign of daylight.

I told him about Paul's determination to include me in his investigation and how he wanted Maxie to hit the laptop in search of the skeleton in my backyard's closet. Josh opened his eyes and said, "Where is Paul?" I pointed directly over our heads.

Josh looked up and said, "I can do that." It was a little disturbing how much he wanted to be Paul's Dr. Watson.

Paul pulled out his phone and texted to Josh: *Maxie has advanced internet skills.*

"I can start and she can follow up," my husband argued. "We don't even know where Maxie is right now."

"You need to get to sleep," I reminded him. This was like talking to Melissa when she was eight. "You have work in the morning."

"I'll quit soon." *Please, Mom, just a few minutes!*

Paul said, "Tell him I appreciate it, but that he should only make the most basic of searches and let Maxie handle the rest. His value lies in his rapport with the construction workers and the contractors." That wasn't where I would have placed Josh's value, but everybody has different priorities.

I decided to make his message a little less insulting. "Paul says he's very grateful but he wants you to just start and let Maxie handle the rest tomorrow. He says you're the only one who can interview the construction guys and get anything valuable out of them, so you should concentrate on that."

Since Josh and I were no longer doing anything resembling snuggling Paul could lower himself to approximate eye level. "That's not precisely what I said," he told me. Josh wasn't looking so I could stick my tongue out at him. And I did.

"I'm on it." Josh stood up, which took some doing because

I was still more or less in front of him, and headed toward the coffee table, the last known location of my dilapidated laptop computer, which had no doubt been carved out of actual stone and was running on the power of microscopic hamsters running on tiny treadmills. It's old, is what I'm saying.

He opened it up and pressed the power button, which meant it would probably be up and running before daybreak. I looked at Paul, and out of Josh's earshot said, "Why can't you let McElone do her job in peace?"

The Canadian ghost has the nerve to look surprised. "How am I impeding the lieutenant?" he asked. "I'm doing nothing that will slow down her investigation, and if we turn up anything useful I would hope you'd pass it on to her immediately."

"You just want me to cave in and say I'll help, don't you?" I gave him a knowing glance. Okay, I gave him a guessing glance. You can't be sure of anything these days.

"I honestly don't know where you are getting that idea," Paul sniffed. "You've made it clear that you don't want to be involved in this investigation and I am complying with your wishes. Melissa and Josh want to help and I am seeing to it that they can do so without involving you."

"Yeah, sure you . . . wait. Melissa?" I thought I'd told her to concentrate on schoolwork and leave the sleuthing to Nancy Drew. And Paul.

"She has helped before," Paul said. "I will not assign her any task that is the least bit dangerous. In fact, this entire case should be completely safe, since there is no evidence of violence yet and even if it transpires that the person in the car was murdered, it happened forty years ago."

From across the room I heard my husband say, "Okay, it's running. Now what am I looking for?"

Paul pointedly bypassed me in his communication and texted to Josh. My husband read the message, nodded and looked back to the spot where Paul had been earlier. "Okay. I'll let you know what I find."

Paul texted him again and Josh looked up once more. "You're welcome," he said.

I stood up. "You boys have your fun," I said. "I'm going to bed." I tried not to look toward my plastic-sheeted kitchen door as I headed for the stairs. I took my time going up because I wanted to clear my head and get into a sleepy state of mind. I took a quick detour to the movie room, which no one had used that day, looked around, confirmed that it still looked the same, and walked back out again.

Up the stairs. I'd try to stay awake reading for another half hour and if Josh didn't come up, I'd text him and remind him that five in the morning gets here a heck of a lot faster than one might expect. So I kept my phone with me while I cleaned up, took off my makeup, got my hair into a sleeping position (that is, one that wouldn't interfere with turning my head one way or another on a pillow—in other words, down) and changed into my sleeping attire, which tonight favored the flannel, as winter wasn't here yet but had sent a postcard announcing its imminent arrival.

To this day I don't know why I walked out of the bedroom to the hallway. I don't believe in intuition—although these days I do believe in ghosts so I guess everything is at least a little bit up for grabs—and I didn't want to interact with guests in my pajamas. But I thought maybe Josh was coming up or that I'd see him on the lower level and that would make me feel better about the evening. Except the hallway and the front room downstairs were both empty. I didn't go to the top of the stairs to check, but I didn't hear anyone moving around downstairs. Adam and Steve were still out, and Katrina had come back to let herself into her room about an hour before. I didn't hear Melissa roaming around above me, since she's not exactly a stomper.

But there was the window at the end of the hall, overlooking the backyard.

I did want to see how much progress had been made since the crime scene mob had quit for the day and gone home. I just wanted one part of this mess to look like it was heading back toward normal.

So I walked down the length of the hall and moved the curtain to one side so I could look out my back window and see some sign of stability.

The motion-activated back light was on, indicating there had been someone at least walking around back there. I wasn't especially concerned because I've seen that light go on for a stray cat walking by. But this hadn't been tripped by a stray cat.

The Continental was back, sitting on the sand next to the hole from which it had been violently extracted the night before, if you believed Katrina Breslin.

I stared at it for a moment and shut my eyes tight. Maybe

it was a hallucination or a mirage or something else that would indicate I was losing my grip on reality.

Nope. When I opened my eyes that big hulk of a rusted-out Lincoln was still there, taunting me.

"Oh, give me a break," I said out loud.

Chapter 12

I actually debated calling McElone because it was going to keep us awake too late. But I was brought up with a respect for those doing their jobs and for the law of the land (well, most of the laws, anyway—I had a rebellious period in my teens and early 20s) so I didn't see a way around letting the local chief of detectives know that someone had played Musical Cars in my backyard again.

First, I went downstairs and informed my husband and resident dead detective that someone had once again towed a not-very-small object onto our property without anyone noticing. This led to a good deal of going outside and looking, which confirmed what I had just told them and surrendered no further information. Men. They won't just take you at your word.

That, in turn, had led to summoning McElone, who no doubt was at her own home with her husband and children. She, having been given the power to delegate by the good people (and some jerks) of Harbor Haven, sent another detective under her command, Sgt. Gabriel Yablonski, to investigate with the explicit instructions that he make sure the area was cordoned off—again—and that he not report back to her until at the very earliest eight the next morning.

Yablonski was a fairly dapper fellow who couldn't afford the best suits so compensated by wearing extremely classy ties. This one was orange. I didn't especially care, but it did catch the eye. He was carrying a tablet computer and looked at the photographs taken by the crime scene crew the day before. Standing out on the sand in the cold and the wind, he walked all the way around the Lincoln slowly, comparing it to what he could see on his tablet. I didn't see how the object itself was all that much more attractive than its photographs, but then I'm not a detective, and you can ask any of my clients if you don't believe me.

Josh and I were watching from the den, just inside the French doors. I wasn't going out there in this temperature unless I had to, and Yablonski had made it clear we were not essential to his work. "You think he's trying to figure out if this is the Continental's evil twin?" Josh asked.

I laughed a little, partially because it was a decent joke and partially because I was glad my husband wasn't acting like a complete detective fanboy the way Paul, outside and practically on Yablonski's shoulders, was. "Maybe he's questioning the car," I told him. "Wants to see what it knows."

We didn't get to riff much longer—which is probably a good thing—because Yablonski finished his interrogation of the sedan and trudged up the beach to our deck. Josh opened the French door for him and the detective walked in, tracking sand into my den, which was not appreciated. Paul phased through the wall so it was unnecessary to hold the door open any longer than it took Yablonski to bring himself and a small dune inside.

"Well, that should do it for tonight," he said once he'd shaken even more sand out of the cuffs on his pants. "We'll send someone over to cordon off the area very shortly, but we'll try not to be too loud. Just a couple of questions, if that's okay." He gestured into the room as if he were the host and we were the guests. He wanted us to sit down for the interrogation.

"I'd appreciate it if you'd wipe your shoes before we sit," I said. "Whatever you bring in I have to clean up." I pointed at the bunker he'd created just inside my door.

Yablonski looked down and winced a little. "Sorry about that. I should have done that before I came inside."

Yes, he should have, but there was no point in pushing it right now. "Just please, if you wouldn't mind doing it now," I said.

"Alison is very particular about the house because it's also her business," Josh said. I shot him a look that indicated he need not have apologized, essentially, for me, but he wasn't seeing that.

"I understand," the detective said as he vigorously scraped his shoes on a mat I have just inside the French doors. "My mistake."

Paul, now hovering just a foot or so off the floor, folded his arms. "Enough about the floor," he said. "There is important business to discuss regarding this case."

He got a look for me too, but it was not as sustained because I didn't want Yablonski to wonder why this crazy woman was staring at a fixed point in the air.

Josh and I sat on the sofa we'd been sharing previously and Yablonski took an easy chair opposite us. He placed his tablet computer on the table between us and no doubt had it recording the conversation so he could refer to it later.

"That almost certainly is the same car that was discovered in your backyard yesterday," he began.

"*Almost* certainly?" I asked. "You think somebody has a stockpile of 1977 Lincoln Continentals lying around for the expressed purpose of keeping my backyard stocked with one?"

"Alison," Paul scolded. "The man is doing his job."

"I have to be certain about any possibility," Yablonski answered. "We don't know why the car was there to begin with, why it was removed and we definitely don't know why it was brought back. I have to be sure about every detail so I can tell Lt. McElone in my report. She's still the lead investigator on this case."

I thought to thank my lucky stars for that, but then I remembered my stars hadn't been particularly lucky the past couple of days and figured I shouldn't ask for more trouble. "How do you know it's the same car, then?" I asked Yablonski, largely because Paul had instructed me to do so.

"I compared the car out there with the photographs of the one that had been there yesterday and there are a couple of dents and scratches in exactly the same places, as well as rust damage in the undercarriage and the trunk that matched pretty much exactly," the detective, who now was answering rather than asking questions, said. "I took a quick glance at the registration number on the dash but it had been removed, probably with a file or something, and that was true of the other car as well. Somebody didn't want us to know where this car was from."

"As I understood it, Lt. McElone has said she would check for the registration number," Josh said. "How can she do that if the number hasn't been there all this time?"

Yablonski, who seemed to understand he was now conducting a clinic in being a police detective, held out a hand to indicate Josh should slow down his thinking. "There are other places that have ID numbers, inside the engine block and on certain parts," he said. "We'll be able to identify the car all right."

"How about the person they found inside the car?" I asked. "He doesn't have any number on his engine block, I'm betting."

"He or she," Yablonski corrected me. "I don't think we have a definitive answer on that just yet. The ME is working on it as we speak. But if you don't mind, I still have a couple of questions to ask you." Our luck, he remembered he was the cop. "First of all, how many people are staying in this house at the moment?"

"Including us and my daughter, six," I said. "I have three guests this week."

"Are they all in the house tonight?"

"Actually, no. Adam and Steve Cosgrove are out somewhere, probably at dinner or somewhere in town," I told him.

Yablonski looked slightly amused. "Adam and Steve?"

"Don't start."

He didn't. "So it's you two, your daughter and one guest in the house tonight?" he asked.

"That's right. Katrina Breslin, who was questioned the first time they found a Continental in my backyard, is here, I'm pretty sure." It occurred to me I hadn't actually seen Katrina in the house after she'd gone for dinner.

Yablonski waited. "Can you ask her to come down?" he asked.

"I'm not sure I want to knock on her door if she's sleeping," I answered. I knew Katrina had been up until at least two in the morning the night before, but for all I knew she'd clocked out at eight tonight to compensate. People's sleep patterns are their own business.

"Just tap."

Josh and I exchanged a *McElone-wouldn't-make-me-do-this* glance but I didn't see a logical out, so I walked out of the den and up the stairs to Katrina's door. There I tapped lightly, believe me, and waited. There was no answer. I tapped again, maybe a hair harder. Still no response. I shrugged my shoulder toward no one at all and turned to go back down the stairs, and almost had an embolism when I saw Paul hovering there, just in the air where there was no landing.

"Don't do that!" I hissed at him.

"Do what?" He looked sincerely confused.

"Forget it. What did you come up here for?"

He pointed to the door. "I'd rather not look inside if she's sleeping, but I'll do so if you think it's best," he said. It was a kind, if bizarre, offer.

"Nah. I'll just let Yablonski know what happened and let him act on it."

"Are you certain she's in there?" Paul asked.

I didn't answer him and went back to the den to report to Yablonski. He nodded as if what I told him was completely expected and said he'd tell McElone all he'd discovered tonight, which in my opinion wasn't very much. Yablonski did glance up at the landing as he left, no doubt wondering if Katrina was hiding out or entirely absent. I chose to decide she was asleep, which was exactly what I wanted to be.

But when I got back to the den to retrieve my husband I found him furiously texting with the 0-pound ghost in the room. Paul, who had his phone out to communicate with Josh, was clearly responding to something when I got there. He was texting as he spoke despite Josh being unable to hear what he said, and since he wasn't looking up I was pretty sure it wasn't for my benefit. Paul just liked to hear his own words out loud. He says it helps him think.

"The most likely possibility is that the car was removed to check for evidence left behind, but it's also possible that the emerald found in your ceiling and the pouch I saw the lieutenant remove from the crater in your yard are related," he said as he tapped his phone. He used both his thumbs, which is something I've never really gotten the hang of; I tend to type as if it were a traditional keyboard but my fingers are too large for the tiny display. This leads to a great many autocorrect mistakes.

"When's Volume Two of that text coming out?" I asked Paul as I walked into the den.

He looked up, startled. "Alison."

At the same time, Josh said, "Honey, we're planning strategy."

"It's late, fellas. You can play Hardy Boys again tomorrow." I beckoned to my husband.

He stood still.

"I'll be up in a few minutes," he said. Now, Josh is never mean and he almost never gets angry at anything. So he wasn't giving me a cold stare like some men would when their wives treat them like children. I'd have to scale back. But he did look determined and he shifted his eyes toward Paul and back, even if he missed by eight feet because he had no idea where Paul was actually floating. He didn't want to lose face in front of his new invisible friend.

It was almost kind of cute.

There was no point in insisting. I didn't want to destroy whatever nutty male bonding thing they were doing because Josh has always been a little wary of the ghosts. He finds the idea of them amusing but until now had never really communicated with either of them, or with my father, whom he knew in life.

"Okay," I said. "But I'm going up. Don't be too long, all right?"

"Of course not," my husband said. "I'll see you in a few minutes."

I went up and got ready for bed. Again. Only this time I made it. And when Josh came in I heard him being as quiet as possible to keep from disturbing me, which was sweet.

It was three a.m.

Chapter 13

When you own a one-person retail business that relies on its clientele (as they all do) you don't have the luxury of calling in sick. The only other employee of Madison Paint was Josh's nonagenarian grandfather Sy, and no matter how engrossed Josh was in the Case of the Sometimes Vanishing Car, he knew he couldn't possibly ask Sy to man the store for an entire day alone. And since the early morning is the busiest time of the day in his business, Josh had to be there when the store opened at six.

So after about 90 minutes of sleep, he stopped to talk to Bill Harrelson and Jim (Fill in Last Name Here) when they arrived. My husband looked like he'd been run over by the Continental, but I saw him outside talking fake-jovially (only I would know the difference) to the men and then trudging over to his car to make the drive to Asbury Park before the sun actually came up. He was texting, no doubt to Paul (who had not yet appeared from his lair in the basement this morning), as he walked. Slightly unsteadily.

I had mustered all my self-discipline and had not told him I had seen this coming. We'd been married less than a year.

It was worth noting, however, that while my mostly asleep ears were listening for my husband's footsteps on the stairs, I had not heard Katrina come back but had heard Adam and Steve. So maybe she'd been asleep in her room after all. I also noted that Bill Harrelson was favoring his left arm, shaking it like it was achy or tight. I didn't know what that was about and couldn't see the arm itself through the jacket he was wearing.

The first thing I'd done that morning (after getting maybe three hours of sleep myself) was look out the window and confirm the Continental had not taken another unexpected nocturnal trip; it had not. It was out there proudly flying its flag inside the yellow crime scene tape on wire posts jammed into the sand. The gaping hole from which the car had emerged only two days ago (was that possible?) was still there, too. Apparently the beach elves who could have filled it in with sand and made the problem go away were on strike.

The second thing I'd done, as my kitchen was still in full lock down mode and encased in plastic sheeting, was drive quickly to Dunkin Donuts for sufficient coffee and tea for myself, my husband (who didn't drink coffee or tea, so he was easy), my daughter and my three guests. The Mandorisis would bring their own morning beverages. The inevitable cops who would no doubt descend on my back property were, I had decided, on their own.

When I'd driven back and parked in the driveway, within sight of the crime scene, Menendez and her crew had not yet arrived. This was surely not considered an urgent emergency by the Harbor Haven cops, and I didn't blame them. A car that had been buried during the Carter Administration kept leaving and coming back? Hardly seemed a current threat to our citizenry. Maybe the thing just liked to go out for fries and a milkshake at night when there was nothing to do.

I couldn't shake the feeling, though, as I walked from the car to the French doors carrying hot beverages, that the Continental's grille was grinning at me.

Now that Josh had taken off and I could hear Melissa rumbling around in the attic two floors above me (something about the way the house is constructed, I guess), I reminded myself to put out the morning beverages and a box of assorted doughnuts as a *please-don't-blame-the-hostess* offering on the sideboard in the den.

Before any of the guests showed up downstairs, though, Maxie (of all people) appeared in the den by way of the ceiling. She was wearing the concealing trench coat until she got all the way into the room and then lost it, revealing her outfit beneath to be that of painter's overalls and work boots. She was carrying a large artist's pad.

"What are you doing up so early?" I asked, broadening my definition of *up* to include the fact that her feet didn't exactly make it all the way to the floor.

"Work to do." Maxie was being terse to indicate she was busy and harried. Maxie, in addition to being a dead spirit, also believes herself to be a character in any one of many vintage movies. I think now she was Rosalind Russell in *His Girl Friday.* "Sketches to show you."

Sketches? She had taken the hypothetical (I had hoped) kitchen/den project to the next phase. I can't say I was excited by that revelation. "Isn't it a little early for sketches?" I asked.

"No! You have no idea of the scope and depth of this project. We need to finalize the designs before we can start acquiring materials." She floated down farther to right over the coffee table where Yoblanski had placed his voice recorder the night before. She laid down the pad and opened it to display her designs. That coffee table was working overtime these days. Maybe soon someone would put some coffee on it just to remind it of its intended function. "Take a look at this."

Almost against my will, I looked. Maxie's drawings were extremely professional looking. I did not find that a surprise at all; I knew she had been very serious about her profession when she was alive and had not hesitated—even when she should have—to make suggestions about my house during the years she'd been haunting the place.

The designs themselves were no less Maxie than I would have predicted, and that was the problem.

Maxie's concept for my kitchen—and I could tell it was my kitchen because at least she'd left the stove in the same spot it now occupied—was essentially to throw a bomb into the room and then rearrange the debris with an eye toward pleasing art critics rather than anyone who might want to cook a meal.

The refrigerator had somehow migrated across the room and gotten smaller. There were cabinets, but instead of hanging from the ceiling as they had they were now all stacked in one area of the room closest to the back door, which was had taken on a rather distinctive purple color. It was easy to see why the cabinets weren't attached to ceiling, as Maxie had eliminated the drywall in favor of open space, exposing the beams, one of which was about to become steel at the hands of Tony and Vic. Each wall was a separate color ranging from aqua to black. Light was supplied with a series of bare bulbs attached to the ceiling beams. The center island was eliminated in favor of a rolling wooden table that had no storage space under it. The barstools I used around the island were replaced with . . . nothing.

"Maxie . . ." I began. I really was trying to be sensitive to her feelings; I knew how much she was invested in this emotionally.

"You don't like it." The disappointment in her voice was palpable.

"You moved one of the windows." Maybe practicality could convince her.

"It was in the way of my design."

"Do you have any idea what this would cost to do?"

Maxie looked at me blankly. "I'm not charging you for this. What would I do with money?"

"You're missing the point. I get there's no fee for your services. You don't seem to understand that I'd have to pay for the workmen and materials to get all this to happen. Moving a window? Redoing the plumbing? I'm already paying for a steel beam in the ceiling. Where's the rest of this supposed to come from?"

Maxie reached for the ceiling in exasperation. "This is what I was afraid of!" she shouted. "I try for one minute to express myself creatively and all you want to do is nitpick.

Okay. Okay." She turned her head to one side and spread out her hands, putting on a show of calming herself down. "You didn't like that one. That's okay. I have another."

She flipped the page on the artist's pad to reveal what I'm sure she'd refer to as her backup design, which was no doubt intended to be less outrageous ("more boring," in Maxie-speak) and appease the customer, who in this case was me.

No major structural changes were made to the room in this one, which was refreshing. But the island was still gone and replaced with next to nothing. There was something resembling a card table in the far corner where I suppose Josh, Liss and I were supposed to eat as long as we never invited anyone over. The bulk of the floor space was devoted to plants, including two palm trees that were intended to grow through the ceiling and into the backyard, which would be a shock for palm trees that hadn't intended to be transplanted into a New Jersey winter. It was also going to be something of a surprise for the kitchen ceiling, which was not pictured in Maxie's sketch. So maybe what I said about "no major structural changes" needs a little revision.

"How are we supposed to cook in this room?" I asked the creative genius.

"You never cook," she pointed out. Apparently that was supposed to justify turning my kitchen into a greenhouse.

"No, but Melissa does, and I do eat. There's barely any space on this to do that, either."

She started to point to the drawing of the card table. "No," I said. "That's not nearly enough. Suppose I have guests for dinner."

"Why do you want to do that?" Maxie is not much for socializing, or doing much of anything else, with people she doesn't like, and she doesn't like most people.

"Occasionally my mother does like to come over or hadn't you noticed that?"

"There's enough room for four people at that table." Maxie said. Her argument was losing a little conviction, which I was grateful to see.

"There's no ceiling on the kitchen," I noted, indicating that space in the drawing.

"I figured we could raise the roof to accommodate the palm trees," she said. "It's really unique."

"That's true, but it's equally impossible. There are two bed-rooms on the second floor above this room, and then the attic, which has Melissa's bedroom. We're going to need a ceiling here."

Maxie snatched the sketchpad off the coffee table like a dog going after a piece of steak that has accidentally hit the dining room floor. "I can't work if I'm not being appreciated!" she shouted, and vanished through the still-extant ceiling. Given her tone I figured I wouldn't be hearing from her until the spook show, and if she was mad enough maybe not even then.

I wasn't alone for long. Tony and Vic showed up in my driveway and eventually could be heard coming through the back door, something I was not yet able to do. Contractors—and I have done a little work in the area in addition to seeing my father do the same the whole time I was growing up—take over a house as their own and there's remarkably little the client can do about it. I was the client. I couldn't do anything about it. But the work was in progress and I appreciated that, so I tried very hard not to resent the intrusion into my life even as I was hoping it would end very soon.

Tony stuck his head through the kitchen door. "We're going to get started," he said. "Might be a little noisy. We're jacking up the house so we can take out the beam."

I knew this was coming. "Do what you have to do, Tony."

He nodded, then looked back at me. "Jeannie wants you to come for dinner tomorrow night," he said. "She says it's your reward for putting up with me all day."

"My reward for putting up with you all day is putting up with you in the evening?"

Tony laughed. "I told her you'd say that." He disappeared back into the kitchen.

Before the door stopped its minimal swinging, Paul had risen up through the den floor. It was like living in a very odd French farce where people kept coming in and out of rooms but doors never slammed shut because most of the people could just phase through solid objects. And I was so used to it by now that I barely even took notice.

Paul looked like something very exciting was going on in his case. His goatee was slightly irregular, indicating a lot of stroking had gone on. His clothes were a little disheveled, and since physical properties could have no effect on them that meant he was not concentrating on his appearance. It was as if he were incredibly tired, which wasn't technically possible. He couldn't even yawn. Yawning happens when your brain needs more oxygen. Paul's brain, I believed, had been returned to Canada and was certainly not in need of extra air.

Before I could comment, he said, "The person whose bones were found in that car in your backyard was murdered."

Chapter 14

"I don't want to hear about it," I told Paul.

We had retreated to the basement because I didn't have my usual kitchen sanctuary on which to rely. Paul is comfortable among all the detritus and the furnace and frankly, aesthetics weren't the first thing on my mind at the moment.

To his credit, he nodded. He understood that I wanted no part of this adventure. "Certainly, Alison," he said. "But I think so much more clearly when I can say everything out loud and have someone to listen."

"Go talk to Lt. McElone," I suggested. "After the spook show I'll drive you over. She can't respond very well but you can tell her absolutely anything you like."

He tried to stop me with a look. "It's not the same thing," he said.

I kept walking. "Talk to Maxie," I countered. "She can hear and see you and she's done this sort of thing before. If all you need is a sounding board, she's the perfect fit." There was a spot behind the furnace I preferred not to look at because seeing what was there would facilitate a complete afternoon of cleaning and possibly a visit from our local exterminator, a guy named Gus who chewed tobacco. I'd rather pass on Gus when I can. No offense, Gus.

"Maxie is engrossed in the design work she is doing for you and can barely be distracted often enough to do the two shows each day," Paul pointed out. "You are my best option. Or I could consult with Melissa." We'd both heard the somewhat heavy steps above our heads. Teenagers in the morning are not light on their feet.

"I don't want Liss involved in this," I said. "She's got enough to do with sixth grade and she's helped solve enough murders for a thirteen-year-old. Move on."

He looked at me and smiled his little polite British/Canadian smile. "You're the one I have left," he said.

From upstairs I heard at the basement door, "Mom?"

"Up in a second," I answered. Then I turned to Paul and said quietly, "Talk fast."

He did. "I spent some time early this morning in the hole from which the Continental had been extracted."

"In the hole?" I asked.

"Best way to see things up close," Paul said. "And since I have no physical presence, it was much like being here is for me right now." I positioned myself away from the corner of the furnace I had been avoiding with my eyes. Now it was behind me. "And once I was in that environment and able to blend into the walls of the earth around me, it was clear that the person in the car had not chosen to be interred with it in the nineteen seventies."

"How was that clear?" Sometimes you have to focus Paul or he will lecture on a topic for what seems like three or four days when it's really only two.

"For one thing in the car there were two spots of blood, very dried, but one less dark than the other, so probably not as old," he said. "There were digging implements thrown into the hole, presumably after the car, and there were spent bullets in the driver's seat, particularly the headrest."

"Were they like the bullets Menendez found in the ceiling beam upstairs?" I asked.

"No. Those were from a larger handgun and these were of a smaller caliber. Even after all these years it was clear they had been fired. But the shooter had not been firing inside the car. That would have been far too tight a space, and the casings would probably have been left on the floor of the Continental. These were scattered but lodged in various areas. Two of them were lodged in the earth around the car, but the car's windows showed no damage from bullets. I believe the shooting was done while the victim was in the car but before it was completely interred. The killing took place before the car was buried. The man did not die of asphyxiation or natural causes."

"What did Josh text you about after he talked to Bill and Jim?" I asked. I might as well know how my husband's obsession might be preying on his mind. There was a whole day to go before he came home to tell me about it.

"He said Mr. Harrelson had told him there was no way to get a full-sized excavator or bulldozer with enough power to haul a Lincoln Continental out of the ground without making deep imprints into the sand and creating enough noise to wake the household, including me, although I'm sure Mr. Harrelson did not refer to Maxie, Everett or myself."

"So how does Bill think it was done?"

Paul looked away; he hates it when he doesn't have a satisfactory explanation for something. It disturbs the vast logical areas of his mind. Paul would have made an excellent Vulcan. "He had no idea," he said finally. "But I believe it is fairly clear; someone wanted to remove an incriminating item from the car and then return it so the police could be led in the wrong direction." He looked at me sideways. "Your husband is a good operative. He said he noticed Bill was favoring his left arm and asked about it; Bill said he had injured it on the job yesterday." I'd noticed the same thing but felt this was a bad time to prove I was a helpful investigator.

I wanted to make sure Paul understood my position in this investigation, which was outside of it. So I worded my next question very carefully. "So what are you going to do next?"

Paul took a moment and acknowledged the message I'd sent by briefly closing his eyes. It didn't help because his eyelids are largely transparent so I could still kind of see the pupils looking at me. But that was the response I'd wanted because it indicated he understood my stance. "If you don't mind I will take you up on that ride to the police station after our first show in the morning," Paul said. "But I think someone should tell Lt. McElone about what I have found."

"You didn't take the bullet casings out with you?" I said, ignoring the implication that since Paul couldn't talk to

McElone it would have to be a living adult who didn't actually run a paint store during the day.

"Of course not. One doesn't disturb a crime scene. Those shells are valuable evidence."

"Look. The wrecking crew from the crime lab will be back here today because I think they see this as their home away from home now. So I'll point out the casings to them. But that's all I'm going to do, okay?" Paul started to raise his hand to correct me so I added, "And give you a ride to McElone."

"Thank you, Alison." He lowered his hand to his side. "Do you have any suggestions?"

Did I . . . what? "Suggestions?"

"Yes. When you consult on a case I always like to hear your input. Do you have any theories on the car in the beach and the murdered person inside it?" Paul tilted his head to one side a bit so he could look more open to my comments.

"My input is that I'm not consulting on this case," I reminded him. "You needed a sounding board. You sounded. That's it. I'll talk to the cops later and I'll drive you to McElone. That is the limit of my participation."

"Heading out, Mom!" Melissa called from upstairs.

"Hang on," I called back and headed up the rickety basement steps.

Liss looked a little surprised but I ran over to her and gave her a very sincere hug as she was heading toward the door. She smiled a bit. "What's that all about?"

"I appreciate you," I said.

She looked just a little bit more bemused. "Thanks. I appreciate you, too. See you later." And off she went, just as if she were a sixth-grader getting a ride to school. I reminded myself that it would be my turn to drive the carpool tomorrow. I had once tried to convince the mayor of Harbor Haven to get a school bus route at least for the little kids, but now that mayor was in prison so it hadn't worked out that well. It's a long story.

Paul was right behind me when Liss closed the front door. "You're holding back," he said.

I felt a sharp intake of breath because it hadn't occurred to me that he'd come up through the floor in the front room. I spun and faced him. "Don't *do* that!" I insisted.

"Do what?" Tony stuck his head out through the kitchen door.

"Not you," I said. "We gonna be finished today?"

"I make no promises." His head was unstuck through the door and I heard the plastic sheeting go back up. The front part zips like the back of a dress. Tony zipped it like I assumed he did for Jeannie when she gets dressed up.

"You're holding back," Paul repeated.

"Is that your new mantra?"

"I didn't even have an old mantra. Come on, Alison. You wanted to say something when I asked you about the case and you made an excuse to come up and give Melissa a hug. Tell me what you think." Paul can have a tone like a beloved college professor coaxing the right answer out of a bright but shy student. It's really annoying.

"I don't know what you're talking about." I made a sharp right turn and headed down the hall. First the library, then the movie room. No. Wait. I hadn't put out the coffee, tea and doughnuts yet. I turned again and went toward the French doors, where I'd left everything.

"Yes you do," Paul countered. "You never change direction in this house; you always have your next move planned ahead of time. Alison. I understand you're not working on this case and I will not ask you anything more about it. But you had something you wanted to say and I'm asking you to say it now. We won't discuss it again."

I started lugging the Box of Joe (only Steve preferred tea and nobody had asked for decaf) to the cart, which I'd left out the night before in anticipation of the Mandorisi infestation in my kitchen. Then it occurred to me that the cart was on wheels so any lugging was unnecessary. I put the coffee box (that didn't sound right) down and went for the cart.

"Okay," I said to Paul. "This once. You want to know what I'm seeing? I see a guy who's so intent on finding a case to investigate that he's ignoring his own rules. You always say that we can't jump to conclusions without enough facts." I picked up the box of coffee again and put it on the cart, next to non-dairy creamer and various sweeteners. I had a pint of milk in the auxiliary fridge and put that out with spoons and napkins near the recyclable cups.

"I don't believe I am doing that," Paul said. He didn't sound defensive but he did seem somewhat surprised that I was challenging him at his own invitation.

"You are." I had bought tea already steeped, since there was no access to the kitchen and therefore the stove. I hoped Steve wouldn't mind. "You found some shotgun shells in an eight-foot hole in the ground. But instead of considering the idea that they might be there because someone used them who knows how long before or after the car was buried, you jumped right to the conclusion that the person in the car was murdered. You don't have a working explanation for how the car was removed and replaced but you tell me it's obviously a sign that something incriminating was in the car that had to be cleaned out. It was forty years ago, Paul. How is that plausible? The killer just happened to be walking by and saw the car, so they decided they had to bring in the heavy equipment instead of getting inside and taking whatever the item might be? You're not thinking logically because you like having a case and this one seemed interesting to you."

Paul stood there—well, hovered there—and stared at me for what seemed like a very long moment. "My goodness, Alison," he said. "You're right."

Chapter 15

"So these spent bullets were found in the same hole as the car?" Det. Lt. Anita McElone has a talent for looking weary. has a talent for looking weary. It's part of the job, I guess. I was sitting in the "visitor" chair in front of her desk, which was now inside a small office rather than in the bullpen where the other cops had desks. There were advantages to being chief of detectives, even when there's only one other detective in the department.

I had agreed to come see McElone because Menendez, who had arrived around nine in the morning, had taken the shells out of the hole after I'd pointed them out where "I" had found them. She'd reported it to McElone, then carefully placed them in an evidence bag (where most of my backyard was now residing) and sent them along to the lab, wherever that was, for examination.

"Yes," I confirmed for her. "They were in the hole near where the car was. That's really all I know."

"You keep saying it like that," McElone said, her eyes narrowing a bit. "You say, 'they were found' and 'they were in the hole.' You don't say, 'I saw them,' or 'I found them.'"

I felt it best to remain silent, not because anything I said could be used against me in a court of law, but because there was no way saying anything right now was going to help me in any imaginable way. Paul, who was hovering over the lieutenant's right shoulder, nodded his approval. As always, he was watching McElone's every move the way a toddler watches her mother for indications of how to behave.

McElone's mouth twitched. "Is this a ghosty thing?" she asked.

"You don't really want me to answer that question, do you, lieutenant?"

"This time I do. I have physical evidence in front of me. I need to know that if I go to an assistant prosecutor with it I can say how it was found. Now is there something you need to tell me?" McElone is as by-the-book as cops come but she's not without compassion. She wants to do things right because that gets the crime solved and the criminal successfully prosecuted.

So I couldn't lie because I'm not going to get on the stand and say I found something if I didn't. When I got hit with a bucket of wallboard compound and started seeing ghosts, perjury was not part of the deal. "My friend Paul found the casings," I said. That was entirely, objectively true. Now if we could leave it at that . . .

But we couldn't. "And Paul is . . . ?"

There wasn't any way to avoid it. "Dead. Paul's dead. But you shouldn't hold that against him."

McElone closed her eyes for a moment, then opened them again. "Then I can't use the rounds in a court of law," she said.

"Sure you can. Nobody touched them before your crime scene team took them out." I didn't see how prejudice against the deceased should mess up McElone's close record.

"No, but since I don't know how they were found— officially—I can't be sure they weren't just placed there this morning." She looked down at her desktop, which was disturbingly immaculate. McElone has a real thing for neatness, which leads me to believe she has deep-seated psychological issues. But she's definitely functional in society.

"Won't the crime lab be able to tell that from, like, erosion and stuff?" When you live with a thirteen-year-old, even one as articulate as Melissa, you pick up speech patterns.

"Probably. But I need testimony from the person who found them about how they were found and in what condition. Can your friend take the stand in a trial? Would anybody even know if he was there?" McElone scrolled through something on her computer screen, probably to take her mind off the fact that the spent bullets had left the list of things she could use in a case of . . .

"What's the crime, anyway? Do you know what happened to the person in the car?" I asked. I hadn't realized it, but McElone was acting like she had a tangible case on her hands when until now it had been a possible incident of someone with incredibly bad taste asking for an unusual burial.

"You didn't answer my question. Would anyone see your friend if he showed up in court?"

It came out faster than I meant it to; in other words, I didn't get a chance to think before I talked. "Well, he's right behind you now and you don't know it, so I'm guessing they wouldn't."

McElone spun around on her chair like someone had said Al Capone was holding a tommy gun on her. Which I guess was kind of how she saw this situation. "He's here now?" she said. I had to hand it to her—McElone's voice sounded no different than her usual, when she would tell me I was an incompetent investigator and a pain in her neck. Or other area.

"Yeah, but it's nothing to worry about. He loves watching you work. He thinks you're a great detective."

Paul held up his hands. "Stop making her uncomfortable, Alison."

I was only enjoying it a *little* bit. "In fact, he says he learns a lot by observing you."

McElone swiveled back around and tried to make holes in my forehead with her eyes. She failed, but it was close. "How often do you send ghosts in here to watch me work?" she demanded.

"Just yesterday and today," I answered. Also true. Although Maxie had definitely been here once or twice before.

McElone swallowed visibly. "Don't do that. Don't ever do that. If I can't be comfortable in my own office I can't function properly. You understand? Never send a ghost in here to watch me."

It occurred to me that I hadn't so much *sent* ghosts as given them a lift to her office, but I let that go. "I promise. Now, you answer *my* question. What crime are you investigating?" Changing the subject seemed a worthwhile path to take.

"Don't challenge the lieutenant," Paul said.

I didn't think that was what I was doing so I ignored him. I simply sat and waited for McElone to respond.

She didn't hesitate. "I don't recall being told by a superior officer that you were to be included in any discussion of my investigations." That was McElone as pure as you could distill her. She didn't have to acknowledge that she'd reacted with some visible discomfort just a few seconds earlier at something that hadn't caused me nightmares in years (although there were a few rough months at the beginning) and just jumped directly into her standard argument. That boiled down to, roughly, *I'm a cop and you're not.* It could be effective, but now I was wondering why I'd bothered coming in today and wanted to get something to make my visit seem at least a little worthwhile.

"I bring in some perfectly helpful evidence your crime scene people missed and you don't even want to tell me what it is I'm helping you solve?" I said, my voice rising just a little. "That's two used bullets and four unused bullets found on my property and I don't even get to know why? Do I have to walk out of here talking about how my *ghost* found the used ones?"

"What do you mean, *your* ghost?" Paul said.

McElone flinched a touch. "Don't raise your voice," she said.

I folded my arms. "Well?"

She leaned forward with her forearms leaning on her desk (probably the most that had ever rested on that pristine surface) and her eyes did not have a great deal of warmth in them as she looked at me. "Fine. The fact is, your . . . friend . . . is right. We have a homicide on our hands based on the preliminary report we've gotten from the ME. And it's a really, really cold case because he says that body was buried and hasn't been touched since sometime in the last century. You happy now?"

I bit on my lips a little. "I don't think *happy* is the word I'd use."

"Since this only happened on your property by coincidence, long before you owned the place, my very best advice would be to forget the whole thing, tell your pal not to get in the way and let me do my job," McElone added. "How's that?"

"I never had any intention of investigating this case, lieutenant. I'm perfectly happy to leave it to you," I said. "I wish you the best of luck with it." I stood up and lifted by bag off the back of the chair, slinging it onto my right shoulder.

"Good. How about your friend?"

I couldn't resist the impulse to look up at Paul now that McElone had brought him into the conversation herself. He was nodding his head, but more in a thoughtful way than an affirmative one. "He's nodding his head," I told the lieutenant.

"I'm thinking," Paul protested. "I haven't agreed to anything."

"Good," McElone said. "The last thing I need is to be looking around my office for someone I can't even see."

"I promise he won't be here. Thanks for your time," I said. "When do you think I can have my yard back?"

"Shouldn't be long this time. Try not to find anything else."

I left her office and shut the door behind me. Paul was following me so I put my earbuds on and plugged them into my phone. That way I wouldn't look like a complete lunatic when I started talking to him. Paul would not be able to contain himself after that exchange, I knew.

Sure enough, as soon as we got to the bullpen he caught up with me and stayed by my side.

"*Your* ghost?" he said.

Chapter 16

"Who would have been around here forty years ago?" Josh asked. "Do you even know who owned the house then?"

"Not really," I said. "But then it's not my business, is it? And since the lieutenant asked me to back off, it's none of yours, either."

Josh, Melissa and I had met my mother (and by extension my father) at a new Harbor Haven restaurant called Harvest, a farm-to-table affair that was doing its best to be ecologically and agriculturally responsible while managing to raise prices over the average restaurant by only about ten percent. I believe there is a price we pay for saving the planet, and ten percent didn't seem all that high when you put in those terms. Besides, Josh was paying.

"Mom," Melissa scolded. "You can't make that kind of decision for Josh."

My husband patted her on the arm. "It's okay, Liss. I get where your mom is coming from, but that doesn't mean I can't keep being interested in the case. I mean, there it was in our backyard all this time and we never knew it. I feel like it's kind of been waiting for us to find it."

I touched Josh on his left hand. "I didn't mean to sound like that," I said. "But the lieutenant was clear. She doesn't want anybody else investigating this murder, and I don't blame her."

Josh smiled the crooked smile I thought was weird when he was twelve and had different feelings about now. "It's okay, Alison. But you're going to have to convince Paul, I'm afraid."

Paul, who had hitched a ride with us and was positioned just to Mom's left and up a couple of feet, touched his nose. It's something I've seen people do when they're uncomfortable, and there was no doubt Paul wasn't exactly cozy in this setting. He doesn't mind strangers but feels like he's more conspicuous—he's not—in a crowd. The fact was Paul wasn't any more noticeable to the general public than my father, who was examining the miter work in the crown molding, or any of six other ghosts who happened to be present in the restaurant at this moment. One older gentleman was swooping from table to table and desperately sniffing at each plate despite being unable to smell anything. He clearly missed food more than most spirits.

"I don't see how my finding more evidence will serve as an obstacle to the lieutenant," Paul said. "If I continue to investigate and turn up nothing I have done her no harm, and if I manage to find something that will help her investigation I believe that will be a service to her and the police department."

"You're just bored," my mother told him. "I understand that. But you can't follow Lt. McElone around all day and make her feel uncomfortable. That's not fair either."

"Not to mention," I added, "anything you find she can't use in court. You're setting her back, not helping her forward."

Melissa was relating Paul's part of the conversation to Josh. He appeared to be listening to her very closely and nodded, although he did not—probably as a concession to me—take out his phone to monitor any text messages Paul might be compelled to send. The cheap cell phone I'd given Paul for texting didn't look like much, but it would probably have caused something of a stir if it had suddenly begun floating in midair over Mom's head.

"That is not my intention," Paul answered. "But I think there are things that Maxie, Josh and I can do behind the scenes that could help the lieutenant without making her feel badly about it."

"What about me?" Melissa asked.

"You have school and we don't have a client," I reminded her. "You're out on this one." Especially since this had officially become a murder investigation I had decided there was no chance my daughter was going to get involved. I didn't care if the violence had taken place forty years earlier and long before she was born. Murderers tend to be a vindictive type of people and I saw no reason my budding teenager should get on one's wrong side. Not to mention that the escapades of the Continental the past couple of days indicated somebody right now was interested in this case, and probably not in a mild isn't-that-fascinating kind of way.

But Liss huffed a bit and concentrated on the sea scallops (from Barnegat Bay) she had ordered. She couldn't maintain her snit enough to conceal the fact that she was examining them closely. No doubt she was picking up tips on how to prepare seafood, something she doesn't do very much (okay, never) at home because I have a serious aversion to such things. Yeah, call me crazy. I live on the Jersey Shore and I don't eat fish. Insert joke here.

"I think it will be helpful to ask Maxie about the property records on the house," Paul continued as if I hadn't made it clear I didn't want to discuss the murder in the car. "It is important, as Josh has pointed out, to know who the owner was when this crime took place."

Josh listened to Melissa's transcription and looked up closer to Dad than Paul. "Thank you," he said.

We had decided on Harvest because the Mandorisi brothers had not actually finished work in my kitchen, although they'd gotten fairly close. Tony reported that Menendez, who had spent much of the day outside behind my house, had wanted another look at the beam where the four extra bullets had been discovered and that had slowed their progress. The brace holding up the ceiling was still in place, the old wooden beam had been removed and the surrounding area smoothed and sanded. The installation of the steel beam would take place the next day and then Maxie, if I could stand it, would begin her cosmetic work in the kitchen. The damage on the den side of the kitchen door would be minimal, Tony had said, but some repairs would certainly be necessary.

For the moment, though, the kitchen was more impassible than it had been even the day before because of the heavy braces being used to hold up my house while one of the ceiling beams was, for all purposes, missing. So here we were, discussing a decades-old murder case that had emerged from my land among plants that had been in the ground this morning. There was something satisfyingly ironic about it.

"I think Maxie will tell you she's busy deciding how to make my kitchen look as bizarre as possible," I told Paul while facing my mother so it wouldn't appear I was having a discussion with the ceiling. "But you feel free to give it your best shot." And then Pat Benatar's *Hit Me With Your Best Shot* flew into my head as punishment for some odd misdeed I couldn't remember or hadn't noticed. It stayed there the rest of the night. So whomever I wronged, we're even now.

"I can handle the computer research," Josh said. "The property ownership is a matter of public record. That shouldn't be hard to find."

"You are going to bed at a decent hour tonight, young man," I said. "I'm amazed you didn't drop a paint can on your foot today after the fifteen minutes of sleep you got last night."

My father dropped down from the ceiling chuckling. "You sound like you're everybody's mother tonight, Baby Girl," he said. My father, who is the sweetest man who ever lived and no longer does, has a real talent for finding the wrong thing to say with the best of intentions.

I chose not to respond. Josh, who did actually still look like he had rolled reluctantly out of bed six minutes before, nodded. "I'm looking up that one thing and nothing else," he said. "I really do have to get some sleep tonight."

I was having a vegetable fricassee from so many towns in my area that I can't possibly list them here. But it was very nice and included corn, tomatoes, red bliss potatoes and any number of things I don't recall right at the moment. "That's right," I said. "You do." One has to reinforce one's point to emphasize the importance every once in a while.

"I can do some of it," Melissa said, not looking at me. "It's just internet stuff. There won't be any *danger*."

"No, but there will be time taken and you have stuff to do," I reiterated. "This isn't going to stop you from acing your tests."

I didn't look at her but I could pretty much hear Melissa's eyes rolling at the injustice of my totalitarian reign. Still, I was the landlord and the procurer of foodstuffs in the household and she would simply have to deal with it. Sometimes it's good to be the queen.

Paul had heard enough of the family bickering and decided to refocus us on the true importance of the topic at hand. "Someone was murdered either on that spot or killed and then brought to the spot forty years ago or more," he said. "A more complete medical examiner's report would be a very large help. Alison . . ."

I knew he was about to ask me to contact Phyllis, who has a contact at the ME's office. Their relationship is . . . well, I know Phyllis never pays anybody for information and she'd never do anything truly untoward, but she really seems to like this particular guy and what happens between asking for a report and getting it is none of my business. But now I felt the need to say what if felt like I'd been saying nonstop for days now.

"I'm not involved in this one, Paul." I made a point of looking down at my dinner and not up at the ghost. "You're not getting the ME's report through Phyllis unless you ask her yourself and personally I would pay cash money to see that happen."

"I could do it," Josh mumbled. I didn't answer him because I couldn't think of anything.

The ghost who had been trying to sniff everyone's plate had gotten grumpy about it and taken to picking people's napkins off their laps and dropping them to the floor. He was reaching out toward my mother's when she looked at him and said, "Now, stop that." She swatted at his hand although she couldn't really make a physical impact. The ghost looked astonished and pulled his hand back. He stared at Mom and decided to deflect his attention toward another table.

"My intention was to plead Melissa's case," Paul said. "She could do a bit of online research without putting herself at any risk, and you could monitor her time very closely if you think it might infringe on her studies. That has to be her first priority."

"I'm not letting my daughter get involved in this case, Paul," I said. "Deal with it."

"I'm right here at the same table with you," Melissa reminded us. She waved a hand. "See?"

Josh did not reach for his phone—he knew better—but he did lean over and talk quietly to Liss out of my earshot.

Then she looked at Paul. "Since this is a forty-year-old case, isn't there less information you might be able to find? We don't even know who the victim is and that means we don't know who the suspects are."

"She's so smart," said my mother, who apparently doesn't know a husband making an end run when she sees it. She has no basis for comparison; my father is so transparent, in any number of ways.

"It's true that we know very little," Paul answered, and Melissa immediately began relaying the words to Josh. "But much of what we can find out should be simplified by the time that has gone by. The property records can lead to possible identities for the victim, as can the registration on the car if that can be found. A medical examiner's report will indicate what kind of bullet, if any, was used to shoot the person inside the Continental. That can be traced to gun records."

"Do I have to put my fingers in my ears and start humming?" I asked. "How will I eat?"

Of course that was when the phone in my pocket buzzed. Thinking the message might be from one of my guests, who were not used to having me out of the house at this time of the evening, I grabbed it and took a look quickly. And naturally the person getting in touch was Phyllis, who had probably put a reporter in the restaurant on the odd chance that her name was mentioned, ever.

"Oh, what is it?" I sort of groaned to myself.

Melissa, looking concerned, turned toward me at the same time Josh did. "What?" they said in unison. Honestly, it couldn't have been better if they'd rehearsed.

I waved a hand. "Nothing important," I said, hoping I was being truthful.

I was still deciding about that when I read Phyllis's text message:

Got preliminary ME report on body in car—man shot 4X. C me.

It took me three readings to understand what she meant. "I have to go see Phyllis," I said. Looking up at Paul I added, "I hope you're happy."

He was disingenuous enough to look stunned. "Happy?" he wondered aloud.

"Do we have to skip dessert, then?" Melissa asked.

"Don't be crazy," I told her. "They have ice cream from local dairies."

Chapter 17

"We don't know who your victim was yet, but he was definitely male and he suffered four separate gunshot wounds from a pistol or handgun of some kind." Phyllis Coates rarely engages in small talk. No. The fact is, for Phyllis, this *was* small talk. "No definite determination of the caliber yet." I thought the newfound bullets might be a help in determining that, but McElone would never use evidence she couldn't authenticate.

"This place is a fire trap," my father noted, his eyes wide. "How does she manage to keep getting approved to run a business here?"

It was a fair question. Phyllis appeared to have kept every single piece of paper she's come into contact with since she'd left the *New York Daily News* more than twenty-five years earlier. And maybe some from before that. They were spread around her office in piles from floor to Phyllis's reach, which was about six feet off the ground. Phyllis is a huge personality, but she's not tall.

I had tried—believe me—to talk my mother into going

home from *Harvest*. I had, in fact, attempted to talk my husband and daughter into letting me drop them off at home before I came to the already-cramped offices of the Harbor Haven *Chronicle* to have what I hoped would be a brief meeting with my friend. I knew there was no chance Paul would be left out, but he takes up remarkably little space in a car or an office.

Suffice it to say, the whole gang was here now and breathing space in Phyllis's little office, filled to bursting with paper and, as my father had pointed out, a danger to all those who entered it. I had successfully convinced Phyllis to talk to us (when she'd been expecting only me) in the bullpen area of her workspace, which made it possible for all of us who were still doing so to continue breathing.

"What more can you tell us?" I asked Phyllis. I wanted Paul, Josh and not as much Melissa to get the information they wanted so I could go home and tend to my guests, and maybe even sit down for a few minutes. It's a dream, I know, but I keep striving toward it.

"A few things, nothing huge." Phyllis tends to talk in nips rather than bites. She is an advocate of punchy, terse prose. She talks like a newspaper would if a) people still read newspapers and b) one of them came to life. "For one, the victim was probably between thirty and fifty years old. About five-ten. Maybe two hundred pounds, maybe a little less. From a few cloth fragments they found, probably dressed in jeans and a denim shirt. Definitely not expecting to end his day buried in a Lincoln Continental. Shot from a low angle. They're actually exploring the idea that the shooter was standing in the hole before the car was lowered in, but that's probably too deep. Still, someone near the floor, lying down, maybe."

"Are they running a DNA test to see if they can identify the remains?" Josh spent a good deal of time watching police procedural shows on TV before he was foolish enough to marry an innkeeper. Who has time for television?

"The ME sent out some samples, but those could take weeks. And if the guy in the car didn't have a record and wasn't in the FBI's database, which didn't exist in the seventies anyway, there'd be no way to trace it. The best they can hope for is to find some relative with similar DNA and identify this guy that way, but it's the definition of a long shot."

Josh frowned. That's not the way it works for the team at *NCIS*. "How about records of people who were reported missing around the time the car was buried?"

Phyllis pointed at him to indicate he'd said something smart and Josh smiled. He doesn't know Phyllis very well, but he respects her journalism and he really likes being told he's smart. "If we can narrow down the dates that the guy might have been shot we have a better chance to nail that down," she said. "They can analyze the rust in the car and see what tapes were in the 8-track player—oh yes, there was an 8-track player—to at least determine the year. Then I can go through police records to see if there's a likely match."

"What tapes were there for the 8-track player?" That was the one area of the mystery so far that I found interesting. My musical taste, aside from the stuff Melissa tells me I'll find interesting, runs to the oldies.

"What's an 8-track player?" my daughter asked.

"I couldn't find that out from my friend at the ME," Phyllis answered. "He doesn't have the evidence they took out of the car. He just has the bones. Anita would have the stuff from the car; you should ask her."

Trying to get more data from McElone was definitely not at the top of my to-do list. "Anybody who wants to find out is welcome to try," I said.

"I'll do it," Melissa piped up.

"No, you won't."

Melissa's mouth flattened out into a horizontal line. That's teenager for, "I am displeased." So are most expressions.

My mother, who had been uncharacteristically quiet up until now, said, "I'll be happy to talk to the lieutenant." I gave her a look with numerous questions included in it. "Nobody puts a dead body in my daughter's backyard and gets away with it."

"Great," Phyllis said. "Anita will talk to me but she knows I'm going to publish what she says so she'll be careful. With you she won't be as guarded."

Candidly, I figured McElone wouldn't talk to Mom at all. My mother does not even live in Harbor Haven. McElone doesn't really want to talk to me, but Mom comes with layers of irrelevance to the lieutenant. As long as I didn't have to have the conversation, it was okay with me. Besides, if I'd said any of this to Mom she'd have given me six arguments pointing out how I was wrong, and Dad would admonish me for "sassing your mother." I acted against my usual instincts and did not speak.

"Is the car still in your backyard?" Phyllis asked.

"Allegedly," I told her. "With this car there are no guarantees. For something that last got gassed up when they were still putting lead in the Amoco, this thing gets around."

Josh smiled. He finds me amusing, which is one of the reasons this marriage is going to work out. My first husband found my humor—what's the word he used?—oh yeah: "Annoying." Not so much now. My current husband looked at Phyllis and said, "We're told it will be towed away tomorrow morning."

"Get a flashlight inside there tonight," Phyllis advised. "It's probably been picked clean by the cops and whoever took it for a joyride in the middle of the night, but it's worth checking one more time. Mostly look for pieces of plastic or teeth."

Mom looked a little distressed. "Teeth?"

"Yeah. The guy had three missing and there was no bullet that seemed to have traveled in that direction." Phyllis noticed something on a filing cabinet besides the seemingly mountainous pile of papers on it—whatever happened to that paperless society we were promised?—and brushed at it. Whatever it was fluttered its wings and flew to the ceiling, out of sight. "It's possible he just had some major dental problems, which might make identification easier, but it's also possible the person who killed him did a little quick orthodontia on him as an incentive to talk about something before pulling out the artillery."

Melissa's jaw tightened a little bit. She's a feisty girl, but she is still a girl, not a woman. I'll admit this wasn't my favorite mental image, either.

"And the police didn't find the teeth?" Josh asked. He wasn't any less squeamish than the rest of us, but seemed to be channeling his inner Columbo at the moment so he was diving right ahead.

"Nope. Not a trace of one as far as they can tell. But they weren't a hundred percent certain they had a homicide on their hands then. They might look a bit more thoroughly when they get the car back." Phyllis gave me a sideways glance. "Or they might leave it there longer to be sure they don't jostle anything that hasn't already been jostled."

"Bite your tongue," I said.

"What about the emerald?" Mom asked, no doubt to get the conversation away from teeth. "Is that what all this business, the shooting all those years ago and the car moving around, has been about?"

Phyllis made a *who knows* face. "It depends on the quality of the emerald," she answered. "Size, clarity and inclusions will all make a difference."

"Inclusions?" Melissa asked, largely because none of the other living humans in the room go there first.

"Yeah." Phyllis brushed some dust off the papers on the cabinet and the dust met up with other dust on the cabinet surface itself. It was a dust redistribution effort rather than a cleaning of any kind. "Inclusions are things that might become stuck in a stone while it's being formed. Air bubbles, tiny drops of water or a grain of sand. That sort of thing. The more there are, the less pure the emerald is and that makes it less valuable."

"How much money can you get for a fairly large emerald?" I asked when Paul forced me to do so by suggesting it.

"No way of knowing without getting a reliable appraiser

to see it, which I what I imagine the cops are doing now," Phyllis told me, and by extension, Paul. "Emeralds are rarer than diamonds but they have no industrial use so they're not as valuable stone-for-stone. You have a big one that's pure, you can be looking at some serious change."

I shook my head in wonder. "How do you know all this stuff?" I asked Phyllis.

"I'm a reporter," she reminded me, as if her entire lifestyle didn't scream that. "I know a little bit about everything and a lot about nothing."

We all stood around for a moment contemplating that and then Phyllis raised her hands and wiggled them to shoo us out the door. "You have your assignments," she said. "Get out there and find me a story."

Melissa, who has an agreement with Phyllis to work as an assistant in another year, sidled up to me on the way out. "She knows we don't actually work for her, right?" she asked.

"There's really no way of knowing."

Mom and Josh led Liss out the door and toward Mom's Dodge Viper, which had more seats than Josh's truck. My Volvo wagon was being given the night off due to good behavior.

Phyllis stopped me at the door after everyone else was outside. "Be careful with this one," she said quietly.

"I'm not working on this one," I reminded her for what seemed like the millionth time but was probably only somewhere slightly north of a hundred thousand.

"Right," she said. "But be careful anyway. There's something I don't like about it."

"You mean besides the guy with the missing teeth being shot four times and then buried in a car outside my back door?" I asked.

"Yeah," Phyllis said. "This isn't ordinary."

I could have told her that, but clearly there was something that had rattled her, and rattling Phyllis isn't easy. "What didn't you tell the rest of them?" I asked her.

"The ME tells me that the guy might not have been a hundred percent dead when the car was buried. He wasn't sure, but his guess was the victim was bleeding and in pain and they put him in a car and buried him sort of alive."

"Thanks for that, Phyllis. I'll sleep so much better tonight."

Chapter 18

Suffice it to say the rest of the evening was not exactly a nice warm snuggle under a blanket on the sofa. Mom dropped Josh, Melissa and me (and by extension Paul) off at Josh's truck, which was parked at Harvest. She and Dad, who promised to come supervise the end of the Mandorisis' work in the morning, took off for home and then Josh drove us back to the guest-house, where he dutifully found a large flashlight that was brighter than the app on his phone and went out to take another look in the Continental, presumably looking for dental refuse. I did not follow him outside to search for teeth in the dark, which might make me a bad wife but I believed showed off a level of rationality that was not being exhibited elsewhere.

Melissa and I went inside to check on the guests. Katrina was out and Steve, who was with Adam in the movie room again (this time watching *Topper*) told me she'd had dinner plans with none other than Bill Harrelson. *Go, Katrina!* So we left the guys to Cary Grant and company and walked back to the den to watch from the safe distance of the French doors.

To be honest, all I could see from there was some general movement in the area of the car—which strikingly was still where it had been left, indicating to me that the people behind this whole goofy plot were not as inventive as I'd hoped—and Josh's flashlight moving around in odd patterns. I wasn't actually all that worried about my husband because after all it was just a car and he was being guarded by a very earnest ghost, even if I couldn't actually see Paul from this far away in the dark. The motion-activated lights were closer to the house, and weren't showing me much except for a keen view of the hole, which I had memorized.

"None of this makes any sense," Melissa said next to me in her very thoughtful voice.

"What?"

"The whole thing. Somebody kills a man and buries him in a car. Why? Why not just bury the man? It would take up much less space and they could use regular shovels instead of heavy equipment. It would be much faster. Less chance they'd be found."

I almost interrupted, but I could tell my daughter was just warming up. She has an incisive mind and usually comes to conclusions that are worth hearing so I just waited and listened.

Sure enough, she went on. "Then forty years go by and the car is found by accident. Okay so that's a big coincidence. But then the car is taken away and brought back. How could somebody from the nineteen seventies even know that happened? And why would they bring the car back if they wanted it that bad?"

"Those are good questions," I said. "You understand why I want you away from this one?"

Melissa looked at me, her lips pursed. "Not really. You've let me help with other cases before."

"There was always a good reason to take those cases. Somebody needed our help. I didn't think it would be dangerous. This one's different. It doesn't make sense, like you said. And someone is definitely taking an interest in it. I don't want you near it. I don't want *me* near it."

"But Josh is helping Paul," Liss protested.

"Josh is an adult and he doesn't have to listen to me," I told her.

"You're his wife."

"Yeah. He *should* listen to me, but he doesn't have to. You do because even though you're a genius . . ."

"I'm *not* a genius." She brushed her hair back from her face. It's a mechanism of embarrassment. I was being an effective mother.

"Okay, even though you're really smart, you're still only thirteen years old and you really don't have a complete working knowledge of the world. You have to listen to me because I'm your best bet to get decent information on life. And no, it's not Maxie. You understand?"

Melissa toggled her mouth back and forth. If this were a sixties sitcom she probably would have counted that as a nose twitch and an elephant or something would appear in my den. Luckily, this was not a sixties sitcom. "I understand," she said. "But I don't like it."

"I can live with that."

The flashlight started moving in larger circles and seemed to be getting closer. Josh was coming inside. Which, I'll admit, caused me to exhale just a little. He may be a lunatic, but he's my lunatic and I want to keep him.

Being a gentleman and a good husband, he did in fact wipe his shoes on the mat outside before coming in. I didn't even have to tell him the first time; he just did it. I don't know why it took me so long to marry him.

I opened the French doors and Josh came inside, trying very hard not to show that he was legitimately cold. It's some man thing, I guess. All I know is it was thirty-eight degrees outside without the wind chill and he was wearing a light jacket. "Did you find anything?" I asked him. You have to show some interest in your spouse's hobbies.

"I'm not sure," Josh said.

I waited for extra words to come out of his mouth but they were not forthcoming. "What do you mean, you're not sure?" I asked.

"We didn't find any teeth." That sentence came almost simultaneously from Josh and Paul, who had phased through the wall and was now floating to my husband's right.

"That's a plus," I told him/them.

"But you did find something?" Melissa asked.

"I can't imagine there's anything of significance in that car that the police haven't already seen," Paul said.

"I found something," Josh told me. "I texted Paul but he hasn't answered. Was he out there with me?"

Paul regarded me with a look. "I didn't want to dampen his enthusiasm, but I don't think his find is of any importance."

"He was there," I told Josh. "What did you find?"

He reached into his pocket and pulled out something I

couldn't immediately see. "This. See what you can make of it." Josh opened his hand and showed me a small shiny plastic object that was probably clear when it started out. "Phyllis told us to look for plastic," he reminded me.

"What is it?" I asked. It was half-moon shaped and covered more in dust than dirt.

"It's part of a contact lens," Melissa said. "And I don't think it's forty years old."

"The police are looking for a missing person in the wrong decade," Josh said, the excitement rising in his voice. "We're the only ones who know it."

"It's a small plastic disc," Paul scoffed. "It is in a car that has been in the ground for decades, then removed and returned. It might have come from one of the crime scene technicians for all we know."

"Should we call the lieutenant?" Josh asked. He looked like he wanted to. And that was what did it for me. I'd been waiting for him to lose interest, but he wasn't going to. And even though my experience didn't amount to much, it was wrong for me to let him do this without me. A marriage is a team. You're either in it together or you're not.

"Definitely not," Paul sniffed. "It would be a waste of her time."

"Maybe not tonight," I said. "But we'll talk to her tomorrow."

"We?" Melissa asked.

I nodded, giving in to the inevitable. "I think we have to attack this together."

Chapter 19

The Lincoln Continental, thank goodness, left my property (legitimately) at ten the next morning, exactly at the time we had scheduled a spook show for the library, which has windows that look out on the very spot. All three guests had decided to attend this performance. But despite Paul's best attempts to attract their attention by swinging the light fixture hung from the ceiling (which raised my concern level even higher than usual) and despite Maxie stealing a comb from Katrina's hair and a handkerchief from Adam's pocket, they were mostly occupied with the spectacle taking place outside involving a tow truck and half the Harbor Haven police force. Okay, two members of the Harbor Haven police force, but McElone had chosen to come out and not just send an emissary.

She and I hadn't had a chance to talk yet. I was busy overseeing the overlooked goings-on in my library and she was, for reasons I couldn't begin to understand, watching a tow truck take a Carter-era sedan off the beach. How that was going to help solve crimes was a mystery in itself.

Paul picked up a trumpet I'd found in an "antiques" shop

on the boardwalk and pretended to play it. He doesn't have any actual breath to blow into the valve (which was just as well because it had been in the shop for quite some time) so he just swung it around like what a Canadian Englishman thinks a jazz player moves like.

"How does this look?" he asked.

I shrugged. It was hard for me to picture without the ghost behind it but for a second Steve looked up, noticed the movement and smiled. Then he went back to watching the tow truck. Because, you know, tow truck. Paul noticed the moment and smiled just a little.

Maxie put an end to the show—her favorite part of the festivities—by rustling Katrina's collar to get her attention and then opening and closing the blinds on the window they were all watching. It was a new move in the show, and I'm not certain it wasn't Maxie simply acting out because she hadn't been properly respected despite what I'm sure she considered her best efforts.

I announced the end of the morning's program because the ghosts couldn't effectively. The "crowd" applauded dutifully and then rose to head out of the room, and I assumed to the beach where they could see the spectacle of the tow truck better. Katrina hesitated and stopped at the doorway. She waited for Adam and Steve to exit on their way to the French doors (still the only effective route to the backyard without walking all the way around the house) and approached me when I headed in that direction myself.

Behind me I heard Paul say, "Maxie. A moment of your time, please."

Maxie knew what that meant: He was going to ask her to help by doing some internet research on his case. She let out what would have been a long breath in a breathing person. "I'm working," she said with more than a little testiness in her voice.

"This will take only a minute, I promise." Paul's tone was so gentle I was afraid it would put Maxie to sleep. If Maxie could sleep.

"Oh, *fine!*" The two of them vanished into the ceiling, no doubt in search of Maxie's laptop computer which she kept in Melissa's room but sometimes left on a fairly secure area of the roof. Maxie likes to sit "on" the roof and watch the area from there.

"Can I do something for you, Katrina?" I asked this largely based on the fact that Katrina had purposely blocked the library door so I figured she needed me for something.

"I wanted to . . . thank you," she said. That was unexpected; guests usually wait until they were about to go home before thanking me for their stay. Of course, some of them were more apt to berate me about something they'd been keeping to themselves that I could have fixed if only they'd . . . but that's another topic entirely.

"Well, you're certainly welcome," I said. "For what?"

"For introducing me to Bill," Katrina said, indicating that I should have known what she'd meant. "We went out to dinner last night and it was very special."

After four years in the vacation business I have come to recognize the romantic nature of being away from the daily routine that many of my guests feel when they're in my house.

It's gratifying, really. My job is to provide them an experience that takes them away from whatever troubles they might be experiencing in their usual lives and create a place that seems removed from all that. It's like Disney World but without people wearing giant heads and billions of dollars.

The people aren't wearing the billions of dollars. It's about the huge amounts spent to create a theme park. You get the idea.

But I also have to make sure the guest's expectations aren't so heightened as to be unrealistic or impossible to fulfill. For one thing, the guest will be disappointed. For another, she'll usually blame that disappointment on me.

"Well I'm glad you had a nice evening," I told Katrina. "That's what vacations are for." See, that was a subtle attempt at reminding her she wasn't living her real life right now.

"Oh, I think it might be more than that," she said. "We really hit it off."

That could be dangerous. If Bill Harrelson didn't share Katrina's assessment of their one evening out there could be choppy waters ahead, Captain. This was tightrope walking at its most dangerous: I'd have to reinforce the idea that things were great to avoid bursting Katrina's bubble while gently suggesting that the great things were simply a temporary function of her being on vacation. And I was working without a net.

"That's very nice," I said. "It's good to be able to spend some time with someone you just met."

Katrina looked at me with the most innocent eyes I'd seen since Melissa was five. "What we have is much more important than simply spending a little time together," she said. "This might be the man I've been waiting for."

There was no point in arguing with her. I'd voiced my view and she'd told me what she thought. With a guest, I back off. If someone I knew in my real life suggested they'd met The One after going to dinner for a first date, I might not give up quite so easily.

Except of course when Jeannie had met Tony, because I'd fixed them up. But that was a marriage and two children ago. I retired with a 1.000 batting average in fix-ups.

"I hope so, Katrina." Before she could offer more evidence I nodded toward the door and Katrina stopped blocking my way. I walked out and got to the kitchen door, where I could hear Tony and Vic placing the steel beam in my ceiling. "You guys need any help?" I called through the plastic sheeting (and the door).

"We're doing okay," Vic called back. "The beam will be in by this afternoon." I could do the drywall work myself and then Maxie would do her thing, which made me shudder. I'd have to demand new blueprints from her before she started moving my stove into the den because she wanted a more open look, or something.

Of course, he didn't know my father was in there, having been dropped off by Mom this morning because he couldn't bear to stay away. He had not once come out to tell me how the Mandorisis were messing up, which could only mean their work was impeccable.

"Cool," I said. "I'll be outside."

I didn't wait for Vic to answer and walked through the

French doors to the backyard. I put on a sweater I kept on a coat rack right by the beach doors because, you know, it was November.

McElone was alone on the beach. In the distance I could see the tow truck heading for the street with the Continental hanging from its claw. Adam and Steve must have decided the show was over because there wasn't a trace of either of them.

All that was left out here was the great big hole and the yellow crime scene tape on wire posts stuck into the sand. And the lieutenant.

She walked over to me carrying a tablet computer, on which I assumed she had immortalized the exciting action of taking the Continental away—again—and preserved it for future viewing when there was nothing good on TV. "We got your car out of here," she said, exhibiting a grasp for the incredibly obvious I did not think suited her.

"Not my car," I told her. "What happens now?"

McElone gave me a look I'm sure she meant would chill my blood. The wind was doing a good job of that, but I'd seen the look before and it wasn't having much effect. "Now you go back to running a hotel and let us do our job."

She knew me well enough to have expected the word *hotel* would irritate me just a bit. I used that for subtext. "I have never stopped you from doing your job," I pointed out.

"Stopped, no. Slowed down, certainly."

This hilarious banter might have continued for hours but Paul appeared seemingly out of nowhere. With the bright sunlight reflected off the sand sometimes it's hard to see the ghosts on the beach so I hadn't noticed him approaching from the house, or he'd tunneled under the sand and rose up for effect, which did not seem likely.

"We know who the person in the car was," he said, his voice sounding breathless despite the fact that it was. "Maxie and I have managed to track him down. Tell the lieutenant."

Right on the heels of McElone telling me I was an impediment to her work I did not feel especially empowered to solve a major part of her case for her. So I assiduously avoided looking directly at Paul but managed through peripheral vision to see he was holding the piece of contact lens, which also glinted, albeit through some grime, in the sunlight.

"Lieutenant, we found something in the car last night," I began, figuring Paul was featuring the lens because it had some significance. I reminded myself that he had dismissed Josh's discovery the night before as an unimportant piece of plastic.

McElone's eyebrows dropped a couple of feet. "What do you mean, 'we found?' You went past the crime scene tape and looked in the car? You touched things? What are you doing contaminating my evidence?"

This was not going quite as well as I might have hoped, especially since I might now be facing charges. And I wasn't really open to explaining that I hadn't actually done any of that but my husband had. We had only been married a few months, after all.

"Never mind how. Nobody touched anything without wearing gloves." That was true; Josh had worn a pair of batting gloves he'd found in a drawer that he'd worn in a softball league six years before. Men keep everything, especially if it's sports-related. "The important thing is that we found a contact lens."

"Yes," Paul said in an encouraging tone. "It's the lens that made the difference. Because they weren't in wide circulation at the time, extended use contact lenses actually had markings that indicated the manufacturer and lot number, which could be traced."

I told none of that to McElone. "A contact lens? From nineteen seventy-seven?" she asked. "You sure it's not from one of the techs or somebody who helped move this car the other night?"

"Definitely," Paul said to me. I started parroting back everything he said as he said it, so I wasn't listening so much as taking dictation. "This kind of lens is not the sort of thing you'd find in an ophthalmologist's office today. The materials are different and the markings would no longer be found on the lens. It's a certainty this is not a contemporary lens."

"Markings?" McElone said, ignoring the fact that I don't actually talk like that. "Let me see that lens."

I put my hands behind my back. Paul floated around me and placed the small piece of contact lens, which he handled very gently because it was brittle, into my right hand. I made sure to close my hand without putting any pressure on the lens. "Here it is," Paul said. Because apparently he didn't think I knew the plastic disc in my hand had come from him.

With McElone watching I made a show of reaching into the pocket of my jeans—the left hand pocket because the other was holding the lens—and then "transferring" it into my right hand. I carefully held it out to her. The lieutenant had already put on a pair of latex gloves and opened a small evidence bag. She used a pair of tweezers she must have had in her pocket (McElone is the ultimate scout, always prepared) to daintily move the lens into the bag without cracking it. She sealed the bag and looked at me.

"Tell her that Maxie and I have identified the victim," Paul whispered. Paul whispers like there's a chance he might be heard by someone other than me.

"It's possible that the lens can help name the person whose bones were in the car," I told McElone because I actually *do* talk like that.

The lieutenant looked up from the evidence bag and into my eyes. "You think so, huh?" That's McElone being inscrutable.

I thought I could scrute her, though, and that is almost always a mistake. "There appear to be markings on the lens that indicate the manufacturer and the date they were made," I echoed Paul. "Tracing those records of the time to the person who wore the lenses isn't very difficult because they were a kind of beta testing project." I threw that last bit in on my own because Paul had said the lenses were "prototypes of a kind that were contemporaneously being tested on human subjects." I thought my way was better.

I thought I saw a tiny glint of amusement in McElone's eyes. Uh-oh. "No kidding. In the seventies?"

"No," Paul told me to say. "I believe it would have been approximately nineteen eighty-three. The car would have been six years old."

"You're wrong," the detective countered. "It was eighty-two. The car was only five."

That's where the uncharacteristic humor in her eyes came from. "You've found all this already," I said.

"We've identified the victim through ophthalmology records, yes. Only we did it through a pair of prescription sunglasses that were in the glove compartment." McElone put the evidence into a pouch on her belt. I wondered if it would join the small cloth pouch Paul had seen her withhold from the crime scene team when the car was first discovered. But that didn't make sense. The lieutenant was a frighteningly honest cop.

Paul sputtered behind me. "She did?"

"I don't suppose you're interested in telling me his name," I said.

"It's not my first choice, but knowing you I'll be worn down. And you're going to find out anyway." McElone grunted a little in her disapproval of me knowing anything. "His name was . . ."

She and Paul spoke at exactly the same time and said exactly the same thing. "Herman Fitzsimmons."

Paul looked over at McElone with wide eyes. "Damn," he said.

Chapter 20

"Who was Herman Fitzsimmons?" I asked Maxie.

Maxie's head was not in the room. In fact, all that was currently visible was her rear end and her legs. She was hovering on the den side of the bullet-ridden ceiling beam but hadn't been able to resist sticking her head through the wall to get a better look at the work being done. When she heard my voice she withdrew and brought all of herself back to my side with a look of annoyance. I was getting used to seeing that look from just about everybody.

"What?"

"I said, who was Herman Fitzsimmons?"

McElone had taken her contact lens and gone, having refrained from gloating over knowing exactly what I'd known through the discovery of alternate eyewear. No doubt she thought she'd dodged a bullet in not coming into the house and vowed to herself not to come back if she didn't have to, but I recognized the pattern of these things and figured I'd be lucky if I didn't see the lieutenant again before lunch. Which was in roughly two hours.

Paul, flabbergasted at McElone's ability to never not know

something, recovered nicely from his disappointment and was here in the den with me and whatever percentage of Maxie was present. Lamenting that the rudimentary cell phone I'd given him for texting did not have a function that would allow him to store notes, he was going the old-fashioned way with a reporter's notebook and a pencil. When you have a child in the sixth grade you have tons of pencils in the house because you used to have a child in the second grade.

Maxie had been summoned from the roof and had assumed I'd called her to discuss new designs for my kitchen, a subject I preferred to avoid until I was myself a ghost. She'd arrived with her sketchpad under the trench coat and not her laptop. Paul had insisted she go back and get the computer but she'd left the pad while she did. We were going to have The Conversation whether I liked it or not.

"Herman Fitzsimmons?" When she chooses to think of something else, Maxie is as easily distracted as a moth, assuming there is no flame present, in which case the moth will easily out-attention-span her.

"The man who died in the car back there," I said, pointing vaguely toward the back of my house.

"They pretty much have the beam in place," she reported, pointing at the kitchen door. "Another couple hours and it'll be time to start making the place look like something."

"Herman Fitzsimmons," Paul reminded her.

Maxie emoted a deep sigh. Maxie can be as dramatic as Meryl Streep without the talent. "*Fine,*" she moaned, and floated down to the side table where her laptop had been placed before she began her reverie involving my ceiling. Her voice became a singsong drone like a second grader being asked to recite the times tables. They do that in second grade, right? "Herman Fitzsimmons was a car dealer in Matawan, but he didn't sell Lincoln Continentals. He sold Pontiacs. He was born at Beth Israel Hospital in Newark and grew up in Irvington but he moved to West Long Branch after he got out of high school and started selling Pontiacs."

"So he was reported as missing around the time we think the car was buried?" Paul asked, trying to get Maxie out of Herman's early years to the relevant moment.

She consulted her laptop screen. "Yeah, by his wife Darlene. He married her when he was twenty-three and they stayed together until he vanished at the age of thirty-six. Had a daughter, Theresa, who was only two years old when Herman drove into the ground, so she probably didn't shoot him."

Paul flattened out his lips just a touch to indicate he wasn't sure Maxie was treating this matter with the gravity it deserved. "Was there any indication he had enemies? Ties to organized crime?"

"They don't tend to print that kind of thing in the newspaper, and all I really have on our buddy Herman is what was printed when he disappeared. There never were obituaries for him because nobody knew where he was. They were probably walking all over him at the time and didn't know it." Maxie turned toward me, away from her laptop. Her face immediately brightened. "I have some new designs. You want to see them?"

"Sure. When we're done with this." I pointed her back toward her computer.

Maxie grumbled something under her breath that I chose not to hear and devoted herself again to reciting the intricacies of Herman Fitzsimmons. "So your pal ended up buying the car dealership in Matawan after he only worked there five years."

Paul's eyes seemed to get closer to each other. "How did he manage to finance that?" he asked.

"Again, not in the newspapers. Remember there wasn't an internet then so people weren't posting all over the place about Herman. He won a couple of dealer of the year trophies and he was an up-and-coming name in the local Elks Club and that was about it. Other than that the only mentions are about his marriage to Darlene and the birth of his daughter Theresa. There was an article in the *Asbury Park Press* about five days after Darlene reported him missing. All it said was that he was about five feet, eleven inches and weighed two hundred pounds. He had brown eyes and hair and a mustache, which I'm sure was extremely attractive given it was nineteen-eighty-two."

Paul put up a finger to his chin. I was afraid he would burst into *I Am Sixteen Going on Seventeen* but instead he asked Maxie, "Was he an officer in the Elks Club, and in what town was the club located?"

Maxie hit a few keys on her laptop. "It's actually in Keyport and it's not a club; it's a *lodge*," she said. "He was, and I am not making this up, listed as a Loyal Knight. There's also a lecturing knight and a leading knight, so I guess he was maybe fourth on the list. But the head guy was called—get this—the exalted ruler." Maxie laughed. Paul and I, assiduously not joining in, looked at her. "Man, you guys are no fun at all."

Paul ignored her and returned to head-of-the-agency mode. "Print out a list of the officers in the lodge at the time Herman Fitzsimmons vanished," he said. "Check and see if he had any other relatives beside his wife and daughter. He was still a young man. Did he have parents? Siblings? Anyone else in the area? Were there any allegations that he was unscrupulous in business? Did other dealers resent him?"

"You're looking at a guy who's been dead for more than thirty-five years," Maxie reminded him. "I'm not going to be able to dredge up every detail of his life and I do have other things I have to pay attention to, you know." Her eyes darted toward the sketchpad.

"Please do what you can as soon as possible," Paul said. "I will be attempting to contact Mr. Fitzsimmons." Without elaborating he dropped down through the floor. Paul's Ghosternet sessions are activities he considers better done privately and the basement is his favorite area of retreat.

Maxie looked at me.

"I know, I promised," I said. "Let's see the new designs for the kitchen."

She flew—literally—to the sketchpad and brandished it like a Michelangelo, except that it wasn't on an easel so much as floating in thin air. The yellow cardboard cover opened and she pushed the pages over until she reached the one she wanted me to see.

I had braced myself because I know two things: Maxie can be very sensitive to any criticism of her design work, and whatever she did was not going to fit my vision of the kitchen, which frankly would have been to put it back in exactly the same way I'd had it before, only without the bullet damage in the ceiling.

So my teeth were tightly locked together in anticipation of shouting out something I shouldn't when I saw Maxie's latest effort. And I swear, I gave it an honest and thorough examination while trying not to react.

"So, what do you think?" Maxie said, with what I heard as a challenge in her voice.

"The cabinets are on the floor," I pointed out.

"Anybody can hang them from the ceiling," she said. "It's a statement of originality. You're being unconventional."

"No, I'm trying to avoid tripping over my kitchen cabinets."

To her credit, Maxie avoided rolling her eyes but the effort was visible. "So you want them back where *everybody* has them."

"Maxie, it's not always true, but sometimes when everybody does something it's because there's a really good reason." The hammering from inside the kitchen made it difficult to talk at a normal decibel level, but I didn't want Maxie to think I was shouting at her so I tried to modulate my tone even as the volume rose. "Look, the problem I think you and I have here is that you're trying to create a work of art and I want to have a functional kitchen. Now, isn't there some way we can meet in the middle?"

I make a lot of wisecracks about Maxie, and most of them are well deserved. But at her core she's actually a fairly reasonable person who happens to be dead as a result of circumstance. (Try describing any of *your* friends that way, I dare you!) And she is especially serious about her work.

She seemed to consider what I'd said, nodding to herself and pursing her lips. Then she looked me straight in the eyes. "No," she said.

"No?" Maybe I hadn't understood, although her whole sentence had only two letters in it. Not easy to misinterpret that.

"No, I don't think we can compromise like that," Maxie said. "You just want to put a coat of paint on the walls and move everything back. You don't need an interior designer; you need a tray and a roller. How am I supposed to create anything in that space?"

I closed my eyes. This was the thing I really hadn't wanted to say. To be honest, I'd hoped that Maxie would get bored with the project and give up, in which case I really could do exactly what she was suggesting I wanted to do. But that clearly wasn't going to happen now so I had to resort to Plan B, which was really plan A-, since I was making it up at that very moment.

"What if we work on the plans together?" I suggested. "That way you won't be expending all this energy putting together something I can't use, but you'll be able to see what I need and design around it. I promise I'll be open to un . . . conventional ideas. How's that?"

This time Maxie didn't need a moment to mull the idea over. Her face brightened and she snatched the sketchpad up as she rose. Maxie literally gets high when she's happy. In a moment her head would be, well, through the roof.

"Let's do it!" she shouted. She zoomed over to the coffee table and started laying the sketchpad out. "I have the basic dimensions in my head." Her pencil was already hovering over the pad before I could so much as turn in that direction.

I needed some time to think this whole plan over (since I had barely considered it until ten seconds earlier) so I was grateful that Paul came rising up from the basement at that very moment. "I have some progress to report," he said. Everyone has his own way of saying *hello*.

"Not now, we're working," Maxie said, now lying horizontally, parallel to the floor and facing the table.

"It's okay, Maxie," I said. "We can do both. What's up, Paul?" No matter what, he was buying me time and that was enough.

"I have made not made contact with Herman Fitzsimmons," he said. "I believe we are not on the same plane of existence."

That didn't seem like a reason Phyllis would tear up the front page, although the existence of ghosts would probably be something of a journalistic coup for her. "Okay," I said.

Paul smiled. I'd fallen directly into his trap. "But I did manage to reach the woman with whom he was cheating on his wife."

Chapter 21

"Okay," Josh said in the passenger seat of my Volvo wagon. "Let's get this straight. Herman Fitzsimmons is the man whose skeleton was found in the car in the backyard, right? So Paul says he was having an affair?"

"Yes," Melissa answered, despite not having been there for the conversation I'd had with Paul that set this whole merry-go-round in motion. "The woman's name was Harriet Adamson and she told Paul she and Mr. Fitzsimmons were together for two years before he disappeared."

Melissa knew that because Paul and I had told her when she got home from school. She was telling Josh about it in my Volvo because we were all on the way to Jeannie and Tony's house for dinner having cancelled the afternoon spook show due to the entire potential audience being out of the house. I had texted all three guests that I would be out for dinner unless anyone had an objection. None of the guests had so much as replied, which I figured gave me the green light to go out.

Maxie had not been a happy camper when the information Paul had brought took center stage for the rest of the day. I told her we'd work on the kitchen plans tonight.

"When did Harriet become a ghost?" Josh said. He knows the right parlance for our deceased friends now and almost never says *died* or *dead* when they're around. They weren't present at the moment, but it had just become habit for him. I still slip up when I forget or am especially on edge, which covers much of the time.

Melissa looked at me because Paul hadn't covered this point when she was home. "She died only a couple of years ago at the age of sixty-six," I informed her and Josh. Paul wasn't there so I took advantage of the full range of the English language regarding non-living people. "Liver problems."

"What did she tell Paul about Fitzsimmons's disappearance?" Josh asked anybody who would answer him.

"She remembered it vividly," I answered. Might as well be me because this part would require a tiny bit of adult supervision. "She said Herman was supposed to meet her for . . . lunch . . . at a hotel on Route 35 and he never showed up. Harriet figured she got stood up and got mad. She says now that even if she'd known he had disappeared she couldn't have called the police at that moment because nobody was supposed to know they were meeting. If she made the call Herman's wife Darlene would have found out."

Melissa, to my disappointment, did not look the least bit confused by what I'd said. Maybe it was that I was looking at her in the rearview mirror, but I doubted it.

Josh was concentrating on the road, but his face was telling me the case was occupying some of his mind. "Did the police ever find out about Harriet? Did they question her at the time of Herman's disappearance?"

"Paul doesn't know. Harriet faded out on him, but Maxie is supposedly working on finding the police records of the disappearance if she can concentrate on anything except destroying my kitchen."

Melissa waved a hand at me dismissively. Teenagers know everything. "You're underestimating Maxie," she said.

"That's a thought too terrifying for me to consider."

Josh chuckled. "I'm sorry I can't meet Maxie," he said. "She sounds like a real character."

"She's an entire cast of characters," I told him. I was glad he'd never actually met Maxie. What if he liked her? What would that say about me?

"She's very nice and she cares," Melissa said. "I don't see why that's a bad thing."

"If you have to go outside on the deck to use the stove in February, you'll see why it's a bad thing," I suggested.

"Anyway, about Herman Fitzsimmons," Josh said, perhaps to keep the conversation away from a disagreement between my daughter and me. "Did Harriet say whether Herman's wife ever found out about her? That might mean Darlene had a motive to kill him."

I had asked Paul that question. "Harriet didn't think so. Darlene didn't know her husband was having an affair before he vanished. She was pretty sure of that. Of course in situations like that the mistress is the last to know." When The Swine had been caught red-handed (as it were) and ended our marriage, I'm sure his pal . . . I always want to call her *Barbie* . . . had no idea I was wise to her. It's hard to hear inside a tanning bed.

Josh pulled the truck into the driveway at Jeannie and Tony's house in Lavallette, a testament to Tony's taste and skill as a contractor. He'd worked on pretty much every room in the place and, unlike some home improvement maniacs, actually improved each one. There was no ego in his work. He did not leave a signature stamp. It was just that after Tony was done working on a room, it looked better and probably was more efficient or comfortable than it had been before. When I worked on a room, it was lucky to get out alive.

I shuddered to think of what Maxie might have done here.

We came in, when Jeannie opened the front door, to the usual chaos. Jeanne and Tony have two children under four years old and that means there will be no peace, especially before dinner when little kids get antsy because they're hungry. So tonight was no exception.

Oliver, Jeannie's son and her eldest at the advanced age of three-and-change, was ostensibly watching *Paw Patrol* in a corner of the TV room just off the entrance, but he was really jumping up and down on the sofa, luckily without shoes. Molly, who was still short of 18 months but not by much, was toddling around (as toddlers do) carrying a small stuffed toy that looked to my eye like a banana wearing a vest. A green vest.

She came up to Melissa first, because she's an excellent judge of character, and gave her a hug. Liss is crazy about both Jeannie's kids, but I suspect she has a particular fondness for Molly because she's never had a brother and assumes it would be awful. "Hello, Molly," my daughter cooed. "Is that your friend?"

Molly, whose relationship with words is about equivalent to mine with organic chemistry (a class I took for two whole weeks), said, "Ba." You may interpret that as you like.

"She's very nice." Liss walked into the TV room and Molly followed her as the acolyte she would no doubt become. Melissa is a charismatic personality.

I heard the usual hilarity ensue as Oliver saw her walk in and they bonded as well. But I was suddenly engulfed in the arms of my best friend since forever and Jeannie's hugs can be lethal if you don't see them coming.

"Alison!" Jeannie's mouth was right next to my ear, so there went hearing out of my right side for the rest of the evening. "I'm so glad you're here!"

I had seen Jeannie the week before and we talk on the phone every couple of days, so her enthusiasm—which I'm used to—was a little overblown even for her. "Why?" I asked. Out of the corner of my eye, since I could barely move my head, I sensed that Tony was walking over to greet Josh.

"You can settle a disagreement," Jeannie said. I'm pretty sure that's what she said but her greeting was still ringing on that eardrum. "Tony and I have been arguing all day."

"You have not," I pointed out as she mercifully eased up on the clench and let me remember what breathing was like. "Tony was in my house until two hours ago."

Tony, who was indeed shaking hands with Josh in a gesture that I considered much more reasonable, looked over at me as they each released and said, "I'm really sorry about the extra day, Alison."

I waved a hand idly. "I know you're doing the job right," I told him. "I trust you."

Jeannie must have been ticked off that I was being friendly with her husband when she wanted me on her side. "Tony wants me to quit my job."

Tony looked at the ceiling, apparently for some kind of sign. "No, I don't want you to quit your job," he said, his voice fraying just enough to indicate this wasn't the first time he'd said such a thing today. "I'm perfectly happy with you having your job and the money certainly doesn't hurt."

I knew both of them quite well, so I had a good idea where to get the real information. Jeannie is my best friend, my sounding board and my favorite shoulder—other than Josh's—to cry on. When I filed for divorce from The Swine she had to get waterproof blouses. But the fact is, she lets her emotions rule her and doesn't believe she's doing so. She has seen things in my house that absolutely can't be explained with anything but the knowledge that ghosts exist there and because that doesn't enter into her version of reality, she will find any possible (and often impossible) explanation to preserve her worldview. That's Jeannie.

So if I wanted the true dope on this supposed argument they were having I could ask Oliver, who would undoubtedly tell me about the latest doings on *Thomas the Tank Engine* or I could ask Tony. Which would infuriate Jeannie.

Luckily, I married the right man on my second try. "What's this all about?" Josh asked Tony. Guy stuff. Jeannie couldn't get mad at Josh and she knew it. She pouted over a pot of marinara sauce and stirred with a little too much muscle. Luckily she was wearing an apron.

"I said to Jeannie that I'm getting into a busy time of year and the kids' daycare was getting expensive," Tony explained. "Jeannie's decided that means I want her to be a stay-at-home mom." He turned toward his wife. "And that's *not* what I meant, because we can't afford it and she likes her work."

Ollie broke up the laugh fest by walking in with a plastic stick and pointing at Tony. "Bang, Daddy," he said.

Tony looked down at his son. "That's not a gun, Ollie. That's a magic wand."

"*Bang*, Daddy." He pointed again.

Tony got the message, and even though Ollie was really aiming the wand at his leg, clutched his chest. "Oh!" he shouted, and staggered back toward Jeannie.

Oliver looked terrified and ran back into the TV room and Melissa.

Jeannie looked at her husband, who was still playing the part of "wounded man." "See what you did?" she said.

Tony looked over and no doubt noticed his son was no longer in the room. "Ollie!" he called. "Ollie, I'm okay!" He walked out toward the TV room, too.

There was a rather pregnant pause in the kitchen, which was warm just because of all the cooking and I'm pretty sure the oven was on. And as usual, my husband knew how to diffuse an awkward situation.

"Did Alison tell you I'm working on a case?" he asked.

Jeannie turned to look at him. There ensued a good deal

of explanation, all of which you already know. It transpired that Tony had told Jeannie about the bullets found in the cavity of the ceiling beam and hole and about the car that had until recently been an unseen resident of my backyard, but he hadn't known about the body in the car and he definitely had not heard the name Herman Fitzsimmons before. Somewhere in the middle of it all Tony came back with the news that Oliver was no longer under the impression he'd shot his dad.

When we had gotten them up to speed on the situation, two things had changed. First, Jeannie and Tony seemed to forget they'd been disagreeing about Jeannie's career and second, Melissa had reappeared from the TV room with Molly trailing dutifully after her.

I'd left out much of the ghost-related material during our recitation although I'd seen Tony nodding a couple of times in silent understanding. Tony gets the whole ghost thing. I think he's sorry he can't see them, except that he's afraid of Maxie. It's a long story.

Jeannie had put some pasta in a large pot of boiling water. One of the things Tony had done when he inevitably renovated their kitchen—something I could show Maxie if she wanted to be reasonable—was to install an extra-large stove so she had plenty of burners to work with. "So this Fitzsimmons guy was cheating on his wife but she didn't know about it?" she asked.

That was ghost-adjacent so I didn't divulge my source of information. "We think so but we're not sure."

"Well, if the wife did it she had a lot of help," Tony said. "I doubt she drove an earth mover into your backyard and dug a ditch deep enough to put in her husband and the competition's car."

Jeannie turned on him. "Why? Because a woman can't run heavy equipment?"

"No, because nobody would have been able to do that with just one person and also I don't think she could have done it without being seen before she called the cops to report her husband missing." Tony can deflect with the best of them.

"Besides, Katrina said she'd seen two people moving the car," Josh pointed out.

"So if Darlene didn't do it, who did?" I hadn't so much as called one suspect on the phone, but that was largely because I didn't know who the suspects were, let alone their cell numbers. Canvassing all of the Jersey Shore from the nineteen eighties seemed somehow inefficient.

"Let's all sit down to dinner," Jeannie said, which hardly seemed an adequate response to my question. Without waiting for an answer she looked in the direction of the TV room. "Oliver! Supper!" Ollie, who literally knew which side his bread was buttered on, turned off the television and could be heard doing his three-year-old thing in our direction.

* * *

While we were walking toward the dining room, which I could be certain Jeannie never used for normal family dinners because Ollie looked confused when we passed the kitchen table, Melissa, who had clearly been doing some thinking, said, "I think it's important we find out who owned the house back in those days. There might be some connection. I don't think they just buried the car in our backyard randomly. There's so much open space on the beach." That was true, since a beach is pretty much open space by definition.

"I'll have to get on that," I said, meaning I'd get Paul to get Maxie to get on that. "It can't be hard to get those documents; they're all public record." I pulled out my phone and sent the message with the proviso: *Don't text back unless you have to.* I would have been able to explain it, or simply tell Jeannie the truth and let her fabricate whatever explanation suited her mindset, but it was much less tiring to do it this way.

Jeannie knows the three of us well enough that this was hardly a formal dinner. There was sausage and peppers with the pasta and meatballs in the marinara she'd made—jars are not for my friend. And the oven had indeed been in use, since garlic bread accompanied our dinner. I planned to eat again in three days.

Melissa, who undoubtedly could identify every flavor in every aspect of the meal, politely asked Jeannie about the sauce and was given the answer, "Oregano." She nodded as if enlightened but I saw a glimmer of amusement in her eyes. Find me a marinara that *doesn't* have oregano in it.

"Sounds to me like the most obvious possibility is some business thing," Tony said. "Other car dealers would have access to tow trucks and certainly could find that sort of earth moving equipment. I bet it was a rival."

"To kill a guy?" Josh was skeptical. "If you're mad at a competitor you might talk him down to customers or other dealers. I mean *I* wouldn't do that to another paint store but there are those who might. That's as far as it would go. Who needs to kill somebody who's selling more cars than you?"

There was a time when Jeannie would have found this kind of talk absolutely scandalous in front of her son. But once Molly was born Jeannie's incredibly immersive style of parenting had eased up considerably. Ollie, for his part, looked downright uninterested in whatever it was these nutty grown-ups were talking about and was using the marinara to draw a penguin on his plasticized placemat. Jeannie didn't so much as blink. Before Molly she'd have had the whole room decontaminated and might have considered moving.

"Maybe the guy had mob connections," Tony attempted. "I've heard about people being buried in obscure locations before." Jeannie gave him a look. "What? I watch true crime shows."

"It's possible," I said, "but Lt. McElone seemed to think there was nothing really shady on Fitzsimmons's record. I don't know who to look into at all."

Given a setup like that, how could my cell phone *not* have buzzed with a text message from Paul?

Got the property records. We might have solved this case.

Chapter 22

Earlier in my private investigation "career" I might have dropped everything after receiving that kind of message, made an excuse to Jeannie and Tony and made a beeline for the guesthouse to find out what had been discovered. But I knew Paul and he liked to make dramatic statements that would shortly turn out to be a little exaggerated. Like by a factor of thirty.

So I read the message, made an excuse about getting a text from a guest that didn't require any immediate action, put the phone back in my pocket and returned to the dinner conversation. By the time we had reached the dessert, a chocolate cream pie Jeannie admitted she had bought, we had identified at least seven possible suspects in the death of Herman Fitzsimmons, although only two of them (Darlene and Harriet, despite the latter denying any involvement posthumously) had names attached. Otherwise they fell into categories: Rival car dealers, Harriet's husband—if she had one—mob bosses, disgruntled employees and Sting (hey, it was 1983). Okay, so three of them had names. But Sting is not on the guy's birth certificate.

I thanked Jeannie again for making dinner, reiterated that it had not been necessary (although a break from bring-in food was welcome), reinforced the fact that the next day would absolutely be the last one Tony and Vic spent on my ceiling beam, and then played a couple of games of something I didn't recognize with Ollie and Molly (a rhyme that would haunt them the rest of their lives, no doubt to the point that Molly would eventually go by M. Constance Mandorisi) and got the three of us into the truck for the ride home, which aside from some normal post-mortem was uneventful.

Once we were back at the guesthouse, though, a quick glance at Paul told me he'd been in a state of agitation. "Why didn't you text me back?" he demanded as soon as we were through the front door. I looked forward to using the back door again tomorrow. In all likelihood. Paul had texted me twice more wondering why I hadn't responded but I hadn't even seen those until I was in the truck on the way home. Hey, there was chocolate cream pie.

"Because there wasn't anything I could do and you said you solved it anyway," I told him. "Now let me check on my guests."

Maxie, who dropped in from the ceiling with her trench coat and laptop, must have heard what I'd said. "They're all out," she informed me. "The two guys went to dinner and I think the woman is on a date again. She was getting all dressed up before she left."

I stared at her. "You didn't go into her room, did you?"

Maxie gave me her *oh please* face. "No. She was running back and forth on the second floor between her room and the bathroom and every time she was a little more dolled up. So let's talk about designs." She reached into the trench coat again, no doubt for the sketchpad, but Paul stopped her.

"Case first, Maxie. Show Alison what we found."

Maxie stopped in mid-reach and her face showed boredom the way a ten-year-old might. "Okay," she moaned. "But we're definitely talking design later." I resigned myself to that eventuality and moved on, my husband and daughter following me into the den. I plopped down on the sofa with a force I don't usually have when I don't eat like a horse at Jeannie's house. "But *we* didn't find anything. *I* found it." Maxie claims to disdain the internet research Paul asks her to do, but she's very good at it and doesn't like it when she fails to get what she sees as proper credit. Like, all the credit.

Josh watched as the laptop placed itself on the coffee table and maneuvered to see the screen, which Maxie noted with a look. "He's getting a little friendly, isn't he?" she said.

I gave her a look without saying anything to my husband. He had no idea his head was coinciding with her midsection, and I saw no reason to enlighten him on the subject. "Fine," Maxie said. I think she found the situation amusing.

"The key was discovering who had owned the property in the early eighties," Paul began. The fact that Maxie had done the grunt work wasn't going to stop him from lecturing us on the process. Paul sees us as a serious investigative agency when in fact we are one woman who is devoted to keeping a pleasant guesthouse and two ghosts who have literally all the time in the world and not much to do with it. "That was easy enough to find and it led to other dominoes falling."

I was all in favor of wrapping this affair up as quickly as possible but so far Paul—and by extension Maxie—hadn't told me anything. "So who did it?" I asked. Cut to the chase; that's my motto.

"We don't know," Maxie said. She has a similar motto but it's more about getting the dull stuff out of the way so she can show off her genius. Everyone has an agenda.

"Not yet," Paul corrected sternly. "But it is a matter of time, and not much time."

Josh looked at the computer screen, then at me. "I'm seeing ownership documents filed with the county," he said.

Melissa, who knows not to interrupt the ghosts when they're really jazzed up about something, also knows that Josh can't hear them and has everyone's best interests at heart. "Just a second," she said. "I'll make sure you know what's going on."

Maxie was wearing a sour expression and a black t-shirt (now that her trench coat was no longer necessary) bearing the legend, *I Can't Believe It Either*. Her tone was drier and less patient when she said, "Pay attention. We found the records. You remember I owned the house before you did and I bought it from the Preston family, who owned it for twenty years." I saw Liss translating this all for Josh, who kept staring at the screen intently.

"Thanks for the background, but yeah I do remember that. Are you suggesting that one of the Prestons killed Herman Fitzsimmons and buried him in a Lincoln Continental in the backyard?" That would have been awkward. I went to high school with one of the Prestons' children. I don't go to reunions, but still.

"No." Paul was taking charge of the symposium once more. "The Prestons bought the house in 1986 from a man named Lincoln O'Hara."

"Lincoln? Like in 'Lincoln Continental?'" I asked. It seemed a pretty big coincidence and Paul has always said not to trust coincidences. They happen, but they're usually suspect.

"Certainly not a member of that family but the choice of car might have been a signal of some sort," Paul said. "I am not placing a great deal of significance on it yet."

"So what *are* you placing significance on?" I asked. "Melissa has school tomorrow, Josh has to open the store before the sun comes up and I need to look at sketches with Maxie. Let's get to the point." Never let it be said I can't be abrasive when I'm full.

"A few things." Paul can be oblivious to the mood of others when he's engrossed in work. And sometimes when he's not so engrossed. "First, there is no direct line between Lincoln O'Hara and Herman Fitzsimmons yet established. But O'Hara did work for a company that rented out earth moving equipment and would have had access to some of the inventory if he'd needed it. He was certified to use many of the larger machines."

"So even if he didn't kill Fitzsimmons," Maxie said, "he sure could have helped bury the car. And he lived right here so that would explain why he didn't choose any other place."

"Wouldn't the fact that this was his house incriminate him if the car was found?" Josh asked Paul. "Why leave himself open to that kind of jeopardy?" Melissa showed him where to look to approximate eye contact.

"It wasn't discovered until this week," Paul pointed out. "That's a pretty good track record. Besides, it's easier to conceal serious excavation when it's on your own property. There are no neighbors to either side here who might complain. If it was done during the offseason when there are very few tourists and not many people on the beach, and if it was done at night with minimal lighting, it could be easily concealed. Clearly that happened or there would have been some reports at the time of the incident." He waited for Melissa to communicate his response to Josh, whom Paul obviously now considered an associate. Great. The last sane member of the family was being inducted into the Paul Harrison Dead Detectives Society.

I leaned back into the sofa cushions, regretting at least one meatball eaten in haste. I closed my eyes just because it felt good. "So why don't we tell all this to McElone and she can go arrest this Lincoln O'Hara and I can take it easy on the couch?"

"Because Lincoln O'Hara died in 2007," Maxie said. "And so far Paul hasn't been able to reach him with his Jedi mind powers." She rotated a finger pointed at her temple to indicate Paul was not totally sane. Because as they say, it takes one to know one.

I opened my eyes because it would have been rude to fall asleep, but I'd considered it. Besides, antacids were definitely in my future. Paul looked at me sheepishly. "You understand,

Alison. Not everyone who leaves life ends up like Maxie and I did, and some move on after this stage. Lincoln O'Hara appears to have either skipped this level of existence or evolved past it."

"So we still don't really have a list of suspects," Josh said after being brought up to date. He sounded like he'd been promised a new fire engine for Christmas and was now being told the toy store had sold out of that model. I patted him on the hand and he looked at me questioningly, but smiled.

"On the contrary, I believe we have a very good start," Paul said. "We can speak to Herman Fitzsimmons's wife Darlene. Even if she is not a suspect she will know who her husband's enemies or business rivals might have been. I think we should find out from Lt. McElone the name of the detective assigned to the case at the time and question that person. We can get the file from the police department even if the lieutenant is not in a cooperative mood; it is a matter of public record. But the really interesting question is whether anyone in the area has rented excavation equipment lately, because that Continental was moved out and then back on consecutive nights."

"You don't think they used the equipment that was already in the yard?" Melissa asked. "It was just sitting there; you'd think they'd take advantage of it."

"Yes," Paul agreed. "But the thing is, like any piece of equipment or vehicle, a key is necessary to operate it, and no responsible construction worker would ever leave the machine sitting there overnight with the key still available."

Josh listened to Melissa's repeat of Paul's answer. "So I

guess we can't rule out Bill Harrelson and his crew," he suggested.

"No, I think they should definitely be within our focus." Paul was pacing but refrained from goatee stroking. He wasn't sifting evidence so much as he was strategizing, and that required him to pace. Which is an interesting thing to watch when it's taking place two feet above the floor. "But if we can find any records of such equipment being rented in the area on the nights in question, that would lead us toward the conclusion that they were not involved. Maxie?"

Maxie was shading in a sketch on her pad with a charcoal pencil she must have had in her pocket. "What?" she said without any hint of interest.

Everett, wearing fatigues, phased through the wall just as Paul was snapping his fingers in front of Maxie's face in a gesture intended to get her attention. Everett being Everett, he simply floated back and watched. He knew no action was necessary and he was no doubt aware of his wife's attention issues. Maxie would concentrate on her own priorities at the expensive of pretty much everything else.

"Maxie!" Paul shouted.

She looked up after a moment. "Yeah." She glanced back at the sketch.

"We need to find records of equipment rentals for the nights the car was removed and brought back," Paul said again, or to Maxie's point of view, for the first time.

"I did that already. Look at the laptop."

Josh was closest to Maxie's computer and he reached for it

as soon as Melissa told him permission had been granted. "She has a tab open for one heavy equipment rental company," he reported. He scanned the screen carefully. "There's one excavator out both of the nights we're talking about."

Paul's eyes showed interest. "To whom was it rented?" Even when he's excited his grammar is impeccable.

"Someone named James Constantine," Josh read off the screen.

Paul looked at me. "Do we know of a James Constantine?" he asked.

I started to shake my head but stopped, which was a distinct annoyance to the left side of my neck. "Maybe," I said. "Bill has a guy named Jim working with him."

"Oh yeah," Josh said. "Jim . . . somebody."

There was a short moment when nobody spoke, but Maxie can't possibly exist in such a circumstance. "So," she said, "are you ready to start working up some new kitchen designs?"

Chapter 23

"Jim Constantine?" Bill Harrelson looked bemused. "You think Jim had something to do with the car moving around like that?"

We were standing on my back deck despite it being a slightly damp and chilly November morning in New Jersey. I could see my breath, and while that gave me an advantage over Paul (who was hovering nearby) as Tony and Vic were inside doing what they could to get my kitchen back to an operational state.

I'd come out to catch Bill before he could ride off in his Bob the Builder dune buggy and start moving sand around on another area of the beach. Paul was very interested in how this interview would go, but he would have been present even if he'd thought the whole thing would probably yield no information. Paul is a very hands-on kind of ghost.

"I'm not saying that," I assured Bill. "I'm saying I don't know anything about Jim and you do, so whatever you can tell me about him would help me determine if he might have had a reason to pull the Continental out and then move it around like a Matchbox car for two days."

"I don't know much about the guy either," Bill said, staring off into the sea like Captain Ahab wondering where his pal Moby might have wandered off to. "This is the first job I've worked with him, you know."

"Did your client foist him off on you?" I asked.

"That's not the way I'd have put it," Paul said, scowling a bit. Paul doesn't care for a snarky attitude, which makes his move from Canada to New Jersey all the more baffling.

"No, that's not how it works," Bill answered. "The state hires my company but they don't dictate which crew members we use. I was sent out with these guys by my supervisor for the duration of the job, so I've been working with him about two weeks. I don't ask how they choose. Jim must be new to the company because I'd never met him before."

Paul hovered over closer. I don't know why he thinks he has to keep his voice low when he talks to me, but I guess it's a hard habit to break even when you're dead. "Two weeks is long enough," he noted. "Bill must have *some* impression of him."

That made sense and besides, Paul was the investigator and I was the innkeeper so I tend to defer to his judgment on such matters. When a big accommodations industry case comes our way—well, first I'm hoping it doesn't—I will be the resident expert. Until then, I mostly do as I'm told.

Bill scratched his head while thinking, which I didn't think anybody did outside of cartoons. "He's a little sloppy," he said. "He brings his own lunch. The other guys seem to like him well enough. I haven't had any reason to think anything bad about him so far."

"He was behind the controls when they found the car, right?" I asked.

Bill nodded. "Yeah, there was some crazy bet going on that they were going to find buried treasure or something. I didn't think it was possible, but there was that car down there. So I guess those divining rods or whatever actually work, huh?"

At Paul's prompting, although I would have wondered myself, I asked, "Is that typical on a job like this? That you would just start digging an enormous hole in somebody's back-yard because your crew is playing with the idea of buried trea-sure? Was that Jim's idea?" The last part of the question was Paul reminding me what we were actually asking about.

"I mean, the guys always get into little things," Bill said. "But it's just in good fun, a way to take your mind off the job. This is a big thing to do, getting the shore back in shape. If you think of it all at once it can seem impossible. But if they have little side bets and stuff it makes the thing easier to deal with on a day-to-day basis. Jim? He was here pretty much by himself at the time, so I guess he took the initiative himself."

"That's a lot of initiative," I said without any prompting at all. "If he hadn't found a car down there I'd be pretty annoyed that there was this huge crater in my property for no reason."

Bill looked at me a moment, more seeming like he was trying to figure out how to keep his company and the state of New Jersey from being sued. Which was a wise thing for him to do. "If he hadn't found the car the hole wouldn't have been anywhere near as large," he explained. "He started with just a shovel and then hit something that was obviously a lot bigger."

I chose not to debate the point for the moment and keep my legal options open. "Why did they think there was buried treasure here of all places?"

"Excellent question," Paul said. It's the little things.

"There was some legend, one of the guys knew about it. Supposedly a pirate ship in the 1770s was in this area and took on a cannonball or something and couldn't make it home. The idea was they buried a load of jewels and stuff here to come back and get it later, and then they got discovered by the British troops here before the Revolution and got sent to jail or hanged. Nobody ever came for the treasure but word got out."

I looked at Paul and he nodded; he'd have Maxie look into this goofy story. After having spent an hour and twenty minutes the night before looking over and trying to negotiate new kitchen designs, she needed to contribute to the case in order to alleviate my crankiness, which was a reversal in our usual pattern.

"Who in your company told this story?" I asked Bill. That was Paul's question. There's give-and-take in this relationship.

"Ernie Waskow," Bill said. "But I know Ernie and I've worked with him for eight years. There's no way he came and moved the car around for two nights in a row."

"No way?"

"His wife would never let him."

Better to ignore that. "We'll talk to him later. But as you understand it, Ernie came up with the idea but Jim dug the hole, right?"

Bill nodded enthusiastically. "That's how I got it. They thought they were going to find emeralds, apparently."

My head snapped up from the view of my phone, which I had removed from my pocket to check the time. "Emeralds?" Finally, a connection to something else in this strange affair. "They said emeralds specifically?" And in addition to everything else, I immediately forgot what time it was.

"Yeah. Ernie said these pirates had come back from Colombia and they were loaded down with emeralds they'd stolen from some other ship that was bringing back a load of emeralds that had been mined there. I guess Colombia has a lot of emeralds, or did back then, anyway."

Now all we had to do was figure out how at least one of them had gotten into a product of the Ford Motor Company that had ended up interred in my backyard. And why at least one person had died as a result.

"But they didn't find any emeralds." It was sort of a question, I guess, but I figured Bill would have probably mentioned if that kind of thing had occurred on his watch.

"No." He sounded amused. "They found a car that looks like it was on *Starsky and Hutch*."

"With a dead person in it." Definitely not a question. I just wanted Bill to understand the reason I was spending this much time asking him about it.

He stopped looking amused. "Yeah."

"Bill, what would it take to move that car off the beach and not be heard in the night, and then bring it back the next night the same way?" He was the expert, sort of. He'd moved things around with machines more than I had.

He considered. "It really wouldn't make that much noise," he said. "You've probably had cars towed in front of your house and didn't even know it. It's more about the chains than the machinery. If it was me I'd be more worried about the lights, I would think. It's pitch black out there at night without the house lights on, so they'd have to bring their own lights and that would be visible from the house. There wasn't a moon either night, so they couldn't count on that. But if they were careful with the chains and less worried about speed than quiet, it could be done without anybody hearing, especially if they were asleep."

There was a short pause while Paul fed me the next question. "Would they have to bring especially bright lights? Could they do it with small flashlights aimed at specific areas, do you think?"

He raised an eyebrow and tilted his head a little to the right. "It would have to be somebody who's done it a lot, but yeah, they could do it if they were worried about shining spots on the house and waking people up. What I can't figure is why they'd bring the car back after they had taken it away and not gotten caught. Why risk that a second time in order to return what they'd stolen?"

"Good question. Bill, who in your crew would be good enough to do all that work with flashlights and not make a lot of noise with chains?"

Bill looked uncomfortable. "I don't want to name anybody and get them in trouble, Alison. I don't know anything about who moved that car around."

I held up my hands in a defensive posture. "I'm not asking you to incriminate. Who *wouldn't* be able to do it?"

He looked sheepish, torn between worry and pride.

"Frankly, anybody in my crew could have pulled this off without a hitch," he said.

Swell. "Okay, thanks," I said. "I won't keep you any longer. And hey. I hear you and Katrina might have hit it off. Good for you, huh?" I don't know why but people always talk to adults who are starting relationships like they're kids who just started mastering the multiplication tables.

But Bill didn't seem the least bit embarrassed by what I'd said. No, the expression that crossed his face was something more like total puzzlement. "Katrina?" he said.

I know some people like to play their romantic sides close to the vest, but this was pushing things a little far, in my opinion. "Yeah. Come on, Bill. It's okay. Katrina seems very happy and I'm glad for you guys. I'm not making a bigger thing out of it than a nice time during a vacation." Maybe he thought I was suggesting they were headed for a Christmas wedding, which would require serious planning this close to Thanksgiving.

"Katrina?" he said again. His eyes were staring off into space trying to focus on something that seemed very far away.

"That's odd," Paul said.

Okay, this wasn't just a commitment issue. "Katrina Breslin," I reminded him.

Bill looked at me and shook his head. "Nope. Sorry."

"Bill, I introduced you here on this very spot not three days ago." I pointed to the ground in case he didn't know where this very spot was.

The foreman looked at me very carefully. In retrospect I think it's possible he was trying to determine if I was in need of very intense psychological counseling. And I was starting to think he had a point. Then he widened his eyes a bit and took in a deep breath, remembering.

"Oh, yeah," Bill said, and I relaxed a little, although it was still weird. "I remember her. No. Alison, I never asked out Katrina Breslin. Don't know where you got that idea."

I looked at Paul, which probably threw Bill off, and Paul looked just as stunned as I must have. Looked. "That's surprising," he said. Paul has a gift for understatement.

It didn't make sense. I looked back at Bill. "You sure?" It made more sense at the time.

He laughed. "Trust me. I'd know if I was dating one of your guests."

"Surprising indeed," Paul said.

Chapter 24

"Oh, the pirate thing is definitely real." Ernie Waskow said. He brushed the hair out of his eyes. The wind was picking up.

We were standing on the beach about two hundred yards south of my property, where Ernie was taking a break from moving sand around for no discernible reason. I'm a layperson and don't actually get the whole dune-restoration business. I was glad I'd worn a jacket and Ernie was probably regretting his unfortunate lack of a hat. That hair, which was not as thick around the middle as Ernie would have liked me to believe, was doing some serious dance moves every time the breeze decided to change direction.

"These pirates buried a trove of emeralds in the sand behind my house?" Of all the places to choose, that seemed the least likely other than in midtown Manhattan. Except that at least has a diamond district.

"Well, your house wasn't there then," Ernie said, probably wondering how someone this ignorant could get an innkeeper's license. It was a good question. "They had to do something with the gems because their ship was badly damaged and eventually sunk."

"And this was in the 1770s?" I just wanted to get him talking, which did not seem like it would be a problem.

Ernie was a short, solid little man somewhere between twenty-eight and ninety years old. The stubble on his chin was just barely flecked with gray but his eyes were clear and alert. Once I'd asked him about pirates he'd perked up. Before that he seemed to think I was complaining about the noise outside my house, which was interesting because that had more or less ceased once the Lincoln had resurrected itself.

I know; you're wondering what Paul and I decided to do about Bill's statement that he had never so much as asked Katrina Breslin out on a date. After some discussion we'd decided mostly that we'd have to put a pin in that and get back to it later because we had these construction guys to talk to. Translation: Neither of us had an idea and I didn't want to upset Katrina.

"Yeah, the 1770s, probably about 1773," Ernie answered. "The Revolution hadn't really gotten going yet and the coast was guarded by British soldiers who were more concerned with pirates than rebels. When they saw the ship they fired on it and the crew had to take their cargo here to hide it until they got back. But they never got back."

"Did they leave a map or something?" I asked. Pirates who bury treasure make maps, don't they?

Ernie's opinion of me, not stellar to begin with, seemed to take a hit. "There was no map," he said. "They were all of the same crew, they all saw where it was buried, and they all didn't get far afterward. So the treasure stayed here until this week."

"How come the gems didn't all get found?" I asked. "All you got was a Lincoln Continental with a very undernourished passenger in it."

Ernie looked impassive and shrugged. "Probably the real booty is near the site we found," he said. "I think there were a couple of pretty big emeralds in the hole that got dug."

If he thought that he might come back for a better look when nobody was watching. "So is it worth searching the rest of the beach?" I asked. I didn't expect him to confess but his answer might be telling.

"Probably not," Ernie said. "Anything we found would probably be held up in court for years anyway. Nobody knows who really owns it. I just started digging because Jim said there was metal under the sand and that didn't make sense."

Jim said that, huh? "Why was Jim looking for metal in the beach?"

"It's just something he does." Thanks, Ernie. That says a ton.

"Do you think Jim came back that night and took the car, and then brought it back the next night?" Maybe if I couldn't get Ernie to confess I could get him to snitch on a friend. That was what I'd come to.

"I don't know. I have to get back to work." He pulled on his hair again in a vain attempt to get it looking neat. He took two steps toward his dormant earthmover.

I figured I'd get it in while I could. "*You* didn't move the car, did you, Ernie?"

He looked at me like I should be restrained and given

medication. "Of course not. I don't think there's emeralds. Besides." I knew it was coming. "My wife would never let me."

* * *

"My husband—my *late* husband—didn't have any enemies." Darlene Fitzsimmons sat on a very tasteful sofa in her Spring Lake home overlooking the beach. This was not cheap real estate and it was far from a cheap house. I had instinctively wiped my feet before entering, but she was not putting on airs. She had some money (or more to the point her second husband Bernard Coles did) and she didn't see any problem with spending it. Other than the wage gap between us there wasn't much that had put me off about Darlene. She hadn't even objected when I'd asked if I could record the conversation. I'd shown her my driver's license but she seemed to think I was researching a book on her first husband's death. She seemed relatively down-to-earth otherwise.

Paul was not along on this trip because he'd insisted on being dropped off near the Harbor Haven police station where he could eavesdrop once again on McElone, which I thought was kind of cruel (and was me technically breaking a promise), but which wouldn't matter because the subject herself would never know it happened. What McElone didn't know wouldn't hurt me.

"I don't want to be indelicate," I said, which was a sure signal I was about to be indelicate, "but someone did shoot him and bury him in a Lincoln Continental."

"Yes, and that was especially rude," Darlene said. "Putting

him forever in the competition like that. I mean, it's clear he *had* an enemy. That was somebody who *really* didn't like Herm, but I can't begin to guess who it might have been."

Darlene had, being the next of kin, been notified when her extremely late husband's body had been identified by the medical examiner. Being more then thirty years later, it probably hadn't come as much of a shock that Herman Fitzsimmons was deceased. It was more the cause of his demise that had been a surprise for her. "I always just figured he'd had a heart attack somewhere and wasn't carrying his ID," Darlene said. "I guess that doesn't make a whole lot of sense when you think about it, but I needed something that I could use as an explanation."

I was sitting in a very comfortable side chair that I was afraid blocked Darlene's view of the ocean, but I figured she had it memorized by now and anyway she didn't seem to mind. Between us on a small table was the voice recorder, which so far had not immortalized one word that Paul could possibly find useful when I played it for him. Herm, as she called Fitzsimmons, had vanished into thin air. She'd been distraught at the time, but it had been all these years now. No, she had no idea who might have offed a reasonably successful Pontiac dealer in his prime.

But now I was about to take the conversation in another direction and that might possibly provide Paul with some relevant material. "Were you aware that your husband— Mr. Fitzsimmons—was having an affair at the time he disappeared?" I asked. In my sort-of-business, you have to ask people things that they're not going to like answering. But I did find myself involuntarily leaning back in the chair as if waiting for a recoil.

"I wasn't aware at the time, but I found out a little later," Darlene said, as naturally as if I'd asked her what her wedding China pattern might have been. And I'll bet she would have remembered that, too. "The woman—what was her name?—Harriet Adamson contacted me while the police were still searching for Herm and not finding him. I guess she thought I'd gotten wind of what was going on and might have done something to my husband. But it was news to me." She chuckled and shook her head. "I guess it's always news to the wife, right?"

I could write a whole book on the subject. Perhaps one day.

"Were you angry?" I asked.

"Sure. It never occurred to me Herm wasn't being faithful. I was. Faithful. And it wasn't because there weren't opportunities, you can believe me. I might not be much now but I was something back in the old days."

I thought she looked pretty good now, for a woman in her sixties or any other decade. If she'd had plastic surgery it had been done very skillfully. She had stayed trim. She dressed fairly demurely but did not look like a frump. Her legs were up on the sofa, feet hanging off because she was wearing shoes that I probably would have to book three guests for a week to afford. "I believe that," I said.

"Believe it." Darlene gave me a significant look but one with humor in the eyes. "It didn't matter, though. Herm was gone and I couldn't even yell at him. It took me years with Dr. Maples to get past that."

"Dr. Maples?"

"My therapist. The woman's a genius. After Herm went poof, you know, I didn't have much left over. The insurance wouldn't pay off because he hadn't been declared dead yet. The business was in his name but he couldn't run it. I had to sell the dealership to pay the mortgage and raise our daughter. Wasn't a whole lot left over so I took a job at a construction company doing the books and a little light forklift work."

"Forklift?" I didn't *want* it to sound amazed, but there you go.

"Yeah. I did a little bit of that before I met Herm and gave it up, but I still had the skills."

Okay, that was nuts. First, I couldn't picture this woman behind the controls of a heavy piece of equipment, but what was more important was that she was saying she could operate the kind of earthmover someone used to bury her husband in a car.

"Could you still do it today?" I asked. Someone sure as heck was running at least a tow truck service back and forth from my house this week.

"Sure. You never really lose it. But I wouldn't want to risk losing my manicure." That was Darlene joking. She must have known what I was getting at but she wanted to have me think she didn't.

"Any other pieces of equipment you're certified in?" I said. Might as well get it right out there.

"You mean like something that would make a hole big

enough to put a car in with a man in the front seat?" Her tone couldn't have been friendlier, which was weird. "I can run a backhoe, if that's what you're asking. But I think the police would have been a little suspicious if I was seen digging up a piece of the beach on the same day I reported my husband missing, don't you?"

She had a point. "I didn't mean to imply anything," I said. *At least, I didn't mean for you to figure it out.*

Darlene waved a hand. "Don't think a thing of it. I'd suspect me too after all you've heard. But I was frantically calling around that day trying to find Herm."

"It must have been disturbing to get the news, even all these years later," I suggested. Paul would undoubtedly get on my case about not pressing the point, but I doubted Darlene was gearing up to confess.

"I guess," Darlene said. "The thing is, I had gotten so used to the idea that Herm was dead that it didn't really make that much difference to find out for sure. When they told me somebody shot him, well, that was something of a shock. Who'd want to shoot Herm?"

An excellent question. "Was there something about his business at all? Was he getting ready to diversify or move in on someone else's territory? Start selling Buicks?" I'd sort of asked this already, but getting more specific might unearth some information Darlene hadn't thought of before.

Darlene's mouth curled a little; I took that for a sign she was thinking. "Nah. Herm was doing fine and he wasn't that ambitious. Nobody could have felt threatened by Herm."

She seemed to be leaving no alternative but to think that

this was a crime of passion. "You said you spoke to Harriet Adamson after your husband was gone," I reminded Darlene. "Was *she* angry with him?" There's no better way to get a wife going than to suggest that her husband's mistress might have shot and killed him. How Harriet might have gotten access to heavy earth moving equipment would be another topic for another time. If Darlene was a forklift operator, maybe Harriet worked on skyscrapers. Anything's possible.

"No, I don't think so," Darlene said, shaking her head. "Mostly she seemed puzzled. She couldn't figure out why Herm never showed up to wherever he was supposed to meet her. But I'll tell you who must have been pretty steamed at them. Her husband."

Whoa! Back up a couple of steps there, lady. "Harriet was married?" No, genius, she had that other kind of husband where you're not married. Sometimes I astonish even myself.

"Oh yeah," Darlene said, looking at her shoes. I thought that move was designed to keep her from making eye contact with me and betraying her delight at the situation. "And when all this stuff came up with Herm being gone, that came out in the wash. Nat was not a happy man."

I was processing a lot very quickly. "But you're saying that Nat . . . Adamson?" Darlene nodded, so I went on. "He only found out about the affair *after* your husband disappeared?" If that was the case he had no motive to put Herman Fitzsimmons into a very chrome-bumpered grave.

"Well, that's what he *said* but I don't know if it's necessarily true," Darlene answered. "I mean, that could cover up a lot, don't you think? I didn't really connect the dots at the time but now that I know somebody shot Herm, it makes you reconsider. Why don't you ask Harriet about that?"

Was it possible she didn't know? "Harriet Adamson passed away a few years ago," I said.

Darlene Fitzsimmons smiled. "Isn't that a shame," she said.

"What about her husband?" I asked. "Is he still alive?"

"I didn't know *she* was dead so I'm probably not the person to ask."

"Well, thank you for your time," I said. I stood up to leave, having concluded that this was the best I was going to do with Darlene. "I appreciate your putting up with my questions. It can't be easy even after all this time."

"No, it's true." Darlene stood up too and I was taken again with how tall she was, easily three inches over my head. "Dr. Maples and I will have what to talk about this week. When my daughter told me I was absolutely stunned."

My jacket, which was halfway to my shoulders, stopped without any decision made on my part. "You daughter told you about your husband's murder?" I asked. How did that make sense?

"Oh, sure," Darlene said, spreading her hands. "She found out about it before anybody else. She's a police officer in Harbor Haven, you know."

Somehow I knew the answer to the question before I asked it. "Really? What's her name?"

"She took her stepfather's name," Darlene Fitzsimmons told me. "Theresa Menendez."

"Of course she did," I said. "Of course she did."

Chapter 25

"Of course I know that Sgt. Menendez is the daughter of the victim." Lt. Anita McElone stood behind her desk in an unsuccessful attempt to convince me she was not going to sit down and explain. She might not sit down, but she was sure as heck going to explain. "That's why she's been taken off that case. As soon as we had a positive ID on the victim, she was no longer eligible to work on it."

I sat down in the chair in front of McElone's desk. Just because she wanted me to go was no reason to let my feet hurt. "But that doesn't mean she's not involved in some way, does it?"

Grunting with what I assumed was frustration, McElone took the executive swivel chair behind her desk and looked over at her computer screen, still intent on making sure I knew she was busy. I assume the lieutenant is always busy, but that didn't mean she could get out of talking to me. "The woman was all of two years old when her father vanished," she said without much inflection. "I think it's unlikely she shot him and then drove an excavator over to bury him in a Lincoln Continental."

McElone had agreed to see me only because we'd played this game enough times for her to know I wasn't going to leave without a conversation. The truth of the matter was that I'd come to pick up my ghost, who was hovering just over her head and to my right, McElone's left, as we spoke. "Isn't that a pretty big coincidence?" I asked.

"Absolutely. But the thing about coincidences is that they happen sometimes." McElone let some breath out through her lips and looked at me. "Is there something you need that I can answer really fast so you'll go away?"

"Who was the investigator on the original disappearance of Herman Fitzsimmons?" I asked her. She was a cop; she could answer cop things. Paul nodded approvingly.

"I looked it up. His name was Anthony Blanik. He died in 2002. I don't think he's going to be a lot of help."

I didn't necessarily agree with that statement; I looked up at Paul and he held up his hands. Yes, he'd try to get in touch with the late Anthony Blanik. We'd have to wait until he got back to the guesthouse for that.

"Did he file a report? Can I see it?" I had no idea what I thought I'd see in a decades-old police report about an unsolved case but it seemed like something I should ask.

"I've seen it," Paul told me. "If you can get a hard copy we can talk about it later."

"It's public record," McElone said. "If it wasn't so old you'd probably find it on the internet. I'll print out a copy. You can pick it up on your way out." She pointed casually toward the door, the subtle little minx (none of which McElone is).

"Thank you, lieutenant. Now tell me what you're holding back about all this that I should know." The direct approach sometimes works with McElone. Sometimes it doesn't, but you might as well give it a shot.

"I'm not holding anything back," she said. "What I'm doing is investigating the murder of Herman Fitzsimmons." But she couldn't just stop there. "At least."

"Aha! So you've figured out about the second person's blood in the car!" So this was a double murder after all.

McElone's eyes iced up. "How do you know about that?" she grumbled. She didn't even give me time to tell her I wouldn't tell her. "Phyllis Coates. I should have figured." You don't get to be chief of detectives for nothing in Harbor Haven.

"You know whose blood it is?" I asked. I didn't see any utility in letting McElone stew on my getting information from my friend the reporter.

"Not yet. It doesn't match anybody in the system as far as the initial tests can tell us but in a couple of weeks we'll get something more complete and that might show more. Now. About you leaving . . ."

"Let's go," Paul said, floating toward the door. "The lieutenant is busy."

It's one thing when a police detective tells you sarcastically that you're wasting her time. It's another when a ghost you've housed for years takes her side over yours. I was just a little irritated.

Unable to take my frustration out on Paul without letting McElone know he was there I decided to do what I do best, which is to act as an annoyance and see how far that will take me. "So what about the cloth pouch you took out of the hole in my backyard and didn't slip into an evidence bag?" I asked McElone. "How does that fit into all this?" I folded my arms and made sure it was clear I wasn't leaving until I had an answer to that question.

"Alison!" Paul admonished.

McElone looked at me with a combination of anger and respect. She didn't think I'd be good enough to notice something like that, and she was right. Paul had seen it and told me. But I could take credit if I wanted to, I figured.

"I don't know what you're talking about," she said slowly.

"Yes, you do. It was a little pouch, maybe velvet, just like the one that had the emerald in it up in my ceiling. You had it along with the other items you took out of the car and the crater it was buried in, but you didn't put it in an evidence bag. Why didn't you?"

McElone stood up, which was a little scary, given how tall and strong she is. If I'd annoyed her enough she might lose control and hit me with the heaviest thing on her desk, which was probably a paper clip. And I had no doubt she could kill me with it if she wanted to. Paul, given his admiration for the lieutenant, might not even try to save me.

"I think it's time for you to leave," she snarled. "If you think you can sit there and accuse me of stealing evidence."

I held up my hands as if she were pointing a gun at me. I have, alas, had guns pointed at me a number of times since I met my mostly dead friends, so I know the proper protocols. Luckily that was not the case in this instance. "I'm not suggesting anything like that," I said. "I have absolutely no doubt that you are the most honest of police officers."

"Detectives." She wasn't giving me an inch today.

"Right, detectives. I know that for a fact. So if I gave you that impression I sincerely apologize. But it's because I know you're an honest . . . detective that I'm asking the question. You must have a good reason for keeping that one item separate. I'm asking why you did that." As groveling and apologizing go, I thought that was a pretty artful example.

Keep in mind that McElone never smiles, at least not sincerely. She tends to laugh at me when I do something stupid, which isn't the same thing. So my sincere appeal for forgiveness wasn't going to create a warm-and-fuzzy moment between the two of us. Instead, she merely unclenched her jaw and let some of the violence leave her eyes.

"I don't see how, given you're certain I'm so very honest, that it's any of your business," she said.

"You have a point," I told her. "Your only problem is that I'm not leaving until you answer the question." I sat back deeper in the chair to illustrate my point. It wasn't much but it was all I had.

McElone's jaw seemed to clench shut like its spring had snapped. The muscles in her face seemed absolutely steely in their determination. Her eyes, while trying as hard as they could to seem impassive, shot out occasional signs of something between exasperation and homicide.

I sat consciously keeping my face exuding confidence and calm. I was lucky McElone couldn't see what was going on in my stomach, where it felt like the Seven Santini Brothers were moving out some old furniture and delivering an entirely new gastric suite of sofas and chairs, with the occasional side table. And maybe a bowling alley.

I said nothing. There was a long pause that I'm sure seemed silent to McElone during which Paul said, "You're making her uncomfortable. We should go."

"There are security issues involved here and I don't think it's appropriate for me to discuss the matter with a civilian," the lieutenant said. "I'm sure you understand." It was all very professional and reasonable.

"I understand," I admitted. "But I don't accept that as an answer. You had something in your hand that anybody else would agree should be included in evidence of whatever nutty crime went on in the early eighties. But you chose to hold onto it instead. I have zero doubt that there was a legit cop reason to do that, but as you're so fond of pointing out, I'm not a professional investigator or a police officer, so I can't figure out what it is. You also know perfectly well that I'm not going to rat you out to the chief of police because I don't think you did anything wrong. But until you explain this situation to me it's going to bother me and I have enough on my mind, what with dead bodies and old cars coming out of my land all by themselves. So spill."

McElone and Paul had exactly the same reaction, which was surprising in itself, given how she was a police detective and he was dead. They stared at me, apparently amazed I could utter that many words in a row, crossed their arms and then, almost in unison, said, "What?"

There wasn't a chance I was about to repeat all that even if I could have remembered it all in sequence. So I concentrated on the breathing person and said, very calmly, "I'm not leaving until you answer. You can have the maintenance staff clean around me after you leave, but I'll still be here when you get back in the morning."

McElone sat back down in her chair quite gracefully. Under the same circumstances I would have fallen back with an impact that would have been felt a block away, but she was more disciplined than anyone I had ever met and could control every muscle in her body to a disturbing degree. She settled into the swivel chair and very quietly said, "Okay."

It wasn't what I'd been expecting so it was my turn to use that time-honored ice-breaker, "What?"

McElone didn't answer me directly, which was wise of her. She spoke at a very low volume and watched her door with more interest than I would have expected. "There is someone on staff here who might be involved in the case. I am protecting the evidence because there is a possibility—and I hope I am wrong—that there might be some tampering involved. I want to have one piece of physical evidence that I will know for a fact came out of that car in that hole. And that is all I am going to tell you about that. Are we clear?"

I gave that a good deal of thought. "Yes. We are clear," I said. And somehow my respect for McElone had actually increased.

"Good. And I am assuming there is no need to tell you that if one word of what I just said gets repeated to me by *anyone* I will take that as a sign that you have been blabbing confidential information I gave you and I will make it my business to be sure your life is miserable."

"I absolutely believe that," I said. There was not a scintilla of irony in any of those words.

"Now go home and take your ghost with you," she said.

I was midway through standing when those words struck home and I think I stopped in mid-lunge. "How did you know he was here?" I gasped.

"He moved my stapler. Twice." McElone closed her eyes briefly and then opened them. "I told you not to let them spy on me."

"It'll never happen again," I said.

I stared at Paul as I skulked out of McElone's office. "I couldn't help it," he said quietly. "I wanted to see if she'd notice."

"Never again," I repeated to McElone. Then I closed her office door from the outside.

Chapter 26

I berated Paul for his indiscretion for most of the ride home, to the point that he stuck his head through the roof of the Volvo so he wouldn't be able to hear me anymore. Ghosts have some of the most infuriating abilities. But I had a functioning nervous system and I figured that gave me the edge.

Josh called while Paul was playing moon roof and I filled him in on the events of the day so far. We hadn't even gotten to the second spook show and already I'd talked to two possible witnesses, found out Herman Fitzsimmons's daughter was a Harbor Haven cop and squeezed some vague information out of McElone that, although she hadn't mentioned names, seemed to indicate that Sgt. Menendez might be playing fast and loose with evidence she had gathered related to her own father's death, which might mean she'd known ahead of time that was his body in the buried Lincoln. Now I needed lunch.

I had stopped at Between Two Breads on Ocean Avenue and gotten myself a decadent turkey sandwich on sourdough. I'd curbed the impulse to ask Paul if he wanted me to pick up anything for him because that's just cruel and besides it annoys him. Having just admonished him for his behavior I could only hold scolding rights if I didn't do anything wrong myself, which I'll admit is sometimes a trial.

Once I had gotten back to the car Paul had grown weary of my nagging and stuck his head up into the November air, and my husband had called. So you're up to date.

"I'm going to do a little looking around between customers," Josh said. "I have the desktop computer here and it's pretty slow today. I have some questions I think we need to have answered."

"We've got nothing but questions," I admitted. "But I've done this before. Don't make yourself too visible. There's somebody out there who feels antsy enough about this whole thing to move that car around a couple of times. I'm guessing that was to keep the police from finding something out. That kind of person usually comes with two things: anger and a deadly weapon."

"I've seen it happen enough," Josh agreed. "Don't worry. Sy is here to protect me."

"Good. I believe in your grandfather. Give him a kiss for me."

"That's not gonna happen."

We made a few disgusting declarations of emotion and I hung up the phone. Paul lowered himself down into—well, near—the passenger seat at that moment, making me wonder if he could have heard my conversation with Josh. I chose not to dwell on that.

"Are you finished scolding me?" Paul asked. "I realize what I did was wrong and I will not do it again."

"That's right, because you're not going back to McElone's

office without me. Not for all eternity." I was not speaking figuratively.

Paul chose not to argue the point. He'd seen me reverse myself on so many previous absolute proclamations. It's the same thing that has eroded my authority with Melissa. "I think our focus should be on the movements of the Lincoln after it was discovered in the ground," he said. "That seems to be the area Lt. McElone is spending the least time on. I observed her all morning, and she was mostly looking into possible motives for the killing of Herman Fitzsimmons."

"Did she come up with anything promising?" I asked.

"It is difficult to say. I couldn't communicate with the lieutenant."

"Except through stapler signals."

Paul moaned a little. It's not as scary as you might think. "You're never going to let that go, are you?"

"Certainly not today, no. But we're talking about McElone."

He looked considerably more comfortable. "She looked into Fitzsimmons's business dealings and there was one rival dealer who seemed a promising suspect."

"What's his name?"

"Sheila Morgenstern," Paul said. "She owned a car dealership in Belmar on Route 35. There was some communication between the two of them at the time through the Ocean County court system, as Ms. Morgenstern seemed to believe Fitzsimmons was having her excluded from some local professional organizations and service clubs. She filled out forms to sue him for restraint of trade but never filed them."

"Service clubs? Like the Elks in Keyport?" Maxie had mentioned Fitzsimmons was an officer of some kind in that lodge.

"Precisely. Morgenstern was applying to the lodge in an attempt to become the first female member, and she alleged that Fitzsimmons, in his role of Loyal Knight, took steps to keep her from the group. According to some letters between Fitzsimmons and his attorney, he denied any such thing had taken place." Paul's face almost glowed; he was so engrossed in the mystery.

"So McElone's talking to this Morgenstern woman?" I said. "That leaves us with the car and the workmen behind the house. I already talked to Bill and I think we need to see Jim . . . somebody and I talked to Ernie about his weird belief in pirate treasure. And I'm afraid I need to have a very delicate conversation with Katrina Breslin about the relationship she seems to believe she's having with Bill where he doesn't show up."

"Jim Constantine," Paul reminded me. "And I'm not sure if you should broach the subject with Katrina yet. We don't know whether she is delusional or lying, or if Bill Harrelson is trying to cover up his own involvement in this affair."

"I don't get what anybody's motive would be," I said as I pulled into my driveway. Tony and Vic were loading up their van—Tony's van—at the back of my house, which meant (Hooray!) that they'd finished the work on my ceiling beam.

"My best guess would be emeralds," Paul, who couldn't care less about the ceiling beam because the house could fall on his head and he wouldn't feel it, said.

I parked on an angle that would allow the van to pass me on its way out and got out of the Volvo. I walked over to Tony and Vic and gave Tony a hug he probably wasn't expecting. "Hey," he said.

"You're done!" I said. "I can have my kitchen back again!"

"Well, mostly," Vic said.

I let go of his brother. "Mostly?"

"Yeah." Tony wasn't making eye contact and Tony always makes eye contact. "The braces are down and the beam is holding."

I didn't know what was coming but I was sure I wouldn't like it. "But?"

"But I got a call from the Harbor Haven police telling me not to patch the hole in the drywall until they were certain their investigation of those four bullets is over," he said. Then he seemed to flinch, as if expecting me to go off like a small neutron bomb.

"Oh, okay," I said.

Tony looked at me for a moment. "All right. Good. So I'll be back when the cops say it's okay."

I smiled. "I can do the drywall," I reminded him. "Don't forget who you're dealing with."

He grinned back. "Never."

"So I can use my back door now? Because I need to get you guys your check." I took a few steps toward my kitchen door.

"That's not necessary now, Alison." Tony finished closing the van's rear doors. "I trust you for the money."

"Nonetheless." I didn't want Tony and Vic to think I

wasn't paying them on time because I was a friend. We'd agreed on a price that was far below their usual rate and if that was the case I would at least give them their money promptly.

It felt good to walk through the back door again, even as Paul simply floated through the outside wall into the kitchen. Ghosts are such showoffs. I took a moment to assess the damage and its repair.

Tony and Vic had done a fine job, which was precisely what I had expected. The ceiling still had no wallboard on it, to be fair, but where the house itself seemed to have been sagging under the burden of holding up the damaged beam the lines were now straight and sturdy. The floor, which might have been ankle-deep in sawdust, was clean. Yes, the walls needed painting and Maxie and I had to work out a practical (and yet *artistic*) floor plan but for the moment everything was where I had wanted it before and if I was being honest, still wanted it now.

My checkbook was in a drawer in my nightstand, up in our bedroom. I almost never wrote checks anymore and didn't really need to use it all that much. So I was halfway through the kitchen and heading for the staircase when I noticed something just a little strange. Okay, more than a little.

I walked back to the door, Paul having dropped through the floor saying something about trying to find the Harbor Haven cop who'd investigated Herman Fitzsimmons's disappearance. Tony and Vic hadn't left yet, so I could gesture to Tony and he looked up and came to meet me inside the kitchen.

"I was going to come in and see what you thought," he

said. "I wasn't just going to drive off and vanish into the night."

"Funny you should suggest that," I said. "Because I'm wondering about something that seems to have vanished from this very room."

"Ah," Tony nodded. "You're talking about the refrigerator."

"You are amazingly perceptive, my friend. Where's my fridge?"

Tony nodded. "At the moment it's on your deck. I looked inside. Inside there's just a thing of soy milk and an orange."

Vic showed up in the doorway. "You don't mind me eating the orange, do you?"

I did not mind and told Vic so.

"We figured with just some soy milk the fridge wasn't exactly essential immediately," Tony said.

I felt my face flush a little bit. "I'm going grocery shopping later. The question really is, why isn't my refrigerator here in the kitchen, where it belongs? It wasn't even close to the beam. So how come it's gone?"

"Take a look," Tony said, walking to the spot where, if the world were in sync, my refrigerator would be. "There's a hole in the floor where it was sitting and I was concerned about the integrity of the floor. I want to know if you need me to check on it before we take off or if you want to deal with it yourself."

"A hole in the floor?" That was weird. I hadn't moved the fridge in a long time, but every once in a while you need to clean behind it. Maybe I'd just moved it to the side and missed the hole. "Let's see."

Sure enough there was a space where there should have been floorboards and vinyl tile (hey, I can't afford porcelain tile in a space this large), but I don't think I would have called it a hole. It was, for one thing, almost perfectly rectangular, about six inches across and three wide. "This was cut into the floor with a saw, maybe a hole saw," I said.

Vic nodded. "That's what I thought. Why do you have a hole cut in your kitchen floor?"

I had knelt down to examine the slice in my floor more closely. I turned my head to see if Vic was kidding; it appeared he was not. "You think I put this here?"

He shrugged. "None of my business. You're saying you didn't know it was here?"

Tony slapped his brother lightly in the back of his head. "Of course she didn't," he said. "But I can't tell how long it's been here."

"Did you feel inside?" I asked him.

Tony shook his head. "Our hands are too big. You want to give it a try?"

I looked at the opening. "I don't know. You have a flashlight?"

Tony reached on his tool belt and produced one. "I can't say it's going to help much. I took a look before and couldn't see much."

"Could you see if there were spiders in there?"

Tony snickered just a little. "None I could see."

Okay. "I'll give it a shot." I was already on the floor anyway. That's how I justified it to myself.

It wasn't easy. I didn't want to enlarge the gap in the floor, which would have made it easier to explore. And there wasn't really any reason to think there was anything to find, so making a larger repair necessary would have been even more pointless. I gritted my teeth just because I don't enjoy sticking my fingers into spaces I can't predict. Does anybody like that?

I felt like it was a good idea to clear my mind so I actually closed my eyes while I felt inside the "hole." I'm not typically squeamish but surprises are not my best friend so feeling around in a small space where I couldn't see was making me just a little bit jittery.

"See anything?" Vic asked. It was perfectly obvious I couldn't see anything, as the flashlight Tony was shining on the area was adequately illuminating my arm and little else. But I took Vic's question to mean whether I could *feel* anything, and that was a different story.

I could feel lots of things, and none of them was making me happy. I could feel the cross beam in the floor, which was a relief; whoever had cut this hole in my kitchen had at least done so in a way that wouldn't be impossible to repair without Tony and Vic. I could feel dirt, which was hardly a surprise. Even with a basement under it, my kitchen was constructed more than one hundred years ago, and things tend to build up over that kind of time. And the gaps between levels of a building are often full of soil; it was used as a kind of cheap insulation at the time.

"I haven't hit anything I didn't expect yet," I told Vic.

"That's good, right?" he asked. Tony was the college graduate in the family.

"Yes, it's good." I tried not to think of the kind of creatures that might inhabit such a space near the beach. I'm hardly an expert on the local ecosystem and could imagine everything from a garden snake to a lobster under my house. So far, though, nothing living had made its presence known.

"If somebody was hiding something under there, I'm willing to bet it's not too deep," Tony said, no doubt trying to prevent his brother from asking me another question. "They'd want to get back in and get it out. In fact, they might have done that already."

But my fingers had found what they were looking for and I was already sorry I didn't own a supply of the latex gloves McElone and her crew have on them all the time. I withdrew my hand quickly.

Vic looked at my hand, then my face. "So can we move the fridge back now?" he asked.

I shook my head. "We need to call the lieutenant. Again." She was going to love this.

"Why?" Tony asked. "Is there . . . somebody else down there?"

"No," I assured him. "But I think I found the gun that shot the guy in the car."

Chapter 27

"You rent rooms here, right?" Lt. McElone asked. "Because I'm thinking it might be a better use of my time if I just stayed here until we figure this whole thing out."

I almost started to quote her a discounted rate when I realized the lieutenant, standing in my kitchen while Officer Lassen knelt on the floor with his latexed hand in the cutout, was exhibiting her sharp sense of humor. Her tone was so dry you could start a fire with it.

"I didn't think you'd want to hang around with all the ghosts in the house," I said.

McElone gave me a warning look. I thought I was being jocular; she thought I was disparaging her in front of a subordinate. It's all a question of perspective, really. "What do we have there, officer?" she asked Lassen.

"Ms. Kerby is right. It's a gun, okay. It's stuck between the beam and the insulation so it's going to take a little time to get it out without contaminating the evidence."

That had an ominously familiar ring. "This means I can't have my kitchen back yet, doesn't it?" I asked McElone.

"Go to the head of the class." That was payback for the

ghost comment. "This room is going to be sealed off for us to run thorough tests on the floor and the fixtures. There might be fingerprints or footprints. It could take some time."

"This is a thirty-year-old murder," I said. "This is the coldest of cases."

McElone regarded me as she would any dimwitted person who was trying to play with the grownups. "And someone is going miles out of their way to put us off the track," she said. "There's something they don't want us to find. I'm guessing whoever killed Herman Fitzsimmons is still alive and wants very badly to stay out of jail."

"You know anybody who doesn't?" I muttered. I was still smarting from the head-of-the-class remark and simultaneously worried I'd actually acted too familiar with the lieutenant when another cop was in the room. That was bad protocol.

Luckily Tony was there to jump in and divert the bullet. "So we finished our work in here just in time, huh lieutenant?"

McElone's attention was indeed redirected, but I'm guessing Tony wasn't that happy about it. She looked at him with a suspicious look in her eye. "You don't know where this hole in the floor came from?" she said, breaking one of Paul's rules about not giving the person you're interrogating an answer they can use.

Paul didn't comment on it because he pretty much worships McElone and was busy observing her procedure from a perch near the ceiling. It wasn't like he could leave fingerprints or anything.

"No clue." Tony sounded completely relaxed. McElone had met him a number of times before when I was involved in something that demanded her attention. But everybody is a suspect until the case is solved, so past experience wasn't going to buy him any special consideration. "We found it just like that when we moved the refrigerator out of the way."

Maxie, because she has perfect timing whenever she can possibly be inconvenient to me, floated down through the ceiling, for once not carrying anything the observant police officer might see drifting around in thin air. You have to be thankful for whatever you can manage around my house. I'm thinking of putting that in the brochures. "What's *she* doing here?" Maxie pointed at McElone as if she were a rampaging Visigoth. I don't think Maxie ever did anything seriously illegal in her life but she doesn't have a high opinion of the police.

"Alison found the murder weapon under the kitchen floor," Paul explained. He thought he was being helpful, and was as giddy as a six-year-old on Christmas Eve. "The lieutenant is questioning the witnesses." Nothing could please Paul more than that.

"Why were you moving the refrigerator?" McElone asked.

"The space looks open without it," Maxie observed. That wasn't helpful but I couldn't glare my disagreement at her just now.

Besides, I was wondering why McElone was asking what seemed a question with a fairly obvious answer. I was started to get a feeling about her intention and it wasn't a good one. "They were doing work on the ceiling beam with the bullet in it," I reminded the lieutenant. "So they had to move the fixtures out of the way to avoid damage."

McElone cocked an eyebrow. "I was asking him," she said, gesturing toward Tony. One little remark and the woman turned vicious. Of course, I knew she was nervous about the ghosts even though she didn't technically know they were in the room.

"Of course," Tony said. "Alison is right. We didn't want any drywall or wood or other materials to fall from the ceiling onto anything breakable, so we moved everything we could to the other side of the room."

"And you didn't notice the hole when you first moved the refrigerator out of the way?" McElone sounded skeptical. "You were working in this room for a few days; I saw you here."

"Took their time about it, too," Maxie observed. "I could be half done with this room already."

"I can't say for sure, Lieutenant," Tony said. "We didn't move the fridge until yesterday, but I can tell you the hole wasn't there then and it was today."

"How do you account for that?"

I wondered why Tony should account for that, but Lassen interrupted her before Tony could answer. "I've got it, lieutenant." He stood up holding a pistol by the grip with two gloved fingers. He dropped it into an evidence bag and sealed it. "I'm guessing a thirty-eight. Six round capacity. Currently with one in the cylinder."

"Where'd that come from?" Maxie wanted to know. Served her right for missing a staff meeting.

"It was discovered in the kitchen floor," Paul said again.

"Gives me all sorts of opportunities with the floor," Maxie said. She sounded pleased in a way that made the hair on the back of my neck stand up.

McElone walked to Lassen and examined the gun closely. "That seems about right, officer," she said. Then she turned back in Tony's direction. "You don't have a carry license, do you?"

Not a flicker on his face. "No, as a matter of fact I don't. Because I don't own a firearm."

I didn't care for the direction this questioning was taking. "Lieutenant, you can't possibly imagine that Tony killed Herman Fitzsimmons in the Eighties and is trying to cover his tracks, so can you give us an idea of what you're driving at?"

"I really don't think I will, no," she said. "My best guess is the person who did the shooting is dead or quite elderly, because it's been more than thirty-five years since it happened. But that's just a guess. In the meantime, I think I'll leave Officer Lassen to finish his work. Can we go into another room to discuss this?" She gestured toward the kitchen door.

I wasn't in much of a mood to accommodate McElone at that point, but there was something in her voice that told me not to challenge her. That, and Paul, who said, "Don't challenge her, Alison. Let's hear what she has to say."

"Fine," I said to one or both of them. "We can go into the library."

"Does it have a door?" McElone asked.

That seemed like an odd question. "Sure. It was windows, too, and a rug on the floor. Come see for yourself."

"Yeah, good idea," Maxie said. "Give me some time in

here." Like she hadn't spent the better part of four days just staring at my kitchen. But if it kept her out of our meeting in the library I had no objection.

The lieutenant did not comment. She followed Tony, Vic and me through the door and into the hallway that leads to my library. Paul took his shortcut through the wall because he can.

McElone was certainly interested in the library's door; she closed it as soon as all of us—including Paul—were inside. "Now, let's discuss exactly how that weapon could have made it into your house, your kitchen and the floor underneath," she said to me. "Someone had enough time to come in, move your refrigerator, cut a hole in the floor, secure the gun and then move the refrigerator back into place." She looked at Tony. "How long would it take to create a hole like that in the floor?"

"I'm not sure he should answer that without an attorney present," I said before Tony could answer. "His offering an opinion might just make you believe he's the person who did it."

"I don't mind," Tony said.

At the same time Paul was saying, "You're not observing the situation, Alison." But he stopped talking when Tony spoke.

"What do you mean, you don't mind?" I said. "She's trying to make it look like you hid the gun in my floor."

"I didn't, so I have nothing to worry about," Tony said. He looked at McElone. "I think if you had the proper tool, like a Sawzall, it wouldn't take more than ten minutes. It's not a very sophisticated job from what I could see."

"How about moving the refrigerator?" the lieutenant asked.

Vic shrugged. "People think it's harder than it is," he said. "They're on wheels. This was easier because there wasn't anything heavy in it. Just some soy milk and an orange." Like that was relevant. I saw McElone give me an amused glance.

"So that wouldn't add much time to the work either," she said to the two contractors.

"No. You're in and out in twenty minutes, tops, and probably less," Tony said.

McElone nodded. "Thank you. You guys can leave. I'm sure you have another job you need to get to."

Tony gave me a confused look as he and Vic hightailed it out of the library. McElone closed the door again after they left. "I don't suspect your friend," she said. "I never did."

"So what was all that about?" I asked.

"Consider, Alison," Paul said, hovering just to my right. "She wanted you out of that room and in here with the door closed. What does that tell you?" Paul has an annoying habit of leading me to information when he could just tell me and save time and aggravation.

"It wasn't about us," I said to McElone, realizing what Paul had been driving at. "You were concerned about what Officer Lassen might hear. You wanted *him* to think you thought Paul had come in and planted the gun. Why would that matter to you?"

McElone, as was becoming her habit, did not respond to the question. Much like Paul, it seemed she was leading me to finding my own answers. Apparently the two sleuths, while not sharing the same level of life, were conspiring to annoy me by making me be smart.

"He's the officer you were keeping the evidence from," I said. "It wasn't Sgt. Menendez at all, was it?"

"I don't have to tell you anything," McElone said, but there was a hint of a twinkle in her eye. Or it might have been the way the light from the window was hitting her. Knowing McElone, bet on the window. "Right now, what I want you to do is nothing. This is a police matter and you have no skin in the game."

"I had bones in my backyard," I reminded her. "That's something."

"They're thirty-year-old bones. I already heard about you talking to Fitzsimmons's widow. Keep away from my witnesses and let the police do our job." McElone had given me this speech so many times (with the names changed) she might have been better off printing it on a card and just handing it to me when she needed it. "Look me in the eye and tell me you'll leave this alone."

"So far I've had a car pulled out of the ground, bullets found in my kitchen ceiling, that same car moved in and out of my backyard at night, and a gun discovered in the floor under where my refrigerator should be, and you think *I'm* the one who's making it about me?"

"The lieutenant doesn't have to know that we're investigating," Paul suggested, which is what Paul always says right before we investigate and McElone finds out. Except she doesn't so much think of it as *we* investigating as she does *me* investigating. It's a subtle difference but it has juice.

"I'll do my best to keep it out of your house," McElone said. "But this is more dangerous than you think it is, and I have enough to think about without you stomping all over my investigation, okay?"

That was a touching sentiment, certainly, but between my ghost friend and my husband it seemed unlikely I'd be able to stay on the sidelines. Still, the easiest way to get McElone to leave me alone is to agree with her. "You're right," I told her. "This is none of my business. But I do feel a little picked on, if the truth be told." Sorry about that last phrase.

"I get that, but nothing more is going to be centered around you or the house," McElone said with a great deal of certainty in her voice. "You're not in any danger as long as you let me keep this outside."

Officer Lassen, whatever his faults (and I had no idea what those might be), had an impeccable sense of timing. He knocked on the library door and opened it to stick his head inside. "I've finished with the firearm and the others are looking for fingerprints and signs of foot traffic," he told McElone.

"And that's all that was there?" she asked.

"As far as I can tell. Depends on how much you want me to tear up the floor to look. We don't have the budget for a lot of this kind of equipment."

McElone looked at me and must have seen the panic flash across my face. "I don't think we need to do any more excavation unless we get a clear indication there's something else down there." I put the lieutenant back on my Christmas card list. Which reminded me I'd better get a picture of Josh, Liss and me in the next couple of weeks; we didn't have one for our cards yet.

"I'll head back then," Lassen said. McElone nodded her permission and he withdrew from the library.

And that, I am sorry to say, is when my cell phone buzzed.

I didn't recognize the number sending the text and almost deleted it as spam. But something made me glance, and then I was partially glad and partially sorry I did.

If you know what's good for you don't call the police about the gun. Someone might be coming to see you.

Make that mostly sorry.

Chapter 28

Well, the boat had sailed on me knowing what was good for me so I showed the text to McElone, who looked—as was her tradition—displeased.

She immediately got out her cell phone and called someone at Harbor Haven police headquarters, asking for information on the phone number displayed on my screen. She waited for what seemed like a long time while my heart pounded. I don't care much for threats but then, who does?

"Okay," McElone said into her phone and then she disconnected and stashed it in her pocket. "It's what I suspected. A burner phone. We'll probably never find out who bought it and if we do, it'll have been thrown away or destroyed by then."

"You'll forgive me if that doesn't make me feel better," I said. "What I'm worried about is that they warned me not to call you and I called you."

"First, that's the right thing to do," McElone answered. "A crime has been committed, even if it was a long time ago. And your duty as a citizen is to notify the authorities when you have information that could lead to solving that case."

I snorted. I'm not proud of it. "Thanks for the civics

lesson, lieutenant. There are people out there who have killed at least one person and are now ticked off at me for disobeying orders I didn't even get until after I'd already done the opposite of what they'd said. Now what about the idea that somebody might be coming here to hurt me or people I love?" I hadn't even considered the guests. Getting one of them killed: Is that a bust or a boon for a haunted guesthouse? I didn't want to find out.

"I don't think that's a serious threat," McElone said.

"It's not a *funny* threat."

"Easy, Alison," Paul said. "Trust the lieutenant."

I forgot the situation for a moment because my stomach was doing the backstroke in my abdomen and it wasn't because of the sandwich I'd eaten. I pivoted to face Paul, a foot and a half or so above the floor, and said, "Will you stop taking her side? People are coming after me!"

McElone looked downright stricken. It always bothers her that there are ghosts around my house and I think it's more because she doesn't like being watched than anything dealing with the fact that they're dead. If invisible live people were there she'd be just as—please pardon the expression—spooked as now, but that's silly. There's no such thing as invisible live people.

She gathered herself, straightened her shoulders and looked at me. "Don't. Do. That."

We were going to pretend I'd spoken to Paul as a gag to get under her skin. Okay. I could play that game. "Sorry, lieutenant. I'll stop."

"You shouldn't worry the lieutenant that way," Paul said. "I want to be a help, not a source of anxiety."

I exercised great restraint and showed what a good friend I was by not responding to him. I looked instead at McElone. "Even if you don't think the threat is credible, I do. Can you give me any advice on security measures I can take without alarming my guests?" I give each guest a key to the front door but I almost never lock it because they tend not to remember them when they go out. That leads to text messages at one in the morning when a good innkeeper should be asleep. And so should I.

"I'm not discounting the threat entirely," McElone said.

"That doesn't make me feel better."

"I understand. I don't think you're in real danger because there isn't anything you could have done and if there is damning evidence on the gun we'll find it and arrest the person who's threatening you." She looked around the room in the direction of the ceiling. It didn't help her see anything but maybe she felt better. "But in the meantime, I will ask a cruiser to drive by more often than usual and I'd advise you to call me—directly—if anything happens that you think is dangerous. You have my cell number."

"Do I need to go pick up my daughter when school lets out?" I asked.

McElone considered. "It can't hurt."

That sent a shiver up my spine. "Okay." My voice sounded shallow.

"I'll check the outside of the house," Paul said. He was out through the wall before I could even acknowledge that he'd spoken, which I wouldn't have done anyway.

"In the meantime I'm going to get forensics on your kitchen and the gun so maybe we can wrap this whole thing up quickly and you won't have to worry." The lieutenant actually has a very compassionate nature but she doesn't want you to know that. So if you run into her don't mention that I said it.

McElone left just as Paul came in to say nothing around the house, front or back, was out of the ordinary. He said he'd get Maxie working on some of the questions that were lingering, including possible places a person might have been able to rent or borrow heavy machinery in the early Eighties. He suggested I check in with Phyllis on anything the medical examiner might have turned up regarding the bones in the car or the blood on the seats.

Before he could rise into the ceiling in search of Maxie, I asked Paul if he'd managed to turn up Anthony Blanik, the cop who had investigated Herman Fitzsimmons's disappearance when it was first reported. "I've gotten some communication and I think it is from Sgt. Blanik," he said. "It was difficult to decipher."

"It would be so much easier if you guys would set up your own email system," I suggested.

"I don't think the technology exists just yet," Paul said drily. "In the meantime, the mode of communication I use consists mostly of feelings and impressions rather than words, as you'll recall. What I heard from Sgt. Blanik was that he'd mostly suspected Mr. Fitzsimmons's wife was withholding some information but he never found out what it might be. The sergeant died five years ago and appears to be somewhere in Thailand at the moment."

"Does distance matter on the Ghosternet?" I asked.

"No, but he is distracted by what he's seeing and that

leads to a less direct message, and therefore a less clear one. If I can determine the proper time of day to try again I might get more useful data."

"Okay. Go get Maxie. I have an hour or so before I have to pick up Melissa but I'll text her and let her know I'm coming and I'll tell Josh what's going on." Paul vanished—I wasn't looking straight at him so I'm not sure how—and I sent a text to my daughter, who wouldn't see it until she was out of classes. Then I called my husband and filled him in on the latest news in the guesthouse.

"Do you want me to come home?" Josh asked. He sounded, as I would have expected, concerned.

I was about to tell him that wasn't necessary but I happened to look out through the library window. And I saw Sgt. Menendez, who was supposed to be banished from this case, walking purposefully toward my house from the beach side. Her hand wasn't on her weapon, which was something of a relief, but I stopped and stared as she walked.

"Alison?" Josh asked, sounding more than concerned now.

That jarred me back to consciousness. "I'm okay," I said. "I was just looking out the window."

"Now I *am* worried. It's a slow day. I can come home."

"No, I don't want you doing damage to your business. If there's any reason to be concerned I'll call you, I promise." Menendez had a brief conversation with Bill Harrelson, who was near one of the Caterpillars, and seemed to be listening very intensely.

That reminded me I needed to talk to Katrina. Or maybe . . .

It was perfect timing that brought Paul and Maxie down from Melissa's room or the roof (all I knew for sure was it was a level higher than the one I was on, which seemed symbolic). "Where is Everett?" I figured it was best to head off any discussion they might want to start while I was making plans of my own.

Maxie stopped in midair. No, really. "Why?" she asked.

"I want him to follow one of my guests."

* * *

Paul and Maxie have a complicated relationship. They didn't know each other well when they were murdered together and died in what is now my house. I wouldn't really call them friends but they are like siblings who live under the same roof and have learned to put up with each other's foibles. They exchanged a look of puzzlement. "I'll get him," Maxie said. She reversed her direction and headed back upstairs to find her husband. Or whatever he was.

Paul stayed in the library with me. "Do me a favor," I said. "Go outside and see if Sgt. Menendez is still there." She had moved to a position I couldn't see from this window. Paul, without commenting, looked serious and pushed himself through the wall.

I wasn't alone in the room for a full minute when he returned. "The sergeant is no longer on this property," he said. "What was she doing here when she was removed from the case?"

"My question exactly," I said. "She was talking to Bill Harrelson."

The mention of Bill's name seemed to spark Paul. He made

a motion like snapping his fingers but produced no sound. There are disadvantages to not actually having a body. "We have made some progress in our research," he said. "Mostly it was Maxie, but she is so consumed with redecorating the kitchen that I've had to stand over her shoulder most of the time."

"Cut to the chase, Paul," I said. "What did Maxie find out?" I like to give credit where credit is due. I should have waited until Maxie was in the room because she loves getting praised for doing the computer research, but I figured she could hear it from Paul later. My relationship with Maxie isn't any less complex than hers with Paul.

He did not have to refer to notes. Paul has an uncanny ability to remember everything that has to do with a case he's investigating, and nothing about anything else. "First of all, the records regarding heavy equipment rentals in the early nineteen eighties are understandably thin. Even if we knew where the earth mover or other excavation equipment had been rented it would probably be impossible to determine exactly who had done so or what they had taken."

"Okay, so that's a dead end. What else?" Who had time for hearing what they *didn't* find out?

"Wait. We do have a lead in that area. There was a company that owned and rented just the sort of backhoe that might be used to inter a large sedan, and it was owned by William Harrelson, Sr."

William Harrelson . . . "Bill's father?"

"Precisely. He might have had some involvement in the burial, if not in the disappearance and murder of Herman Fitzsimmons. In fact, there had been talk in town, according to articles in the *Chronicle*, that there were allegations Mr. Harrelson had helped Herman Fitzsimmons disappear so Mr. Fitzsimmons could avoid divorce proceedings. Apparently word about his affair had gotten around after he vanished. No one believed he didn't know where Mr. Fitzsimmons was and that haunted him. Eventually he died of cirrhosis brought on by alcohol abuse."

"The *Chronicle*? Phyllis doesn't print gossip."

"She had not bought the newspaper yet," Paul reminded me.

It was weird that Bill hadn't said anything, but then, how weird? If his dad hadn't come home one evening and said, "You won't believe what happened at work today," and then told a story about shooting a car dealer and burying him in the competition's product, he might not have ever thought to mention it.

Maxie and Everett descended through the ceiling, which fit perfectly with the conversation Paul and I had been having, although none of them knew it. "Everett," I said.

"Ghost lady?" In the last years of Everett's life when he'd been plagued with mental illness and homelessness he'd known me by that phrase and I had agreed to let him keep calling me that if it made him feel comfortable. It doesn't bother me.

"Do you know Katrina Breslin?" I asked him. "She's one of the guests here this week."

"I am familiar with the guests," Everett said, floating almost at attention. Everett, in his military mode, does not take any relaxation of discipline for granted. "I know who Ms. Breslin is."

"Good. I would appreciate it if you follow along with her when she goes out on a date tonight."

Everett did not break his stance but he did look at me funny.

"You want me to follow a woman on a date? Do you think she is in some kind of danger? There isn't much I can do."

I explained the Everett and Maxie about Bill's claim that he'd never asked Katrina out despite her being quite clear that she'd gone to dinner with him both of the past two nights and that she thought the relationship had a future even after she went home. "I need to know which of the two of them is lying or mistaken," I told Everett. "If you can follow Katrina when she leaves tonight and confirm where she's going and whether or not Bill is there, that will be enough."

"No it won't," Paul interjected. "Everett, if they are together, see if you can hear what they're discussing. That information could be pertinent to our case."

Everett stood tall, if you can call floating without a body in the middle of the room standing. "If two people are on a date, I will not get close enough to hear their conversation," he told Paul. "That is an invasion of their privacy and something I would not be comfortable doing."

"Good for you, Everett," I said.

Paul looked back and forth between Everett and me, made a frustrated motion with his hands and bit on his bottom lip to keep from speaking. Everett had the moral high ground and Paul would just have to deal with it.

"I will be happy to observe from a distance and confirm whether Ms. Breslin meets Mr. Harrelson, ghost lady. I'll remain to do recon until the mission is complete." Everett's face was without emotion but Maxie just couldn't help but bust out in a grin. She really loves it when Everett gets all military.

"Thanks. Do you want to take Paul's cell phone to text information?"

Paul, forgetting that I was the one who paid the cellular bill each month, looked like he was about to object, but Everett shook his head. "I will return as soon as I confirm the information I'm going to gather," he said. With a house full of ghosts like Everett I could rule the world. Probably better than I don't have a house full of ghosts like Everett.

It was agreed Everett would stake out Katrina's room from the outside and stick with her when she left for what she'd said would be another dinner date with Bill. But Paul clearly wanted to talk about something else he and Maxie had uncovered. So Everett was dispatched to the roof to see when Katrina would return from her afternoon of shopping in town and I looked over at my two other resident ghosts (Lester, who stayed in Melissa's room almost all the time because I was allergic, counted, but was much less often a member of the conversation).

"Okay, what else have you two dug up that I don't know about?" I probably should have asked that question of Maxie alone to make up for the time when I said something nice about her but she wasn't there. Opportunity missed.

"There was another matter," Paul began, but Maxie, intent on the spotlight, floated in front of him.

"Harriet Adamson's husband died of suicide," she said. "And he sold Lincoln Continentals."

Chapter 29

"This seems awfully late in the game to be bringing in more suspects," Josh said.

We were sitting in our kitchen, or what was left of it. The stove and center island were where they should be, as were the cabinets, which had never been moved. But the fridge stayed out on the deck beyond the French doors and the much-examined hole in the floor where it should have been just added insult to injury. We could eat dinner here but Melissa had once again been frustrated in her plans to cook it. We were having Chinese food.

"To be fair, we have no idea how late in the game we are," Melissa told Josh. "We might just be starting to gather information that leads to suspects."

Paul, who had been descending into the basement, stopped and smiled. "That is very astute, Melissa," his top half said. "You are becoming a very good investigator."

Liss smiled and looked shy, which is not how she usually looks. "Thank you, Paul."

He kept dropping down until he was out of sight—he had determined this would be a good time to contact Anthony

Blanik—and Liss turned her attention back to her stepfather, who acknowledged that Paul had said something nice to her with a sideways grin. "I hate to think there are going to be a lot more people we have to consider," he said. "I have a *suspects* file on my computer that is absolutely bursting as it is."

"Still, we have to consider Harriet Adamson's husband Nathaniel," Melissa said. "The fact that Herman Fitzsimmons was buried in a Lincoln certainly seems to point to him, but that could mean someone wants us to think that way."

Finally I had something I could add. "Maxie said Nathaniel Adamson killed himself only eight months after Herman Fitzsimmons disappeared, before he was declared dead."

"There are so many loose ends on this case you could knit a sweater," Josh said, shaking his head. I gave him a knowing look. "Okay, not *you*, but somebody could." I don't knit.

"The question is, what do we do about it?" I said. Josh didn't care that I don't knit, and neither did anyone else I could think of. Maybe my mother but she thinks everything I do is amazing so I'd never know if the whole knitting thing is a source of disappointment for her, and . . . what was I talking about?

"It's probably time to get back in touch with Phyllis." In Paul's absence (he was also trying to get in touch with Nat Adamson, so he might be gone a while), Melissa was acting as lead investigator. I wasn't sure how that had come about, but it actually seemed to make the most sense. "There might be some work on the ME's report. The idea that the person who shot Mr. Fitzsimmons was sitting on the floor. How does that work?"

"Good point," Josh said. "Sgt. Blanik might be able to help with that. We probably should also see if Maxie can dig into the police department's files so we can check on the investigation into the bullets Tony and Vic found in the beam, and whether they matched the gun they found in the floor."

"I'd really like to know why whoever did this is taking it out on our kitchen," I whined. "I remember when you used to be able to make food here."

One mention of the kitchen and you could count on Maxie appearing with her sketchpad. She was not going to be happy with Josh's suggestion she do more computer searching when she wanted to make things in this room look . . . more like whatever was going on in that warped mind of hers.

But this time Everett was with her. "I can see Ms. Breslin is about to leave," he told me. "I am preparing to leave on the recon mission."

"Excellent," I said. "Thank you, Everett." He saluted snappily and left through the kitchen wall toward the front room. Sure enough I heard Katrina's footsteps on the stairs heading in the same direction. Everett was as dependable as an atomic clock.

"When you're done eating, I have some designs based on what we talked about," Maxie said. The fact that she was waiting until the three of us finished our Chinese feast was an indicator of how hard Maxie was trying to curry my favor here. Normally she'd burst in, swipe all the food off the island and lay down her sketchpad to show me the latest in Maxie design.

"That sounds good." Best to stay on Maxie's good side. "But while you're waiting . . ."

Her face closed. "What?" As flat an inflection as you can imagine.

I nodded to Josh, who thought the idea of communicating directly with Maxie would be fun. Because he'd never done it. "We were wondering if you might be able to find out whether the police have looked at the bullets they found in the ceiling here. To see if they match the gun Alison found under the floor. Could you please do that? You can use my laptop. It's right there." He looked mostly at his plate while he was talking to avoid making eye contact with a Maxie who was nowhere near the real one, but pointed to the computer not far from where he was seated.

Maxie, who was looking directly at Josh because he was visible to everybody, took a moment. "Okay," she said, and floated directly to Josh's laptop, which she opened, causing my husband to start momentarily and then smile. She began pounding away on the keyboard while we ate and I wondered how Josh had been able to get such a reaction without the least amount of complaining. I'd never managed it, and a few times I was even nice to Maxie when I asked.

Melissa was hiding a smile behind Kung Pau chicken.

I chose to ignore that and took out my phone to send a text to Phyllis with the eloquent message: *Anything from the ME?* Pithy without being sassy, I thought.

Almost the second I finished sending the text, which was less than a full minute after Maxie had begun searching for records from the police department that were meant to be kept confidential, she looked up and said, "Got it."

I wasn't sure whether to be impressed by Maxie or

horribly dismayed at the state of the Harbor Haven police. Melissa touched Josh on the hand and did a head fake toward Maxie. He looked in her direction. "Wow, that was fast!" he said. "What did you find out?"

Maxie, pleased with the praise, smiled. "It was easy." Melissa started translating for Josh. "The bullets they took out of the hole by the beam don't match the gun. They're a smaller caliber, nine millimeters while the gun is a forty-five. Is there anything else you need to know?"

Since Menendez, back when we were talking, had initially told me the bullets didn't match the gun that had fired at me, the only news was that we now had it confirmed. So I thought I'd try asking a question myself. "It's about the gun I found. Could that be the gun that shot Herman Fitzsimmons all those years ago?"

I hadn't specifically told Maxie how wonderful she was, so it is possible her response had a touch more irritation in it than the one she'd given Josh. "I guess it's possible. There are no ballistics tests mentioned in the documents I found. They might not have had time to do them yet." She looked at my plate. "Are you gonna finish that or can we start in with the designs?"

"Soon," I said, taking a bite I didn't really want just to reinforce my point. "Are gun licenses a matter of public record in New Jersey?"

"No, but that doesn't mean I can't find them." Maxie's tone still wasn't as friendly with me as with Josh, who ironically couldn't hear it, but she was proud of her skills. "What do you want to know?"

"If any of these people owned a forty-five caliber pistol: William Harrelson, senior; Nathaniel Adamson, Darlene Fitzsimmons Menendez; Harriet Adamson; Sheila Morgenstern; Herman Fitzsimmons."

Maxie, who had started clicking away on Josh's keyboard as soon as I'd started mentioning names, looked up. "You think Herman shot himself and then buried the gun in our kitchen?" She'd given up the idea that this was her house alone but did not relinquish all claims to at least partial ownership. It was my name on the mortgage; I knew that for sure.

"No," I answered. "But we can't rule out the idea that he was shot with his own gun."

Maxie tilted her head to the left in a *whatever* gesture and kept clicking away. While she did that Paul rose out of the basement, giving me ghosts in virtually every direction. "I communicated with Anthony Blanik again," he said. "And I believe I might have made contact with the spirit of Nathaniel Adamson."

"I'm looking up gun records," Maxie said. Why would Paul—or anyone else—be speaking to someone other than her?

"What did they tell you?" I asked Paul.

"Sgt. Blanik was somewhat less distracted this time," he said. "I imagine mornings on Bangkok are not quite as much a spectacle as the nights." I could have told him that and I've never been to Thailand. "He remembered a little more about the Fitzsimmons case."

"Does he know if Fitzsimmons owned a forty-five?"

Maxie asked. I guessed she hadn't gotten to that name on my list yet.

Paul looked a little puzzled. "It did not occur to me to ask," he said. He turned his attention back toward me while Melissa continued to give Paul a play-by-play. I added United Nations translator and sports commentator to the growing list of possible professions for her. She'd be great at any of them. "But he did say that he always thought of the case as a homicide. He said there was definitely some professional animosity against Fitzsimmons, especially among his fellow Elks, and he specifically mentioned Sheila Morgenstern. But he believed the best avenue to explore was personal—the affair with Harriet Adamson was apparently well-known to everyone except Fitzsimmons's wife and Harriet's husband."

"Did you ask Nathaniel Adamson about that when you found him?" Melissa asked.

"More or less. It was a delicate conversation. It's been a good number of years, but people who die of suicide are often somewhat sensitive about the times just before they became like Maxie and me. And that is what I found interesting."

"What did he say about his wife cheating on him?" Maxie asked. She was still clacking away on Josh's laptop, and my husband couldn't keep himself from watching the keys go up and down. You'd think he'd be used to stuff like that by now but it never seems to lose its novelty.

"All he managed to communicate clearly was that his wife's indiscretions were not the reason he did himself in," Paul said. "But he had definitely put up some very defensive walls against accessing those thoughts."

Josh waited for the translation. "But he did admit he knew about the affair. Do you think he killed Herman Fitzsimmons?"

Paul, gentleman that he is, texted directly to Josh to keep him feeling like an integral part of the team. I peeked over my husband's shoulder and saw the message, *Not enough data to form a theory yet.* If Paul had lived long enough he might have had that tattooed across his chest. It was sort of his motto.

Josh looked over at Liss and me. "Where does this leave us? We have any number of people who might have been mad at Fitzsimmons but no evidence at all that one of them shot him and buried him in a Continental."

My friend Phyllis possesses an instinctive sense of timing that is truly a wonder to behold. At that exact moment she answered my text.

Second person's blood in the car came from William Harrelson. What have you got?

Chapter 30

"So Bill Harrelson's dad left some blood in the Continental when Henry Fitzsimmons was shot," I said. "Does that mean he killed Henry? Why would he kill Henry?"

We had relocated to the movie room, where Adam and Steve were getting ready to leave for dinner. Steve knew of Federici's, a famous Italian restaurant and pizza emporium in Freehold but Adam thought that might be too far a drive to get pizza when there were lots of places in the middle.

"But Federici's is where Bruce Springsteen's keyboard player worked," Steve said. I didn't explain that Danny Federici had actually played in this very space not all that long ago. It's a long story, but he was a very nice ghost. "It's like a piece of history." Just for the record, they also make a really good pizza.

Adam couldn't find it in his heart to refuse his spouse so the two of them were off in a few minutes, only after Steve had offered the advice (based on what he'd heard Melissa, Josh and me saying) that we should "stick with the gun license. Whoever has that is the killer." A few days at the haunted guesthouse and everybody gets into the act.

"The blood in the car is interesting, but it is not, if you'll pardon the expression, the smoking gun we need," Paul said. "It might place Mr. Harrelson at the scene of the crime without actually being involved. He might have rented the earth moving equipment to the owner of the Continental and cut his finger while doing so. We don't know enough about the bloodstain yet. There are too many scenarios that don't end with him being the killer. That said, there's no better suspect just at the moment. I don't know what his motive might have been, however."

Maxie, hovering near the ceiling and lying horizontally with the laptop on her midsection, said, "You'd think he would have reported the car stolen if he had nothing to do with it disappearing. I don't see any police records about that, but not everything online goes back that far."

"The gun records, Maxie," I reminded her. "What did you find in the gun license records that we're not supposed to have?"

"So far nobody has a license to carry," she said. "But I'm still looking. It's not like I can just Google a name and see if they had a gun. It's more like sifting through every permit that was issued and seeing if the names we had match."

I held up my hands. "Take your time," I said. "That sounds huge."

"I haven't forgotten about the kitchen designs," she warned.

"Neither have I."

"We should ask Bill about his father," Melissa said. "Do you know how to find him?"

I shrugged. "Until Everett gets back I won't even know if Bill is out on a date with Katrina. As it is we don't know where Katrina is, and I have no idea where Bill lives. It's a dead end."

"Take it easy," Josh said, stroking my shoulder in the cushy loveseat we'd occupied. "Nobody's in any danger right now."

"You came and picked me up at school," Melissa reminded him. "You closed your store early. If nobody's in danger . . ."

"We're being proactive," I said. "We're trying to keep everyone safe all the time."

"Uh-huh." I hadn't told Liss about the threatening text message but she knew something was up; it was evident in the way she wasn't asking me what was wrong.

"The only person we haven't talked to in this matter is Sheila Morgenstern," Paul said, no doubt trying to redirect the conversation to something more investigate-y. "There is no direct evidence of her being involved but Sgt. Blanik was adamant that she held a grudge against Henry Fitzsimmons, although he didn't know why. You should try to set up an interview, Alison."

I didn't even argue. That's how completely fogged in my brain was at the time. I hadn't wanted to get involved in this investigation but it kept forcing its way into my house. Suspects and motives were being flung around in every possible direction and from every conceivable angle and no clear pattern was developing. Now the usual pattern—where some homicidal maniac had decided I was to be a target despite not having done anything at all threatening to them—was forming again and I was powerless to stop it. Might as well just bring on the inevitable. I reached for my phone.

"You got a phone number for Sheila Morgenstern, Maxie?"

Of course she did. Within seconds there was ringing in my right ear, and it wasn't caused by a bucket of drywall compound hitting me on the head. Because I know what that feels like.

"Hello?" The woman sounded middle-aged, if such a thing is possible. She wasn't old, certainly, although my concept of "old" keeps going up in numbers the longer I live. And she wasn't terribly young, so I assumed this was Sheila herself and not a daughter or granddaughter.

"Hi," I said, hoping I sounded friendly. I hate making cold phone calls, but doesn't everybody? "My name is Alison Kerby."

"I don't answer this kind of phone call," the woman said, and hung up.

Paul looked at me expectantly, and when I turned to face Josh he was doing the same. Melissa was staring at her phone, no doubt looking up some piece of information she thought was going to help. "She hung up on me," I told the room.

"Figures," Maxie said off-handedly.

"She did not understand why you were calling," Paul said. No kidding, Paul.

At the same time, Josh suggested Sheila had thought I was trying to sell her insurance.

"I can try again, but I doubt she'll pick up this time," I told Paul.

He nodded. "Perhaps try texting. If the number Maxie

gave you is a cell phone—and the odds are it is—she might read the text."

I figured that was easy enough, and if Sheila never called back I'd be off the hook, which was my best-case scenario. I sent: *I am a private investigator looking into a matter and I believe you might have some useful information. Please call back.* And I left my cell number for Sheila to use.

"Aha," Maxie said. "I have a hit on the license to carry a gun."

There was nothing so far from Sheila, so this was the best source of information we had at the moment. "Who owned the gun?" I asked Maxie.

"Herman Fitzsimmons," she answered. "A forty-five, too."

I was confused so I looked at Paul as Melissa finished telling Josh what had occurred. Josh said, "What?"

Paul was stroking his goatee madly. "The medical examiner was very clear that Mr. Fitzsimmons did not shoot himself," he said. "But he was the person who owned a gun of the same caliber as the one that killed him."

"It's pretty clear," said my thirteen-year-old daughter, still checking something on her phone. "Darlene shot her husband with his own gun because he was having an affair with Harriet Adamson."

Chapter 31

Before any of us could respond to Melissa's conclusion, my cell phone buzzed and the number was the one I'd used to call Sheila Morgenstern. I picked up before she could change her mind, still looking at my daughter.

"This is Alison Kerby?" the woman I'd spoken to asked.

"Yes. Are you Sheila Morgenstern?"

There was a pause. "How did you get this number?" It wasn't a yes, but it wasn't exactly a no, either.

"It's a matter of public record," I said, although I wasn't certain that was true. I've learned not to ask Maxie how she gets the information she gathers. As the living person in the equation it would be worse for me if I knew how things are done. They're not going to arrest Maxie. "Is this Sheila? I'm just asking for some information on something I'm looking into." I wasn't going to say there was no chance Sheila would get into trouble because for all I knew she was a mad killer who liked to move buried sedans around in the middle of the night.

"I'm Sheila," she admitted. "I'm not giving you any money."

"I'm not asking you for any," I said. "I'm calling about Herman Fitzsimmons."

This time the pause was considerably longer and more awkward. "Herman?"

"Yes. I'm sure you remember him."

"You could say that. I didn't like the guy."

Finally, someone who would admit to having negative feelings about Herman Fitzsimmons. "You and he were in the Elks Club together?" That was the only connection I knew of between the two.

"Oh, no," Sheila said. "The Elks was an all-male club until the Nineties. I applied because I thought that was stupid. And I think most of the members would have been fine with applying to national about letting in the first woman."

I could see where this was going. "But Fitzsimmons was against it."

There was a distinct growl in Sheila's voice. "You guessed it. He said the traditions in the lodge went back to the nineteenth century and there was no reason to smash that all to pieces just for, and I'm quoting now, 'one little lady who thinks she's an Elk.' I'm asking you."

"So it probably didn't bother you when he was murdered," I said. It was a calculated gamble. I wanted to see her reaction, given that she wasn't shy about voicing her dislike of the victim. Paul nodded his approval but Josh's eyes narrowed with concern.

But Sheila's reaction was not one of anger. "He was murdered?" she said. "I knew he disappeared but I figured he was just on the run from his wife because he was always making passes at other women."

Always? "He made advances at multiple women?" I said,

E. J. COPPERMAN

just to give the room the same information I already had. Then it occurred to me to ask, "Did he approach you?"

"Oh, yeah." Like it was a given. "I owned my own dealership and I guess he thought that was sexy, or something. Weren't that many women owners at that time. He hit on me maybe four or five times at dealer conventions, product announcements, that sort of thing. I told him to his face that I wasn't even a little interested but that didn't seem to make any difference to him. He just kept trying. But he never got anywhere. With me."

I had to ask. "I assume that means he did with other women?" Okay, so that's not exactly *asking*, but my inflection made it a question. Don't quibble.

"Oh, yeah," Sheila answered. It was her go-to response. "Herm had something going with at least three women I knew about, and then there was his wife."

"Darlene," I said, not so much to Sheila as to myself.

"Oh, yeah." No, it wasn't her go-to response; it was her credo. "She was a piece of work, that one. The scary part is I'm pretty sure she actually loved him. But we never met so it's hard to say. Herm wouldn't come to events with his wife because it'd slow him down, if you know what I mean."

A piece of unfinished teak would know what she meant. "Did Darlene find out about Herman's . . . activities?" I was watching my words. My daughter is thirteen and has been involved in a number of murder investigations, but that doesn't make me comfortable discussing absolutely everything in front of her. I know she understands. I just don't like to admit it to myself.

"I don't know," Sheila said. "It never got beyond the go-away-Herm stage with me so I didn't have to tell her anything. One of the others might have called her up one night but I never heard about it."

"Did you hear anything after he vanished?" I asked. Paul had suggested the question.

"Like I said, I figured he found himself some new babe and just took off. He never really seemed to care about selling Chevys too much so it'd be easy for him to get in the car and start a new life, I guess."

That was news to me, although nobody had said Chevrolets were Herman Fitzsimmons's life. "He didn't like selling Chevys?" I repeated back.

"No, not really. He was always asking me about how I'd gotten the Honda dealership, even though Hondas weren't that big a deal back then. He kept showing up at some of the product presentations even when he wasn't invited and talking to the people from corporate, like he wanted to get a dealership deal. But they liked me and didn't want the competition nearby, I suppose. I never asked."

"Did he ever check in with people from Lincoln?" I asked. Maybe being buried in a Continental was Herman Fitzsimmons's last wish after all.

"Not that I know about. Why?"

I saw no harm in telling her. "His body was found buried in a Lincoln Continental."

I think it's possible Sheila Morgenstern is still laughing.

* * *

Calls to Darlene Menendez were not answered and messages were not returned so I couldn't confirm any of Sheila Morgenstern's story or ask about the things Sheila said she didn't know. By the same token, Paul was not able to get in touch with Harriet Adamson via Ghosternet messages. Some nights even dead people have other things to do.

There was nothing left for us to do but sit around and guess, although I did ask Paul to watch through the French doors on the odd chance that Bill Harrelson showed up in my backyard again. Why not? I'd gotten so used to having the crew out there it felt weird when Bill, Jim, Ernie or somebody *wasn't* out there. But so far, that particular brand of weirdness was proving to be the case tonight.

"I still think it was Mrs. Fitzsimmons," Melissa said. We'd moved to the den so Paul could take up his station near the back of the house. Josh and I were on one of the sofas, Melissa was lying on the floor looking at the ceiling—she said it helped her think and she's smarter than me, so who was I to argue?—and Maxie was trying as hard as she could to get me to look at the designs on her sketchpad. And I swear, I was looking. The drawings had gotten much closer to being an actual kitchen than before, but still needed some toning down. "She had access to the gun that killed her husband and the medical examiner's report showed that he didn't shoot himself. She could easily have been sitting on the floor or on their bed when she shot him."

"Anyone could have gotten into the house and stolen the gun," Josh said. "I'm not saying you're definitely wrong,

Melissa. That's a real possibility. But I think Paul will agree that it doesn't prove that's what happened."

"That's right," Paul said, texting to Josh directly. "If the gun were all that was needed, Lt. McElone would have made an arrest already. She has that information."

Josh got the text and smiled. "I think we need to figure out why Mr. Harrelson's blood is in the car. He doesn't seem to have a reason to want to kill Herman Fitzsimmons. What was he doing in the car the night Fitzsimmons died?"

"Why did the car get moved both those nights?" I said, throwing another topic into the mix. "If there was something there the killer didn't want seen, I can understand dragging the Lincoln away. But why bring it back the next night?" I looked at Maxie. "The cabinets still need to be accessible and we can't afford to recess them into the walls. That would require constructing false walls and making the whole room a lot smaller than it is now."

"What if it wasn't about taking out something the killer didn't want seen," Josh suggested.

Even before Maxie could protest that I was stifling her artistic expression everyone stopped what they were doing and looked at my husband. "What do you mean?" Melissa asked. "What else could it be?"

Paul, stroking his goatee furiously, said quietly, "It's possible."

"It could be that the killer was putting something *into* the car that they *did* want the police to see," Josh said. "Maybe they couldn't do that on the scene. Maybe they had to take it elsewhere to plant some evidence in the car that would implicate someone else."

"Like what?" Maxie asked. Yes, Maxie.

Josh looked up and for a moment I thought he might have heard Maxie. It was not a pleasant thought; I needed at least one person who was ghost-free in my life. But he didn't answer her directly. It was more like he was continuing his thought.

"For example, we don't know which blood stain in the pictures is from Harrelson. Do we know for sure that the second person's blood—the sample that was identified as William Harrelson's—was in the car before it was taken away for one day?"

That made me blink a couple of times. "I don't see how it makes sense," I told Josh, but I saw Paul nodding in agreement out of the corner of my eye. "If Bill's father was involved with this it would have been more than thirty years ago. Do you think someone held onto a sample of his blood for all those year just in case someone found the car they buried?"

Paul was already in full Sherlock mode, head down, right hand at the goatee, moving back and forth in a style of pacing that Arthur Conan Doyle would never have imagined (although maybe he would, because he was a serious believer in spirits). He didn't say anything but he was clearly in deep thought about what Josh had proposed.

"The blood sample was marked, 'William Harrelson'?" Melissa asked.

"I don't know," I said. "Phyllis wasn't that specific, but she said that's whose blood it was."

"She didn't specify senior or junior," Josh said. "We've just been assuming it was the father."

Okay, it took me a moment. "You think it might have been Bill's? But he was a little kid when the murder took place."

"It's never the crime that gets you," Paul said. "It's the cover-up."

"Okay," Maxie said. "Suppose we just build the wallboard out a little to make the cabinets look recessed?"

"The cover-up?" I said to Paul as Melissa leaned over toward Josh. "Why would Bill have anything to do with covering up a murder that took place before he was out of grade school?"

"His father seems to be the person who leased out the backhoe that helped bury that car in the backyard," Josh answered when he was up to speed. "If there was involvement beyond that, Bill might be especially interested in protecting his father's reputation. When did Harrelson, Sr., die?"

Melissa got out her phone. "That one's easy," she said. After less than a minute she announced, "William Harrelson Sr. of Tinton Falls passed away in 2009."

"This could be about saving his good name," Paul said. He looked at Josh. "He's very good at this. Is he absolutely sure he wants to run a paint store?"

I was about to point out that as an investigator I'd never once been paid in actual money but I didn't have time. In a true Hollywood moment Everett flew in through the front wall at a very high speed, looking as close to frantic as I've ever seen Everett look.

"Come quickly, Ghost Lady!" he said. "Ms. Breslin is with the construction manager, and I think she's in great danger!"

Chapter 32

Anyone who passed by Josh's truck on Rt. 34 that night would have thought it was comfortably inhabited by two adults and a young teenager. From my perspective, however, the truck was stuffed with six people, three of whom—Paul, Maxie and Everett—weren't exactly there, but were making enough noise to be audible in space, where no one can hear you scream.

"They met at nineteen hundred thirty hours at a restaurant called Deep Dive in Hazlet," Everett reported. "The establishment specializes in the local seafood and is dedicated to using only those items produced locally."

"Ugh, fish." I have a problem with eating things that swim. It's not ethical; it's more in the area of hating fish.

"What about fish?" Josh asked.

"Let it go," Melissa told him. "It's not important." Josh nodded.

"It had obviously been agreed upon ahead of time," Everett continued as if I hadn't just been incredibly juvenile. "And Mr. Harrelson arrived first, so he was waiting for Ms. Breslin when we arrived in her car." Everett had hitched a ride with

Katrina, the best way for him to get where she was going at the same time as she did.

"Was there trouble right away?" Paul asked.

Everett looked serious, which he usually does, but more on edge than I was used to seeing. "No. They seemed quite pleased to see each other. I did not approach so closely as to hear their conversation, but they appeared cordial throughout the meal. It was afterward that there appeared to be some change in the mood."

"What happened?" I asked. We were racing toward the scene as Everett had directed but we hadn't yet been told why he'd been so agitated when he'd arrived (via another car that had come through Harbor Haven after a bus that had left Hazlet in our direction and then finally through sheer Everett power, the equivalent of running) back at the guesthouse.

"They left the restaurant together," he reported. "I did not notice anything disturbing but when they were in the parking lot it was clear there was some disagreement about the next part of the evening. Ms. Breslin was trying to walk to her own car but Mr. Harrelson appeared to be insisting she come with him in his own."

"How does that translate to great danger?" Josh asked when he heard the transcription from Melissa.

"Mr. Harrelson was becoming angry or frustrated," Everett answered. "He grabbed Ms. Breslin's wrist and would not let her leave in her vehicle. At that point I determined she needed some assistance but I was not carrying anything I could use as a weapon and could not create enough force with my body to physically stop him from forcing her away."

"Did she get into his car?" I asked.

"She did, but not happily," he said. "Not happily." He shook his head. "I was too far away to get to the car before he drove it away."

I heard Paul make a discontented noise. He'd told Everett to get close enough to hear the conversation and did not agree with his argument about respecting Katrina's and Bill's privacy. Everett, if he noticed, did not react.

"How are we going to find them if they drove away?" Melissa asked Everett.

"I rose up high enough to gauge the direction in which Mr. Harrelson was driving, and Maxie has zeroed in on his home address through her research," Everett said. "We believe he was driving that way and I hope we are right. It should be about two clicks ahead."

Maxie gave the address she'd found to me and I programmed it into my phone's map app. There was no further conversation while Josh followed the directions toward Bill Harrelson's address. It took about three minutes to get to the house. Exactly three minutes. But it's not like I was tense or anything.

The house was a small but well-tended split-level on a rise, with a fenced-in backyard and an attached garage whose door was closed. From the street where Josh was parking, there was no way to see if Bill's car was inside it or not.

"I guess I'll go up to the front door and knock," I said, given that the ghosts couldn't knock and Melissa, who no doubt would have volunteered, was lucky I'd let her get into the truck. "Anybody want to run some reconnaissance for me?"

"I will," Liss said, of course.

"Someone who can float through walls?" I clarified.

"I am on my way," Everett said with great force. I noticed that as he quickly pushed his way out of the truck, Maxie followed directly behind him with not so much as a word. Impulsive Maxie was taking a back seat to Loyal Maxie.

I took my time getting out of the truck after making it plain to my daughter that there was no way she was joining me on this adventure. Josh got out on the driver's side and instructed Liss to keep a close eye on her phone. We'd get in touch immediately if we needed backup, and if we did, it would not be in the form of a thirteen-year-old girl. Liss looked grumpy but didn't argue. She knows all my tones of voice and recognized this one as meaning she had absolutely no chance of changing my mind. Besides, we left Paul behind to keep her from forgetting my tone of voice. I promised that if there was something to detect I would text him.

And then I opened my message file, picked out Paul's contact info and typed in the letters SOS. If I needed him all I would have to do would be to hit Send.

Maxie made it back to Josh and me even before we made it all the way across the street. "There's a car in the garage," she reported. "Everett says it's his."

"It's Everett's car?" I asked.

Maxie sighed to indicate that I was not amusing if I was attempting to be, and stupid if I wasn't attempting to be amusing. "It's the construction guy's car, the one Everett saw him driving before. He's—Everett—inside looking for the two of them."

"Okay." I looked at Josh. "Let's play this calm, like we're just looking for Bill because . . . why?"

"Let's tell him one of the backhoes is missing and see how he reacts to that," my husband suggested.

"That's pretty good," Maxie said. "Maybe Paul is right about the whole paint thing."

I decided not to respond to that and climbed the steps to Bill Harrelson's front door. Josh wanted to be in front of me, I could tell, but the odds that somebody was going to shoot first and ask questions later just because we knocked were probably pretty bad. And I had at least some experience doing this sort of thing, no matter how enthusiastic Josh was about this investigation. I would be the face and the voice for the person who answered the door, whom I assumed would be Bill.

Long story short (if that's still possible), I knocked.

It took a while for him to open the door. You know how in movies someone knocks on the door and immediately the person inside opens it and the scene begins? Makes you wonder if that person just stands on the inside of their entrance all day waiting for someone to knock. But I digress. In this case, it was close to a full minute and two more rounds of knocking before Bill Harrelson opened his front door and looked at my husband and me.

Bill's professional smile immediately lit his face. "Alison. Josh." He did allow himself to look confused. "How did you guys get my home address?" Then Bill remembered he was trying to be the helpful guy who by no means forced one of my guests to get into his car and come to his house. "What can I do for you?"

Now, you'll recall that we had a perfectly good plan in place for this very moment. And Josh was in the process of opening his mouth, having noted a momentary pause, when I just blurted out, "We're looking for Katrina Breslin and we think you brought her here against her will."

"Wow," Maxie said. "I'll get Everett." She vanished into the house.

Among the living there was a stunned pause from both men and if I'm being honest—which I am—I'll admit I was pretty taken aback at my own behavior as well. Then Bill broke the silence by rasping, "What?" It wasn't original but nobody else was coming up with anything better.

"I think you heard me," I said. "Where's Katrina? And this time, don't tell me you never asked her out. We have witnesses." Okay, only one witness, and he was dead, but beggars can't be choosers.

I'm not sure whether Bill or Josh looked more astonished. But there was a subtle difference between the two expressions: My husband seemed amazed that I had scrapped the plan and spoken so boldly to the construction foreman.

Bill looked more like he had been caught in a lie and was trying to determine how to get out of the situation.

"She was here for a little bit but she left," he stammered. "How did you get this address?"

I wasn't in the mood to tell him about my deceased hacker friend or to listen to what was so obviously not true. "How'd she leave?" I said. "You made her come here in your car. There isn't much we don't know about this, Bill. But one thing you haven't told us yet is where Katrina is and that's key. So if you'll allow me . . ." And I walked right past him into his house. Now even *I* was amazed at my brazenness.

Josh, rather apologetically, followed behind me. Bill made some sounds but none of them were recognizable words. Whatever was going on here, he wasn't very good at improvising and that was the weakness to exploit, I was sure Paul would say.

Before we could even take in the whole of Bill's front room, which wasn't very large, Maxie phased through the ceiling. "She's not upstairs," she reported. "I haven't looked down here because I figured Everett was around but I don't see him." Then she was gone just as quickly through a wall that must have led to the kitchen.

"She took an Uber." Bill had just managed to come up with an answer to my question. It was a lie, but at least he was back in the game. "It just wasn't working out so she called for a car and it came and took her home. You should call and leave a message with her."

"Wow, you're really bad at this, Bill." It seemed like Josh was catching some of my sass and using it as his own. "You just told us you know for a fact that Katrina won't answer her phone if we call her right now. So why don't you stop trying so hard to come up with a plausible lie and tell us the truth?"

"I'm telling you the truth . . ." he began.

"Don't waste our time," Josh said. He gestured and the two of us took separate routes around the room and toward the door at its far side. "We know your blood was in the Lincoln that was taken out of the ground with the dead man in it. We know you've been stringing Katrina along but we don't know why. What we're concerned about right now is her safety. So just tell us where she is and we can sort the rest of it out later."

I cringed a little at the info dump Bill had just been given. Telling him we knew about the blood in the car was a mistake; it took away a weapon we could use and increased Bill's sense of danger at the same time. Neither of those things was good.

"She's not here," Bill said, but his eyes had definitely bulged at the mention of the blood.

"I texted her four times on the way here," I told him. "She hasn't answered and I was clearly worried when I got in touch. I don't know Katrina well, but I'm certain she would have gotten in touch if she could. So you're not fooling anybody, Bill. You're just putting off a bad end to this scene."

It wasn't a large room so Josh and I met at the door quickly. I pushed on the door and it swung open into what was a medium-sized kitchen with a tiny breakfast nook in one corner. I was hoping Maxie wasn't taking notes. Josh watched Bill as I walked in.

Katrina wasn't there, either. I had no plan beyond going into every room, opening every closet door and looking under every possible piece of furniture until I found the guest I'd inadvertently sent to this house. All I could have told you at this point was that she definitely wasn't under the kitchen table.

The problem was, there was no other way out of this room

than the door we'd just used and Bill Harrelson was standing in the doorway. He didn't look threatening as much as he looked threatened but there is that saying about a cornered animal, and I could look it up to complete that for you if I managed to get out of the kitchen, and then the house, alive.

Josh was certainly sensing my anxiety. He made certain to be at the door ahead of me and looked like he was planning to push Bill out of the way, but the foreman, who looked pretty formidable, simply let him pass. That left me.

Bill made no menacing move at me as I approached the kitchen door. But he did move toward me just as I attempted to walk through and back into the front room. I flinched a little and the sound of my foot skidding on the floor made Josh turn around, looking like he'd realized he'd made a terrible mistake. I stopped in my tracks, sure this one was going to cost me. There was no sign of Maxie or Everett to come and stop Bill as he approached.

But all he did was lean in toward me and whisper in a barely audible voice, "Don't do this to me. They'll kill me."

Chapter 33

Bill moved out of my way before I could whisper back. He did not put his finger to his lips but it was quite clear he could not discuss his situation—whatever it was—in a normal conversational volume. Josh looked at me with the obvious question in his eyes and I had no facial expression that would communicate the answer he needed. Instead I simply showed him that I was all right and moved into the front room, intending to make a left turn toward a hall that must have led to a bedroom.

That was the moment that Everett rose up out of the basement, making me think of Paul, who always rises up out of the basement. For a second the incongruity made me stop and that was long enough for Everett to say, "Ms. Breslin is not in the basement, Ghost Lady. I have been in every room in the house and have not seen her. Maxie is currently checking the garage."

I stopped my progress to the hallway and Josh, sensing I'd gotten some new information, stopped behind me. With what I'm sure was a confused expression on my face I turned to face Bill. "She's not here, is she?" I said.

Bill must have gotten the wrong impression. Seeing me stop and turn so soon after his strange statement, I'm guessing he thought I was now playing along with his bogus scenario. "That's right," he said, "Katrina took an Uber home like I told you. There's no reason to worry. So if you want to get back to your house . . ." He just let his voice trail off like that, suggesting in the most polite terms he could that Josh and I should get our butts out of his house.

"No, I don't think so." I didn't want Bill to have the wrong idea; I still wasn't on his side and I wasn't just going to pack up and go home because he said so. "I think you've either taken her somewhere or she's just someplace we haven't looked yet. So why don't you tell us why you were seen forcibly putting Katrina into your car."

What flashed through Bill's eyes was not anger or betrayal. He wasn't appalled at what I'd said or my audacity in saying it. What I saw there at that moment was fear, pure and simple. I was going to force his hand, he thought, and that was not something he could afford to do under the current circumstances.

"I don't know what you're talking about," he said.

But I wasn't feeling especially charitable toward him at the moment. I feel responsible for my guests while they're staying in my house, and he had at the very least played with the emotions of one of them and at most . . . I didn't want to think about at most.

"Yeah, you do," I said. "You met Katrina at a restaurant called Deep Dive. You had dinner which I assume consisted mostly of fish." I managed not to shudder at the thought.

"Then you went out into the parking lot, you had some sort of argument with Katrina and you grabbed her forcibly by the wrist and made her get into your car. You drove here together. Am I about right so far?"

"I did not force her into the car," Bill said. "I'm not that guy. We didn't have a disagreement about coming back here, just about her taking her own car. I thought it was best if I drove because I knew the way, that's all. I didn't force her to do anything."

"That's not the way my witness saw it. But I'm still trying to figure out why you lied about seeing Katrina at all and more importantly, where she is right now. You want to start by answering that one?" Josh closed in behind me. He was letting me conduct the interrogation but he wasn't going to be left out if Bill proved to be dangerous.

Bill spoke very slowly. "Katrina. Isn't. Here. You have to believe me on this."

"As far as I can tell, he's being truthful, Ghost Lady," Everett said. "But I am prepared to defend you if necessary. There is a fireplace in the den with several implements that would make excellent weapons."

Josh didn't back off at all. He hadn't heard Everett, but it wouldn't have made any difference if he had.

"But you sent me a text threatening me about the gun, didn't you?" I said to Bill. "You were the only one who could have walked in and planted that gun and those bullets. You panicked when it was obvious the gun had been found and you threatened me."

Bill said nothing, so I was right.

My phone buzzed. No doubt Melissa wanting an update. I did not take it out of my pocket.

As much as I wanted to push Bill farther, there had been something about the way he'd said, "They'll kill me" that was holding me back. That was real fear, not some ploy to gain time or sympathy. The question was how to maneuver without asking who "they" might be.

I heard a voice behind me say, "Ask him about his father." I didn't have to turn around. Paul's voice is as familiar to me as anyone's after four years. But I also didn't want to alarm Bill by acknowledging the voice he didn't hear or the man he didn't see. I was annoyed that he'd left Melissa in the truck by herself—she wasn't behind me too, was she? No. She wasn't—but this wasn't the time to scold Paul about that, either.

"Your father rented some earth moving equipment to the person who shot Herman Fitzsimmons in 1983," I said to Bill. "Is that how you got involved in all this?"

The foreman's attention seemed to focus, and not in a good way. He snapped his gaze toward me with some anger in his eyes that made Josh tense up. "What do you know about my father?" he said in a low voice.

"Just what I said. He owned a business that dealt in rentals for heavy equipment. There's a really good probability that he was the guy who leased the backhoe or another earthmover to whoever wanted to bury Herman Fitzsimmons behind my house in a Lincoln Continental. Is your father still alive?" We knew perfectly well he was not.

"That's good," Paul said. "You're getting a reaction." I

didn't see how the reaction I was getting was *good*, but I guess it's all a matter of perspective. Mine was from that of someone who could still be hurt and killed, and Paul was beyond that sort of thing.

"My father passed away in 2009," Bill growled. "You can't pin anything on him."

I didn't want to pin anything on Bill's father but a medal for helping me stay alive, but there was still work to be done in that area and besides, being dead wasn't always a deal breaker in my world.

"I'm not trying to accuse him of anything," I said, despite that being what I'd done a few seconds earlier. "I'm just trying to understand. What's your interest in all this?"

Bill, it should be noted, was not holding a weapon of any kind. In my corner I had my husband, Everett and Paul. So I felt fairly secure challenging him a little bit. It was the "they'll kill me" comment that had me worried because he could have talking about literally anybody.

"I just got the call to come and work on the dunes," he insisted. "Jim Constantine said there was treasure buried in the ground and then he found that car down there. Before that I didn't know anything about my dad renting anybody any equipment thirty years ago."

Maybe Jim was one of the "they" he'd mentioned. For somebody whose name I couldn't remember he seemed to have played a central role in digging up Henry Fitzsimmons and his off-brand coffin. "Did Jim know the car was there?" I asked.

"Look, I'm not pushing it," Bill said. I didn't understand

exactly what he meant but his tone was final. "I don't know anything about this whole business. Katrina isn't here. Why don't you go looking for her somewhere else?"

And that was when Maxie appeared, as usual, through the ceiling. "I found her!" she shouted. "She's in a shed in the backyard!" Everything in this whole disturbing affair was taking place in a backyard.

Given my new information I turned on Bill just as Everett said, "I should have looked there," and vanished through the back wall.

"So you don't mind if I look in your shed behind the house?" I asked Bill.

He went absolutely pale and for a moment I thought he was going to pass out on the floor. "What made you say that?" he asked. Then he looked around like people do when they know about the strange circumstances surrounding my house. "Are there ghosts here?"

Of course Bill had been hanging around my house long enough to recognize the signs, but there was an odd urgency in his voice that made me think it wasn't what he meant. "Why do you ask that?" Josh said. "We can look out the window and see the shed back there as well as anyone else. Maybe I should go back there and take a look." He took a step toward the kitchen, where there was a door to the backyard.

"No!" Bill shouted. "Look, you don't know what you're getting yourself into."

"So tell us," I suggested. "Then we'll know."

But Bill had obviously turned a corner. He walked to a

side table and opened a drawer, from which he extracted a small pistol.

I should have been expecting that; this was about the time a gun usually appeared in my experience.

"You want to see the shed?" he said. "Okay. Let's go see the shed."

Bill gestured with the gun toward the kitchen, indicating Josh and I should walk in that direction. We hesitated for a moment and he yelled, "Move!"

"Go ahead," Paul said. "Maxie and I will be right behind you."

"I'll be in front of you," Maxie said, and shot herself through the wall in the same direction Everett had gone.

Josh looked at me; of course he hadn't heard the ghosts. "Don't worry," I said very quietly, and started moving in the direction Bill was insisting on. Josh's face, angry and anxious to do something to stop Bill, did not change, but he bit on his bottom lip and walked with me through the kitchen and out the back door into the yard.

"If you're going to shoot us, taking us outside isn't really the smart move," I said to Bill as he held the gun discreetly on us. Actually it didn't seem *that* stupid a plan, but I wasn't going to tell him that. The yard was surrounded by a stockade fence, so any neighbor seeing us would have to be at least one floor up and have a burning desire to see into Bill Harrelson's backyard. Besides, it was getting dark and the yard wasn't lit very well. We couldn't count on a call to the police from someone watching Bill's property.

"I'm not going to shoot you if I don't have to," our captor told us. "That's really not who I am."

"From here it looks like exactly who you are," Josh said out of the corner of his mouth. My husband isn't great at suffering gun-toting fools gladly.

"Shut up." Eloquent as well as charming.

In case you're wondering, it doesn't take long to walk from the back door of a suburban New Jersey house to the far reaches of the yard, even a fairly large one like Bill's. We found ourselves at the shed, which was fairly large and sturdy, in less than half a minute.

Bill reached into his pocket and found a ring of keys, one of which he managed to isolate even while holding the gun (although to be honest, he wasn't actually aiming it at Josh or me the whole time—it just felt like rushing him would be a very bad plan). He used it to open a padlock on the latch to the shed door and then maneuvered Josh and me to one side as he opened the door.

"Don't worry," Paul said. Easy for him to say.

Inside the shed, illuminated by a single light bulb in a ceiling fixture, was Katrina. She was not tied to a chair or chained to the shed wall. In fact, once the door was opened she tried to rush out but was stopped by Bill and his trusty pistol. Then she saw Josh and me.

"Oh no," she said. I get that a lot, but Josh?

"Get inside," Bill said, mostly to my husband and me. He waved the gun.

As the door opened wider I saw Everett inside the shed. He was reaching for a shovel hung on the wall, but I knew he wasn't wearing anything large enough to conceal it, so he wouldn't be able to get it outside the shed. I had to buy him a few seconds.

"I don't think so," I said. "I feel safer out here."

Bill looked more exasperated than anything else. He pointed the gun directly at Katrina. "You want me to kill her?" he said. "If not, get in."

Katrina, even after all this, looked shocked. "Me?"

I bet on my ghost friends. Even if we were locked inside, they'd find a way. And I really didn't want Bill to shoot Katrina. I walked into the shed and Josh followed me. If you can think of what we should have done please feel free to get in touch and let me know, but that was the best option I could see at the moment.

"It's all right, Alison," Paul told me. "Let him lock you in. We'll have you out very soon."

Josh, who hadn't heard, asked, "Is this what investigating is like all the time?"

"I don't think for everybody, but for me, yes," I told him.

Before Everett and his shovel could make it back out the door to clobber Bill, our captor had closed the entrance solidly without a word. We could hear him putting the lock back on. Everett went through the wall, sans shovel but with something in his pocket I couldn't see as he flew by. Paul was already out there.

"What are you doing here?" Katrina said. "Why didn't you call the police?"

It seemed like a good question, but how could I have called the Hazlet cops and said I knew a woman was in danger because a ghost had seen her forced into a car? Also, until we'd arrived and Bill decided to be armed, we hadn't known anything for certain. But this wasn't the time to justify what had clearly been a mistake.

At least the light stayed on. Being in here in the dark would have been intolerable.

"Hang on," I said. "Bill forgot to take my phone." I reached into my pocket and pulled it out.

"Don't you think I thought of that?" Katrina said. "I can't get a signal in here."

That was odd. There was no reason the simple shed would block a cellular signal unless . . .

"He must have some kind of a signal jammer he's using to block it or he's insulated the walls and ceiling with something that would stop it from getting in here," Josh said. "This might not be the first time he's kept someone in here. That's why he didn't care if we had our phones."

Swell. I couldn't even text Melissa, who was definitely wondering where the heck we were by now. Of course Paul or Maxie could go to the truck and get her up to date, but I was hoping they were working on that lock.

"What happened?" I asked Katrina.

"I don't know," she answered with a slight sniffle. "Everything was going so well and then he said let's go back to my house because it's right nearby. And I said I'd take my car and follow him so I could just go home whenever I wanted, and that's when he got crazy."

Josh immediately looked concerned. "Crazy?"

"He said no, he wanted to drive and he'd just bring me

back to my car later. That sounded a little strange to me, so I said again that I'd just follow him. And he grabbed my arm, tight, and told me to just get in the car." Katrina showed us her left wrist, but in this light I didn't see any mark on her arm. I took her word for it.

I was about to answer her when I heard something going on with the lock. Maxie, who had stayed in the shed with us, said, "I'll check," and flew through the front wall. There was a definite scraping sound that I thought might be metal on metal. Was Everett trying to chop the lock off with an ax or something?

"What did Bill want?" Josh asked Katrina. "Why was he so insistent that you come back here with him and not take your car?"

Katrina looked at Josh with wide eyes. He's very easy to talk to and exudes trustworthiness without trying to do it, which means he really deserves the trust. "At first I thought he was trying to get me to spend the night, you know," she said. "I mean, I wasn't totally against the idea but I wanted to be able to leave if I felt like it. But once we got here it was obvious that wasn't on his mind at all."

"What was?" Josh said.

"He wanted me to talk to the police," she answered. "I didn't know about what, but he wanted me to say that I'd been . . . with him . . . for two nights this week."

"The two nights the car was being moved around?" I asked.

"I guess so. I'd seen him earlier in the evening the first time but we didn't . . . I mean, we just went to dinner."

"He wanted to use you as an alibi," I said. "It must have been Bill who towed the car out and back so he wanted you to tell Lt. McElone you were with him so he wouldn't be a suspect."

"Then why would he deny he was seeing Katrina at all?" Josh asked.

Katrina's jaw opened and hung a little. "He said we weren't seeing each other?"

At that moment the metallic sound from outside stopped and I heard something hit the ground. The door swung open to reveal Everett, holding a metal file he'd found in the shed, with Paul and Maxie behind him. Everett was grinning broadly.

"I told you we would get you out, Ghost Lady," he said.

Chapter 34

The first thing I did when we were out of the shed was text Melissa. I wanted that girl out of the area as quickly as humanly possible, and since I had no idea whether Josh or I would make it out that fast (or, if Bill and his pistol found us, at all) she absolutely did not need to wait for us.

Get a Lyft and charge it on your emergency credit card, I sent. *Go home now.*

In a more convenient world I would have called my mother to give Liss a ride home but she lived too far away to get here quickly. I cursed myself for even considering letting my daughter come on this nutty errand and hit the *Send* button.

(Actually, the first thing I did was accidentally hit the *Send* button on that SOS text and send it to Paul, who looked stumped.)

I would have put the phone away even as Josh was saying, "Is there a way out of the yard without going through the house?" but I noticed a text from Phyllis.

Got word on the owner of that Lincoln. Call me 4 more. I

briefly pondered four more what until I realized what she meant and decided I didn't have time for a phone call now.

"No," Paul said. "The whole yard is fenced in and there is no gate other than the one over there." He pointed toward a panel of the stockade fence that had hinges on the yard side. "But it is locked on the outside. We could probably cut the lock the way we did this one." He nodded toward Everett, who was still holding the file.

I relayed all this to Josh, who shook his head. "It would make too much noise. Can we remove the hinges on this side?"

It took a short walk to get to the panel in question and I looked at the hinges. "We could if we had exactly the right screwdriver. It would have to be pretty big because you're going to need some leverage and those screws are large. I didn't see one like that in the shed."

"Looks like our best shot is to go in through the house and try to make a dash for the front door," Josh said. "I can't say I'm crazy about that option with a guy who has a gun in there."

"Don't think you could hop the fence?" I was kidding; the fence was wooden and at least seven feet tall. But Josh looked at it and considered. "I'm joking."

"You should wave a flag or something when you do that."

I ignored that. "How long do you think before he comes looking for us?" I asked anybody who wanted to venture an opinion. "Do I have time to call the Hazlet cops?"

"And tell them what?" Katrina asked. "That a man is holding us hostage in a suburban backyard?"

"He has a gun and he is threatening us," Josh pointed out. "I don't think we have to worry about looking foolish."

* * *

"I don't get this at all," Katrina said. "He kept telling me I'd have to wait until someone else got here. Was that you?"

I shrugged. Who knew what Bill's weird plan was?

We huddled together in a corner of the yard that seemed least visible from the house, close to the back wall of the building but to the side where it would be hard for Bill to see us from any of the windows in the kitchen or back bedroom. We couldn't see in, either, so it was hard to say whether he was inside or not.

We spoke in low tones. "No, it must be someone other than us. Bill said something about having to do this or 'they' would kill him," I told Katrina. "Do you have any idea who 'they' are?"

"I don't know but he was talking to somebody on the phone and he seemed really nervous," she answered. "But that was before things got really crazy and he locked me in the shed. All I know is he called somebody and said the car thing wasn't working out. I don't know what that means, but whatever answer he got seemed to shake him up a lot. That's when he said we should go outside to clear our heads and the next thing I knew I was locked up in there." She shook her head, trying to jettison the memory of twenty minutes ago.

"Call the police," Josh urged. "Or I can. Either way we might have a better chance trying to wait it out here than to storm through the house. I can't protect both of you and myself at the same time." The usual male response: Women must be protected. Of course, there was a guy with a gun who had threatened to shoot us, so I'd take any protection I could get.

"We can help if it comes to that," Paul said. "But an intervention from the police might actually speed the resolution of this case." That's Paul. He's not only male; he's also so focused that it borders on crazy.

"It makes sense," I said. I reached for my phone.

"Making sense is overrated." The voice was coming from the back door of the house, and it certainly was not Bill Harrelson's. It was female and had a vaguely familiar tone. I couldn't see the speaker yet but I could hear her footsteps and they were coming in our direction. Calling the cops seemed out of the question now, but I quickly dialed McElone's number—she's on speed dial—and put the phone on mute. She'd be able to hear without making noises that would put us in even more danger. If that was possible.

The footsteps increased in volume until the woman turned the corner and looked at the group of us. And in this case, I was betting all of us—including the ghosts—were visible. Because although the speaker, Darlene Menendez, was looking just at Josh, Katrina and me, she was not alone.

Behind her and slightly to her right was another ghost.

"Harriet Adamson," Paul said. "That's who you are, isn't it?" I guess he recognized her aura, or something, from the Ghosternet.

"And you're Paul." Harriet looked him up and down. "Nice looking young fella, weren't you?"

Oh, and did I mention that Darlene was holding a gun?

"There are too many things that don't make sense and are still true," she said. "Like that Herm was cheating on me."

"And he was cheating on me at the same time," Harriet said.

"Apparently with a number of women," I said. "So you shot him when he was supposed to be going to see Harriet here."

"Harriet where?" Both Josh and Katrina started looking randomly around. I don't know why people who can't see ghosts will do that. It's not going to help. In any event, this conversation was going to be complicated.

"Just go with it," I told Josh. I knew he would pick up on that immediately. Katrina, however, was not as understanding, having not been married to me and seeing (or not seeing) what goes on in my house for some time now.

"Go with what?" she asked and I just didn't answer. It didn't seem the top priority right at the moment.

I'd only mentioned Harriet to see if Darlene was aware of her presence, and I saw no reaction from her, which indicated I was right: Darlene could see Harriet, and probably all ghosts. So Paul, Maxie and Everett couldn't use the element of surprise.

But Darlene wasn't listening; she was considering what I'd said. Finally, she nodded. "I'm not going to confess to anything in public, even here and even in front of your three ghosts," Darlene said. Like they were *my* ghosts.

Yup, she saw them. That was a major bummer.

"You can see ghosts," I said out loud. It was surprise more than communication.

"Of course," Darlene told me. "Did you think you were the only one?"

I didn't even think I was the only one in my family, but that wasn't the point. "Did you kill Harriet?"

"No," Harriet said. "I drank myself to death."

"I told you, I'm not confessing anything to you," Darlene repeated. But there was something about the way she was refusing to confirm or deny my accusation that struck me as wrong. Why would she sound like that if she hadn't . . . and I flashed on Oliver and Tony. Oh, of course.

"You didn't kill Herman," I said.

"What?" It could have been Paul. Could have been Josh. Could have been Katrina. Probably was all of them.

"You're protecting someone else. Someone who would have been shooting from a very low angle." I was finally putting it all together. "Sgt. Menendez killed her father."

"It was an *accident*." From what I'd seen, you could count on Harriet not to think before she spoke. "She was only three."

"Sgt. Menendez?" Josh was trying to keep up.

Josh and Katrina hadn't heard, but they heard Darlene say, "Your theory is interesting but you're not getting me on tape saying so."

"I don't have a recorder on me." It was true; I'd even left the voice recorder I use for Paul at home because . . . well, there was Paul. "Have you been covering for your daughter all these years?"

"It's none of your business."

"Let me guess," I said. "She got hold of her father's gun somehow."

"Darlene had it out." Good old Harriet. "She was mad at Herm because of me."

"And Theresa picked it up and shot him by accident, right?" I said. To anyone who would confirm. "That's really irresponsible gun ownership, Darlene."

"Don't say a word." Darlene's tone was threatening, although I couldn't imagine what she might be able to do to Harriet. Still, Harriet shut up.

Josh gets ornery when someone threatens our lives; go figure. "What did you do with Bill? I didn't hear a gunshot."

"Mr. Harrelson is alive and well and preparing his van," Darlene said. "He'll have some work to do when we are finished here."

I didn't care for that innuendo much so I decided to distract Darlene with facts. "It was Bill Harrelson's blood in addition to Herman Fitzsimmons's in the Continental," I said. "Obviously that couldn't have been there since 1983 because Bill was just a little boy then. So when you heard the Continental had been found you somehow got it taken away long enough to put some of his blood—and I'd love to hear how you got that—in the car and then bring it back. You were blackmailing Bill and you probably still are. He was talking to you on the phone before when Katrina heard his end of the conversation and he was terrified you could hear me question him. Had you arrived here already or were you listening in on your cell phone?"

Harriet smiled. "Getting Bill's blood was easy. I just used a razor blade on his wrist when he wasn't looking. And he's always not looking for me. The tricky part was getting his hand in the car." Okay, so Harriet, in addition to being dead, was crazy. Good to know. But it did explain the way Bill had been favoring his arm the day before.

I turned and looked back at Darlene because talking to Harriet wasn't going to get me anywhere. I wasn't optimistic about the chances with Darlene, but keeping her from shooting us was probably the best use of my time. Stall. "Why'd you bury old Herm in a Continental, anyway, and how'd you get Bill's dad to give you his car?"

Darlene smiled. Clearly she was proud of her handiwork even if it was a subject she was not keen on discussing for fear of the imaginary wire I was wearing to incriminate her. If she was here to shoot the three of us I didn't really see the utility in keeping mum, but Darlene did. "I'm not going to tell you anything at all." She turned sharply to admonish Harriet. "And neither are you!"

"Neither is who?" Katrina asked. Katrina had only been living with ghosts for a few days. It takes most people at least a week.

"So let's get you all back into the shed," Darlene said, pointing with the gun. "It'll be so much quieter and neater that way."

I saw Josh's triceps tighten up.

The only thing to do was pretend Darlene hadn't spoken. "Here's how I see it," I said. "Your daughter accidentally killed her father. You didn't want to call the police and tell them that. Why not?" No answer, so I went on. (See: Gun.) "You got somebody—Harriet?—to help you get the body out of your house. There wasn't much in the way of forensic science in those days to find the traces once you'd cleaned up. And then somehow you got to Harrelson, Sr. and made him help you bury the car, with Herman, behind what wasn't yet my house. Why there? Why pick on me thirty years ahead of time?"

"Oh, seriously," Darlene said. "Can't you just go into the shed and get shot like you're supposed to?"

"Once the car was in the ground you reported your husband missing and the police investigated," I continued as if nothing had been said. (Hey, it was working so far.) "Sgt. Blanik didn't think it was that clear a missing person case but he couldn't find any evidence so he had to close it as unsolved. And for three decades everything was good. You married Mr. Menendez and your daughter grew up to be a Harbor Haven cop. I bet you hadn't seen that coming."

"Get. In. The shed."

My tactic was wearing thin. I wondered if Josh had anything he wanted to try because I was coming up blank.

When in doubt, just barrel on through. "But then Bill's crew—and that must have been a surprise—dug up the Continental looking for emeralds. How did emeralds get into the car, Darlene?" Maybe she'd answer *that* question.

"I don't know." And oddly, I believed her. But she didn't add anything else. I took it as progress that she wasn't repeating her order to go inside and get shot. It's the little things that keep you going in life.

Josh must have been thinking along with me because I

felt him move very slowly away from my left shoulder. If I could keep Darlene's attention on me he might be able to circle over to her and get the gun out of her hand.

Paul was watching Josh too and provided a partial distraction. "I have been investigating your late husband's murder," he told Darlene. "He seemed to disappear literally without a trace until his body was discovered in the Lincoln. You knew how to use a forklift, and assumedly a backhoe as well. You were capable to operating that type of earth moving equipment. Was it originally your plan to do the whole job on your own?"

"I'm not saying anything," Darlene said, which was itself a contradiction.

"Who is she talking to?" Katrina asked. Then her attention was redirected toward the back door of the house. And a strange, nostalgic smile came across her face that was absolutely inexplicable given our current circumstances.

She was beaming at Bill Harrelson, who was walking out toward us holding a coil of rope. I've done my share of home improvement and a little light construction but at the moment I couldn't think of one positive usage for a coil of rope.

"Bill," Katrina said, and then she remembered what was going on and the smile turned sad.

"Everything's ready," Bill told Darlene. "Why aren't they in the shed?"

"Because you didn't plan for ghosts," she told him. "Get them in there now."

"Ghosts?" Bill looked at me. "That's real?"

I shook my head disapprovingly at him. "How'd they get

you, Bill?" I asked. "What can Darlene possibly have on you to get you into this position?"

"Nothing." A fourth grader couldn't have been less convincing.

"He did enough to get himself arrested and he knows it," Darlene said, aimed more at Bill than at answering my question. "He put out a couple of fake gems so his boys would find the car that he thought would clear his dad. But now he knows better. His father helped kill Herman, indirectly, and Bill here helped cover it up. Not so indirectly."

"Stop it," Bill told her.

"I'm just reminding you of your responsibilities." She gestured toward us.

Josh had stopped moving when Bill arrived because Bill was coming from an angle that would betray Josh's plan if he kept going. Darlene handed Bill the gun anyway, which moved the focus of our effort toward getting it away from him. So that hadn't worked out great, no fault of my husband's.

"Maybe Bill knows." If something didn't work on Darlene it didn't mean I couldn't use it on Bill. "How'd the emeralds get into the Lincoln and my ceiling beam?"

"Pirates, I guess," Bill said. "Maybe the legend was true." He gestured with the gun as he had before. "Now get back into that shed."

It was fairly dark in the yard now and getting chillier by the minute. I wished I'd brought a heavier jacket to get shot in. The porch light from Bill's back door was shining but it wasn't exactly bright back here. The ghosts were getting harder to see. I wondered if that was better for my side or for Darlene's and decided three ghosts are better than one.

"No," I said to Bill. "The pirates would have been there two hundred years or more before the car got there. How'd the emeralds get into the car? I'm sure you know, Bill. You're the foreman on the job and those men were operating under your supervision. You planted a couple of stones, didn't you? Because you *wanted* that car to be found."

Bill's eyes widened by about an inch—which is a lot in eyes—and he steeled himself not to look at Darlene. "That's not true."

"Yes it is," Josh said, circling back toward me. "You wanted to clear your father's name after all these years because you'd heard the stories about how he must have been in on the disappearance of Herman Fitzsimmons and how he should have been in jail. You'd seen him drink himself to death over it. And you wanted to make that go away. But you had a problem: It was true."

"But a metal detector can't find emeralds," I pointed out. "Why plant gems if the car was going to be found anyway?"

Bill was sweating and it wasn't at all hot out. "I don't know where the emeralds came from," he insisted.

"Yeah, you do," I said. "Was this a side thing? In digging up the beach you found some of the fabled gems left by pirates and you wanted to use that for cover? Or did you just buy some fake emeralds because of the legend and leave them in there so you could tell the police the pirate story and distract them from the idea that you were trying to get the car found?"

"Enough," Bill said. "Get in the shed."

"You don't want to do this," Josh continued. Out of the corner of my eye I saw Katrina take a couple of steps toward the shed because Bill had told her to do so. "This isn't going to help clear your dad's name and it's going to get you into jail for the rest of your life."

All that was true, but it wasn't actually helpful because Bill was now angry in addition to being afraid of Darlene. I was hoping we could keep this going long enough for the encroaching darkness to make the ghosts practically invisible and exercise our advantage in numbers over Bill's advantage in firepower.

"Enough!" he shouted. "I'll shoot you here if I have to." Personally I didn't see how the scene of the shooting was of all that much difference to the shoot-ee, but the timing was essential in that the later it got the better chance we had of there being no shooting at all.

But Maxie wasn't helping by being more conspicuous than I wanted her to be, which was pretty much par for the course with Maxie. "You're not shooting anybody," she said to the man who couldn't hear her.

Harriet did take note, however, and flew over toward Maxie. "Yeah he is, and I'll make sure of it."

There were so many questions unanswered, like why Herman had been in a competitor's car and why it had been necessary for Darlene to blackmail Bill into his role in this bizarre business when she knew how to run excavation equipment herself. But there wasn't going to be time to ask them and not get answers from Darlene. Maxie had called the question somehow just as the light was fading in the backyard.

Maxie was, in fact, raising her fists to take on the advancing Harriet when they became too difficult for me to see. I thought I saw Everett head toward the shed, presumably to find something he could use as a weapon. Bill was apparently having the same difficulty, although without the added problem of trying to get a fix on transparent people. He started flailing around with the gun in his right hand, variously aiming at Josh, Katrina and me and causing each of us to back off when it seemed he was going to fire.

"There's no time to get them into the shed!" Darlene yelled at him. "Shoot now!"

Something hit me hard from the left side and I felt myself falling to the ground, where I landed ungracefully but unharmed. I heard the report of the gun and then Josh's voice in my ear, whispering, "Stay down. Roll around so there's never a stationary target."

"What about Katrina?" I asked as quietly as I could.

"I'll see." And then his arms weren't around me anymore. Which wasn't as good.

I did as he said and rolled back and forth on the grass, not giving a moment's thought to how I was going to get those stains out of relatively new denim and a cotton blouse, which hopefully was being somewhat protected by my fake leather jacket. All the time my mind was focusing on Josh and where he might be. Aside from the small area around the back door the yard was pretty much pitch black now. Seeing anything more than a couple of feet away was a useless exercise.

But I could hear things: Mostly the sound of struggle. Maxie and Harriet must have been going at it pretty seriously.

Josh said something to Katrina, who it seemed was trying to advance toward Bill, about hitting the deck. Paul said something about the rope and Everett answered with an, "Affirmative" that really didn't help me understand any better. Darlene kept telling Bill to shoot but the one round was the only bullet I'd heard go by. Bill cursed once and then I heard something hit the ground in his direction. I squinted and could barely make out the gun.

That was enough; I had to crawl toward the weapon and secure it and then I could take control of the situation. I had made it about three feet on my knees when the gun was raised from the turf by a woman's hand I took to be Darlene's, and that wasn't good. I froze, not wanting to give Darlene an audible clue about my whereabouts. Then much of the sound—except for Maxie grunting a lot in her struggle with Harriet—died down.

And I heard the sound of wood breaking and saw flashlights gathering from somewhere. Maybe fifteen feet away came the desperate cry, "Mom!"

I wanted to leap up then and scream at Melissa to get out of here, to stop being in danger. She was my only priority and I was petrified that she might somehow find herself in front of the gun in Darlene's hand. But something kept me on the ground and stopped me from screaming out at her, and it wasn't just that I was upset with my daughter for disobeying me and staying here when she should be on her way home.

The voice wasn't Melissa's.

"Mom!" she shouted again. "Put down the gun. Now!"

Sgt. Theresa Menendez, holding her four-battery flashlight

straight at her left shoulder and her police-issued weapon in her right, marched into the backyard with five other flashlight beams to her sides and behind her. I was focused on finding Melissa, but she did not seem to be present, which was a huge relief. Meanwhile Menendez was doing her best to contain her mother, Darlene.

"Drop the weapon and put your hands behind your head, Mom. Do it right now." Menendez's voice was firm but she was trying to sound soothing. "Let's not make this worse than it has to be."

"You don't understand," Darlene told her. I could see her in profile because of the angle of the flashlights. "They're trying to say you murdered your father."

I could hear the conflict in Menendez's voice as Josh crawled over to me and placed himself between me and the gun. He held me closely. I felt my neck relax a little. Maybe we *weren't* going to get shot. But maybe Darlene was. "I did, Mom," Menendez said. "I was a little girl and it was an accident but I shot him. I don't remember it really, but that's what happened. And we're going to have to deal with that, but there are a lot of officers here now and if you don't drop your gun we're not going to get the chance. So please. Mom. Put down the gun."

Darlene twisted quickly, like a spasm, and when she did I saw that Bill was already in handcuffs and putting up no fight at all. I couldn't see any of the ghosts because flashlights just go right through them but I heard Maxie grunting a little less. Then she said, "Now be a good girl and go back to being dead."

Harriet, doing the ghost equivalent of breathing heavily, said nothing. But I could hear her straining in some way and I'll admit that gave me some satisfaction. It was one thing to try and kill me, but to lie to Paul on the Ghoster-net? Unforgiveable.

"You don't *understand*," Darlene protested as Bill was led out of the backyard. "They would have taken you away from me!"

Her daughter clearly knew that letting Darlene slide into a breakdown would not end well for anybody. It was up to Menendez to talk her mother down and she had to do it quickly. The other cops didn't have the same kind of attachment to the woman holding the gun.

"Maybe, but they can't do that now," she said. "But you need to focus on now, Mom. You need to put that gun down— very carefully—on the ground and we'll take a ride to the station to work this all out, okay? Put the gun down. Right now."

Darlene looked at her daughter. "Terry. It's you." She started to turn toward Menendez.

"Don't move, Mom." The voice was firm but insistent. "Don't turn with the gun in your hand. These officers don't want you to do that. They want you to put it down on the grass."

"I have a shot," I heard one of the officers say.

"Don't take it," Menendez said with authority, although I was certain she had no jurisdiction at all outside of Harbor Haven. "She's going to put the gun down."

"What?" Darlene asked. I couldn't see her face very well at this angle but in profile her left eye looked profoundly confused.

"Mom. Do you see the gun in your hand?" I thought it clear Menendez had gone through some negotiation training.

Darlene looked at her hand. "This one?"

"Yes. Don't move it. Don't do anything except put it right down on the grass, slowly. Okay? Then it'll be all right, I promise."

Darlene looked at her daughter and there was no way to know if she comprehended even where she was standing at that moment. She didn't move or speak for a long pause. But then she said, "All right," and bent over to place the gun softly on the ground in front of her. "Was that okay?" she asked Menendez.

Theresa Menendez exhaled as she holstered her weapon and carefully picked up the one on the grass using a ballpoint pen. She immediately put the pistol into an evidence bag from her pocket.

"Yes, Mom," she said. "You did just fine."

Chapter 35

"Did I or did I not tell you to keep your nose out of this investigation?" Lt. Anita McElone shook her head at my sheer idiocy and sat down uncomfortably on an easy chair in my den. I hasten to point out that it wasn't the chair or my den that was uncomfortable; McElone just won't ever be at ease in the guesthouse. I've come to accept that and even, if I'm being honest, to find some amusement in it.

"You always tell me that," I countered. "How am I supposed to know when I should listen to you?"

The detective let out a deep theatrical sigh and broke eye contact as if just looking at me was too aggravating to consider. She looked instead at my mother and asked, "Was she always like this?"

"Oh yes," Mom said with a pride in her voice I don't think McElone had been trying to elicit. "She's so smart."

You didn't think Mom was going to get that call from Melissa and *not* come back to the house with my father, did you?

I had instructed the ghosts to leave the lieutenant alone and so far they were acting accordingly. But Maxie had that look in her eye indicating she was more interested in finalizing the kitchen design than having to deal with all this cop stuff. Still, McElone had shown up to get statements from Josh and me, it was late at night and Maxie understood that unnerving the lieutenant was only going to prolong the process. She was, in a Maxie kind of way, being reasonable.

Melissa had called my mother from the truck while she was waiting for Josh and me to emerge with Katrina from Bill Harrelson's backyard. She had not obeyed my text and gotten a ride home but instead had conferred with Mom, who agreed to come with my father to Melissa's side, and then called McElone after texting me back and getting no answer. She had not left the truck despite desperately wanting to see what was going on but she was orchestrating help from the Hazlet police even as McElone had been on her way, leaving her husband and children yet again for an evening of rescuing the likes of me.

"Have you been able to sort all this stuff out?" I asked McElone. "I can't make head or tail of it."

The lieutenant reestablished eye contact with a look that made me wish she hadn't. "I don't know if I've mentioned this, but I'm a trained police officer and you own a little hotel. We've managed to work out most of the story, and it's a weird one, which I should expect by now whenever I get a call to this address."

I ignored all the wiseacre stuff she'd just said because there just wasn't any point. "So Darlene found out Herman was cheating on her and was going to scare him with his gun, but his daughter shot him by accident. Right? How'd she find out? Did one of the women Herm was harassing dime him out?"

Melissa, sitting on the sofa with Josh and me, looked over. "Dime him out?" she asked.

"Public phone calls used to cost a dime," Josh explained. "So when someone dropped a dime on you they were calling the authorities to say you'd done something wrong."

"What's a public phone?" Liss asked, but she was kidding, I'm pretty sure.

"No," McElone said as if this hilarious banter had not been performed strictly for her benefit. "Actually Darlene just happened to see Herman in a Dairy Queen parking lot with someone she was pretty sure wasn't her."

"So she immediately went home and got Herman's gun to take her revenge?" My mother looked positively appalled.

McElone shook her head. "Yes, but it was not without planning. She didn't intend to shoot her husband, but when her daughter did that, she saw an opportunity and called her pal Nathaniel Adamson, telling him Herman needed a car to leave town and she wouldn't let him use his own."

"And Mr. Adamson bought that?" Melissa asked. "Mr. Fitzsimmons was a car dealer. He didn't need a borrowed car if he really wanted to leave."

"No, that's true," McElone said. "But Nat probably knew Darlene didn't intend to let her husband drive off. He knew she was angry and vindictive. I'm sure he didn't figure Herman was dead and she would bury him in the car, but when her husband suddenly vanished into thin air and the car went with him, Nat knew not to ask questions."

"Yeah, that's about how Harriet tells it," Maxie said from her corner of the ceiling. "She's really a nice person once you get to know her." Maxie had gotten to talk to Harriet Adamson by beating her mercilessly and then containing her so she couldn't hurt Josh or me. It seemed they had now formed something of a friendship, which was lucky since it would have been really difficult to send Harriet to jail.

"Do you think that's why he killed himself?" Melissa asks questions that most thirteen-year-olds might not ask and it has a way of unnerving some adults.

Not McElone. "Medical records indicate Mr. Adamson was suffering from depression and it was unrelated to the Fitzsimmons thing," she told Liss. "But the question I most wanted to ask Darlene was why she decided to bury her husband in a Lincoln Continental, and not just in the ground."

"What did she say?" Mom asked. I saw my father conferring with Maxie in the upper corner and he pointed toward the kitchen. Maxie nodded.

"She looked surprised," McElone answered. "As if it seemed the most obvious thing in the world. Apparently one of the reasons Herman had taken up with Harriet Adamson was that he envied her husband's Lincoln/Mercury dealership. He'd applied for a franchise and been turned down because Nat was local and he objected. Herman figured he'd get his revenge in, you know, another way. So Darlene thought putting him in the Lincoln, even after he was dead, would annoy him no end."

"Where'd she get the Lincoln?" I asked. "That was just mean."

"From Adamson," McElone said. "He wanted to punish the man who was cheating with his wife and once he found out Herman was dead, he furnished a used car."

I looked over at Paul, who was hovering in front of the lieutenant, intent as always on seeing how she operated. He knew why I was training my attention on him and reminded me, "I couldn't raise Herman Fitzsimmons. Maybe he really *was* irritated through all eternity."

"I'm confused," Josh said to McElone. "If Darlene Fitzsimmons . . ."

"Darlene Menendez," the lieutenant corrected.

"Of course. If she could operate all the earth moving equipment herself, why did she need to get William Harrelson, Sr. involved, and why did she need Bill to move the car after it had been exhumed?"

"She needed senior because even if she could run the machines she didn't own any," McElone told him. "Harrelson rented them out, but Darlene had to be sure there was no record, no paper trail that would implicate her in digging the hole and putting a car in it, which would be illegal even if there *wasn't* a dead body in the car that she just happened to kill. The stuff with Bill, who filled in as many blanks for me as he could, was only to keep him quiet. Once that car came out of the ground he knew what his father had been talking about all those years ago and when the body was found he got in touch immediately with Darlene. He wasn't blackmailing her so much as alerting her and begging not to mention his father's name."

"That should have been enough," I said.

"Yeah, but you have to keep in mind that Darlene is crazy and paranoid," McElone answered. "She wanted to be sure Bill would keep quiet about what he knew, even though he didn't know that much. Once she heard it was his crew that unearthed the car—and Bill admits he was trying to confirm the story his dad told him—she saw him as a potential threat. She was desperate to keep her daughter's name out of this. So she came here that one night and took the car away to put his blood in it. I'm not sure how she got the blood because she is telling one nutty story." Maxie stifled a laugh. I don't know why since McElone couldn't have heard it. "But however she did it she convinced Bill she could implicate his dad in the whole mess, maybe even say *he* had shot Herman, and essentially forced him to keep quiet after she brought the car back the next night."

"And so the construction man was romancing Alison's guest to create an alibi?" My mother looked scandalized and I thought about Katrina, up in her room probably thinking this was the worst vacation she'd ever had. Is it saying something awful about me that I spent a moment wondering how this would affect her evaluation form?

"No, not really, according to Bill." McElone didn't sit back on the sofa; it was something of a small victory that she was sitting down at all. Usually she looks like she had her spine replaced with a steel pole simply to make her stance perfectly straight. "He says he really liked Ms. Breslin and only thought this morning that maybe he could use her to get out of the situation. It would have been easier if he'd just told me what had happened, but that appears never to have occurred to him. The county prosecutor will decide what he'll be charged with, although surely abduction and maybe kidnapping will be included. He threatened both of you with a gun, too." That was in case Josh and I had forgotten and somehow decided to be sympathetic toward Bill. I didn't know about Josh, but that certainly wasn't my inclination at the moment.

"What about Sgt. Menendez?" I asked. "The poor kid was only three."

"She's not going to be in trouble about that; it was an accident and it was over thirty years ago," McElone said. "She should have told us what she knew as soon as her dad's body was identified, but she was conflicted. She'll be on leave for a couple of weeks but I'm sure her work in securing the situation without any injuries will work to her advantage."

"Was that why you were holding the emerald, Lieutenant? You didn't suspect Officer Lassen at all, did you?" Josh has the ability to cut to the chase much more smoothly than I do.

"No. I knew there was something up with Menendez," McElone admitted. "I wanted to see if she would report that emerald missing or if she wanted to cover up as much of the case as she could to protect her mother. She reported the emerald, which was what I wanted her to do, but I had turned it in personally to the chief of police as soon as I left here. But I didn't need you knowing all that. It was a department matter." She gave me a significant look. "I'm not stupid."

"Nobody ever thought you were," Melissa said.

I wanted to close my eyes suddenly. It had been a long,

difficult day and I still didn't understand so much. "Why here, Lieutenant? Why did the car get buried in my backyard?"

"Lincoln O'Hara owned this property then," McElone said. "He wasn't living here and he wasn't renting it out. It was sitting quiet. Nobody was watching. They could take all night to bury the car and nobody would know."

I sifted through all the dizzying details of this episode in my head. "Wait. What about the four bullets in the kitchen beam and the gun we found in the floor? What were they all about?"

"The gun was there just because Darlene had been holding it all these years and got antsy about it being found in her house, so she got Bill to hide it during a bathroom break from the construction," McElone explained. "The bullets are a little more complicated."

"How's that?" Josh asked.

"Well as it turns out, those bullets are a match for the gun that Nathaniel Adamson used to kill himself," McElone said. "At least, they were the same vintage and the same caliber. We can't say they were precisely from the same manufacturing lot, but they're not terribly common these days and they were then. So we're still trying to figure out if Nat actually did do himself in, or if someone else might have helped him along. The incident report from the time isn't being especially helpful."

I glanced at Paul, who immediately dropped down into the basement.

"And the bullets from Nat got to my house . . ."

"I'm not clear on whose idea it was because Bill is talking ghosts, but he says he was ordered to stash the bullets in your ceiling. I guess they thought they wouldn't be found." McElone snorted a laugh of sorts. "They were wrong."

Josh shook his head. "It's hard to get your mind around all of it. One man cheats on his wife and more than thirty years later we're trying to sort out what happened after that. And it almost got us killed." He reached for my hand and I took his and squeezed it a little.

McElone stood up. That took a while, as she is tall and imposing. "But I came here to ask *you* questions," she said. "How did Sgt. Menendez know you were in danger and how did she know to come to Bill Harrelson's house in Hazlet?"

"I can only guess," I said. "But I saw the sergeant talking to Bill earlier and she seemed very serious about what she was saying and hearing. I'm guessing she suspected her mother wasn't taking the investigation well and was following up even after you told her not to do that."

"I think that without her, Darlene would have gotten herself into a situation where the officers would have been forced to shoot her," Josh told McElone. "She talked Darlene down and made her put away her gun. Another officer might not have been able to do that."

Paul flew up through the floor. "Confronted with the facts, Nathaniel Adamson admitted he did not die of suicide," he said. "His wife Harriet shot him and made it appear to be by his own hand. That's one reason they are not traveling together now that they are both on my side of the equation."

So that's why Harriet wanted the bullets to be stashed somewhere she thought they would never be found. Should I give that information to McElone? Would it do her any good?

Harriet was dead, after all. My mother looked at me and cocked her head toward the lieutenant. And since getting through my marriage to The Swine I've mostly followed my mother's advice.

"I have some information on Nathaniel Adamson's death," I said to the lieutenant. "But it's not anything you'll want to put into a police report."

McElone shut her eyes briefly and then looked at me. "Is there any legal action I should be taking in regard to that information?" she asked.

"I don't think that would be possible."

She absorbed what I'd said and took a breath. "All right, then," she said. "I'm heading back to my office." She took a few steps toward the door.

"Lieutenant," I said. McElone stopped and turned to look at me. "I'm a little puzzled. Why did you tell us all that stuff about what Darlene and Bill confessed? Usually you won't even give me the time of day if you don't have to."

McElone's lips narrowed a bit. "You were going to get me to tell you anyway," she said. "I just didn't have the energy to fight it at this time of night."

"Go home and go to sleep, lieutenant," Mom said. "You've done a full day's work tonight."

"First sane person I talked to today," McElone muttered as she left.

Chapter 36

"It looks good," Maxie said.

Indeed, the light aqua paint she had decided on for my kitchen did add some character to the room now that I was finishing the last wall. Maxie had offered to do some of the painting herself but I felt that the sight of a roller working itself on the wall was the stuff of a spook show and not a trip to the fridge for some orange juice. I had let her work on the place after my guests were asleep at night. One of them, a lovely older man named Milt, was not here for the ghosts and would have been a little freaked out otherwise.

It had been three weeks since Katrina, Adam and Steve had packed up and left the guesthouse, and now approaching the new year I had only Milt and another guest who had been sent by Senior Plus Tours, a woman named Margot who loved the ghosts and liked to wade in the freezing cold ocean. I get them all here at the guesthouse.

Josh was in the store (he stays open on Saturdays but takes Sundays off) and things seemed like they were more or less back to whatever version of "normal" was currently unraveling in my house.

"It does," I agreed. "I'm glad we managed to agree on the plan after all." It had taken some long negotiations worthy of a multinational arms treaty but Maxie and I had hammered out a design for the kitchen that included her color scheme and my insistence on having cabinets and countertops pretty much where they'd been before to avoid any serious construction labor and the resulting costs of that. Two cabinets were now hung closer to the island, which was actually useful. Point, Maxie.

Katrina Breslin had filled out a glowing evaluation form for the guesthouse based on her proposition that I had done everything I could to give her a great vacation experience including intervening to save her life. I didn't think I'd actually done that last bit but felt I was not in a position to argue the point. Katrina had already visited Bill Harrelson in county lock-up and said she would continue her correspondence with him, whom she hoped would avoid a lengthy prison sentence. His trial had not yet been scheduled.

"It could have been more interesting but I see where you actually needed it to be a working kitchen for Melissa," Maxie said. That's Maxie when she's agreeing with me but still wants to get in a dig just to keep the score in her favor.

Of course Maxie had also advocated for a second access to the basement directly through the kitchen floor, and while I could see some utility—but not much—in the suggestion it was something I did not feel like expending time and money on right now. That had been a slight point of contention, but when I gave in to Maxie on new crown moldings in an accent color of very muted orange she was appeased.

There was a knock at the back door. I looked up to see Phyllis Coates standing on my doorstep. That was a tiny bit disturbing as Phyllis rarely leaves her office for anything but a hot story, and I wanted to be done being a hot story for a very long time, if forever was not available.

Phyllis doesn't much deal in pleasantries so as soon as she made it inside she said, "I heard the prosecutor isn't trying Darlene Menendez."

"A hearty hello to you as well, Phyllis. Why did the prosecutor decide that? Wasn't Darlene guilty enough for him?"

Phyllis chuckled. "Oh she's plenty guilty of obstructing justice and about six other things," she said. "You got any coffee?" Luckily I did because it was Saturday and Melissa was home so I'd been sure to make a fresh urn. I got Phyllis a cup from the den and she followed me there. "The prosecutor and Darlene's attorney came to an agreement that she was not competent to stand trial. Once the assistant prosecutor heard Darlene go on about having a ghost help her cover up a crime she was convinced."

I handed Phyllis the coffee, black as I knew she liked it. "Yeah. People who see ghosts are definitely nuts."

"It probably didn't hurt that she had a daughter on the cops," Phyllis said, ignoring my semi-snide remark. "Law enforcement protects its own."

I led her toward the coffee table because 1. Phyllis was drinking coffee and 2. Maxie was in the kitchen and not paying attention to living people. Phyllis is a reporter. She has heard rumors about my house but I prefer to keep her away from any sights that would verify those rumors and make her want to investigate further.

"What are you doing here, anyway?" I asked. "You could have texted me that little piece of legal gossip."

"I'm here to see Melissa," she said.

That wasn't a total surprise. Since I delivered papers for her when I was the age Melissa is now, Phyllis has long discussed a part-time job with Liss. I looked at her. "She can't get working papers until she's fourteen," I reminded Phyllis.

"And she turns fourteen . . . ?"

"Next month."

On cue my daughter appeared in the entrance to the den, dressed in sweats and looking like someone who had just slept about ten hours and didn't know why she was awake now. Her feet were in slippers that accentuated the sound of her shuffling across the room toward the coffee urn. She made a sound I can't describe. Then she saw we had a guest and her face brightened up in a nanosecond. "Oh hi, Phyllis," she said. "What's new?"

"Hey, Melissa. Came by to talk to you about work."

Liss had been waiting for this literally for years. She probably believed she had been waiting for it her whole life, but I'm sure there were years when she was in diapers that working for Phyllis wouldn't have appealed quite as much. "When can I start?" she said, rushing to her almost-boss' side.

Phyllis knew well enough to answer correctly. "First you have to be fourteen and then you have to wait until your mom says it's okay."

Melissa looked at me with the same eyes that have been

talking me into things against my will since she was two months old. "Mom?"

"I want to know what the job entails." I looked at Phyllis. "She's not going out chasing crime stories. Period."

Phyllis held up her hands. "No. I wouldn't ask her to do that. That's the fun part. That's what *I* get to do. No, Melissa, you'll be working in the office on administrative things, organizing my paperwork and such."

Melissa, who's seen Phyllis's paperwork, looked daunted just for a second. "Okay," she said after a beat.

"But eventually I'm going to need you to become an assistant editor. You know the paper is mostly online these days. I need to have a social media presence and I don't do that yet. Now, I don't want you being the voice of the paper and taking all the heat until you're older, but you'll be working up to that, okay?"

Liss looked at me, I nodded a hair reluctantly, and she reached over and gave Phyllis a hug. "It sounds great!" she said. I didn't think it sounded that great, but it's been a while since I was thirteen.

"You realize she's going to college in five years," I reminded Phyllis.

"I'll worry about that in five years. A journalism degree can't hurt."

Best to change the subject. "So what else about Darlene? What about Bill Harrelson?" I asked. "Is he going to jail?"

Phyllis snapped into reporter mode, which is her default. "The prosecutor thought long and hard about charging him with kidnapping but he brought charges of criminal restraint and assault with a weapon, which Bill definitely did. He got something of a break because he cooperated against Darlene the business with her dead husband, even though everything he said was secondhand news. He was a kid when Herman Fitzsimmons got himself shot."

"So was the girl who shot him." My daughter is not really focused before she has coffee.

"The whole thing was so much more complicated than it needed to be," I mused aloud. "Theresa shot Herman. All Darlene had to do to cover it up was say he was assaulting her and it was self defense and the cops would have disposed of the body for her."

Phyllis shook her head. "It was 1983. First of all he *wasn't* assaulting her but even if he was, domestic violence wasn't being prosecuted nearly as often as it is today. They would have investigated, they would have come to the correct conclusion and Theresa Menendez would have gone into foster care. Would that have been better?"

"Maybe."

Maxie emerged through the kitchen door. "Are you almost done? I want to get to the molding!" I didn't answer for Phyllis's benefit and Maxie looked disgusted. "I'll start it myself." She headed back toward the kitchen before I could even begin to anticipate the unearthly racket she was about to commence.

Luckily, Phyllis had done her business and that meant Phyllis was ready to move on to the next thing. "Okay then," she said to Melissa. "When you're fourteen and you're applying for working papers you know where to find me."

Phyllis left through the kitchen, so Maxie didn't start in on her painting of the molding—which I decided would be okay because she'd do a good job and I didn't feel like it—until Phyllis was well out the door and backing out of my driveway.

Melissa and I walked into the kitchen to watch Phyllis leave and so Liss could get some milk for her coffee. There are creamers and a small pitcher of milk out on the urn cart, but I had kept both in short supply because we had only two guests and Liss likes milk from the fridge that cools the hot coffee down a bit. As we walked in Maxie, up near the ceiling with a paintbrush in her hand, looked down at us. "What's up?" she asked Melissa. Melissa gets a greeting. I'm lucky when I don't get a snarl.

"I got a job!" Liss told her.

"Cool!" They're like sisters, only I'm pretty sure my thirteen-year-old is the more mature one.

They continued to gab away with Melissa telling Maxie all about her upcoming responsibilities—about which she knew very little—and Maxie carefully painting the ceiling molding that muted orange. I looked around the room and considered all that had happened here since it was under construction and I'd gotten a bucket of wallboard compound dropped on my head. The room looked different, and I hoped better. The bullet wound to the ceiling was repaired and invisible. The walls were a cheerful new color. The place would be useable for Liss to cook dinner for me, her stepfather and her grandparents tonight and she loved doing that.

I sat down next to the center island away from Maxie's

drop cloths. She was a careful and meticulous painter but I still wanted to stay out of her way. Let Melissa and Maxie talk like sisters for a little while longer.

After all it was only five years until Liss would be away in college and I'd be in my forties. But Maxie would be Maxie forever. So I'd let her enjoy the bond she'd developed now and try to make it last a little longer.

Most of the utensils and cooking implements were away in drawers to avoid the paint, but the island was in the center of the room where Maxie (and eventually I when she got bored) would be working so there was no danger of their catching the odd drop of orange from above. I had put the newspaper down and now picked up a section to read. I like real newspapers on real paper. I'm old school.

In order to spread it out on the countertop I had to move a pitcher in which we kept wooden utensils, cooking spoons and such that might have gotten knocked over otherwise. So I pushed it a little bit to the right and picked up the cup of coffee I'd left when Phyllis had appeared, which was no doubt cold now.

That didn't matter because I stopped with the cup halfway to my lips as I stared at the space I'd created by moving the pitcher.

Sitting on the countertop, which I'd personally cleaned the night before, was an emerald. And next to it, what I could only guess was a gold doubloon.

Acknowledgments

Wow. Ten books in a series! It didn't seem possible when this train started out and it didn't seem possible after Book #8, but thanks to the crew at Crooked Lane Books we are still traveling the Haunted Guesthouse track and hope we keep going for a while to come! Special thanks to Matt Martz, Jenny Chen and Sarah Poppe for the great support.

Thanks as ever to Dominic Finelle for the cover illustration that makes this look like a Haunted Guesthouse book *and* makes it look terrific! Dom has been with us every step of the way and that's part of what lures people to the series.

None of this would have been remotely possible without the terrific work of the gang at HSG Agency, particularly my astonishingly good agent (you can ask anybody) Josh Getzler and Jonathan Cobb. Thanks for making me a little less obscure, guys. You're the best and your tireless efforts are never unappreciated.

But as the dedication to this book notes, it's all happening (and it all has happened) because of the loyal readers of the Guesthouse and a few other series under this name and another. I never forget that there's a reader (or maybe two) out there and always feel grateful and amazed that you started off with me and are staying with me. It's ten books so far, guys. Let's see how far this train goes.

E. J. Copperman
Deepest New Jersey
July, 2018